Cambio Bay

BOOKS BY KATE WILHELM

▼ ▼ ▼ ▼ ▼ ▼ ▼ ▼ ▼

CAMBIO BAY

Kate Wilhelm

St. Martin's Press
New York

Design by Judy Dannecker

Library of Congress Cataloging-in-Publication Data
MAY   8 '90
Wilhelm, Kate.
    Cambio Bay / Kate Wilhelm.
      p. cm.
    ISBN 0-312-03800-3
    I. Title.
    PS3573.I434C36   1990
    813'.54—dc20   89-24099

First Edition
10 9 8 7 6 5 4 3 2 1

To Damon

Cambio Bay

1

▼ ▼ ▼ ▼

Coyote woke up one morning earlier than he wanted; he squinted at Sun and said, "Go away and come back later." Coyote rolled over and closed his eyes again, but Sun glared at him so fiercely that he could not sleep. Coyote became annoyed at Sun, and all day he thought and thought; when Sun finally dipped down to Sea for a drink, Coyote had a plan. He began to throw rocks and trees and dirt and chaparral with all his might, piling it up higher and higher, and the next day when Sun began his stroll across Sky, he saw a great mountain before him. He looked all around, but he was sure he had taken the right trail. Finally he started to climb the high mountain, straining and puffing, getting hotter and hotter as he went up until at last he reached the summit. From there he saw Coyote and all the other creatures sleeping soundly in the cool shade below. Now Sun became angry because the climb had been hard, and he was hotter than he liked. He sucked up the waters from the streams and blasted the

trees and withered the leaves and dried up the sweet berries
and lush grasses. "From now on," Sun roared, "this will
be the place of changes. You may find shade and even
sleep late, but when I come, I will be big and I will be
burning." The animals awakened hot and thirsty and they
threw stones and sticks at Coyote and chased him over
the mountain, all the way to the desert. And even now it
is so: Sun climbs the high, dry mountain and becomes
full-bodied and ablaze before he glares down into the shadows; the people call the mountain our Sierra Madre.

A bony arm, freed from the sandhills on both sides,
reached for the sea, and where they met, the froth of tides
and the bones of the mother mountain, a bay was formed
in the shadow of the great mountain range. The Spaniards
called it *La Bahia de los Cambios*, but in time this was short-
ened and simplified, and it became simply Cambio Bay.
To the north the fog visits the land and caresses it in cool,
moist embrace; to the south the desert begins. Cambio
Bay, in the rocky likeness of the northern coast, with the
climate of the southern, is neither; it is the place of changes.

Although on the eastern face of the mountain dawn is
flickering with pale fires, it is still dark in Cambio Bay.
The tide has run out; the bay is sleeping. As always, the
first light to go on in the town is that of Terry Hayes. He
and his wife are stumbling past each other, making coffee,
not talking yet. Terry works at the ranger station high on
Los Padres, thirty miles away. It is too early in the season
for fires, although the mountain burns annually, almost
ritually, it sometimes seems. Now the crew is concerned
with another storm front, the fourth of the spring season,
stalled offshore and due within twenty-four hours. If the

damn mountain wasn't burning, it was being washed away, Terry thinks, turning on the radio in the kitchen. The light in the Eccleses' house comes on next, and is turned off again. Too early. Rita Cronen's kitchen glows through her red curtains, and the Emersons are up now, and so it goes as the tiny town comes to life. Above the houses the mission gleams in the twilight; if there are ghosts, this is the time for them to stir in the adobe ruins, barefoot friars in cowls silently mouthing Hail Marys.

In the Cambio Bay Motel the hiking party from the university is up, in boisterous high spirits, ready for the adventure on the mountain collecting something or other. A group bivouacs here now and again before tackling the dry canyons and ravines. And on the opposite point, a light goes on, one goes off in Miss Luisa's Victorian house. It isn't a true Victorian, but since no one knows what else to call the structure that has grown and evolved as if with inner life, they have said it is. Some say instead "That monstrosity on the hill."

The house is said to occupy land that once held an Indian longhouse, and before that the northernmost outreach of the vast Aztec empire, and before that the dwelling place of Great Chief and Squaw and their child.

A second light from Miss Luisa's house is visible from the village below; her tenant is up, a newcomer, pale and bookish, friendly enough, but different.

Harold Ritchie came straight from the Coyote dream into full wakefulness, flushed with excitement. He had read the story only a day or two ago, and now he had seen it come to life. He almost wished there were someone he could tell, someone to talk it all over with, but he knew he would not do that even if there were such a person. No, the excitement had to be guarded so that it would still carry its energy to the page when he began to write the stories. And, he thought in real wonder, the solution to his problem had come to him also during the night. The stories would work in columns, Harold realized that morning, immensely pleased with his own unfathomable mind that, while he slept, had delivered a solution to the problem that had plagued him on and off for many weeks.

Dawn light was still gray, the air still too cool for coffee on the balcony, but he would have it there anyway and start to line up the stories and their accompanying text, taken from where? He was considering text as necessary, a kind of reality control. He mulled over possible sources for it as he carefully measured the beans into the small coffee grinder that he carried on trips. He was a precise man, knowing well the value of details, that a moment spent in preparation was worth many minutes, hours, days of reparation. With the same care he measured the water, cut the bread—made with nine grains, since he also knew exactly how much fiber he should have, where the best sources were to be obtained, so many grams from whole grains, so many from fruits and vegetables—but already his mind was sorting through possible references he could tap without having to pay permission fees or bother with copyrights. The Bible certainly, old textbooks, if he paraphrased them somewhat, the bottomless well of mythology.

Harold Ritchie was fifty-one. Once his mother had said he was fourteen going on ninety, and he had liked that and thought of himself afterward as a man in pursuit of the magic number ninety. He saw nothing in his future to prevent his reaching that number. He was healthy, and careful, did nothing to excess, and while he did not actually exercise, he did walk a lot. Normally rather pale, with sandy hair and light-blue eyes, on this trip he was getting a bit of a suntan, not much because he had followed the stories about the ozone depletion. Now he blessed his bias

4

against strenuous outdoor pursuits and still took care to avoid the sun during the middle hours of the day.

He had married a long time ago, but found, without surprise, that marriage did not fit him well, like a suit that bound under the arms and hung in baggy disarray in other places. It had been a great relief to give it up; the bond of wedlock had been severed with amicable mutual goodwill, and now his ex-wife's two children called him Uncle Harold, and he was an occasional visitor in their comfortable Atlanta home. He was a professor of English at a small, private, and very expensive college in Connecticut. This year was his sabbatical.

This year he had discovered the mythos of the West, had discovered the magical Coyote and Crow, the Great Spirit, and Great Chief and Squaw . . .

Eventually he had his breakfast prepared: no eggs (too much cholesterol), toast, a sugarless strawberry spread, margarine, an orange and a banana, one glass of skim milk, decaf coffee, one ounce of low-fat, low-sodium cheddar cheese. He added a napkin to the tray and carried it to the balcony, which was, after all, sheltered from the wind, and offered such a pleasant view of the sea that not to take advantage of it would have been asinine. Small and large balconies seemed to jut out from rooms almost randomly, as his own did, and from each one the vista was magnificent: sea, sea cliffs, the curious formations of rocks on the shore and the rocky arm that curved around to form the bay that at the moment looked nearly like a pond.

He ate slowly, preoccupied with the plans for his book. The tale of how Sierra Madre had been formed would be balanced by an account of the geology of the entire state —earthquakes, moving tectonic plates, upthrusts of land, rain shadows, the pattern of ocean currents that turned the northern part of the state into a near rain forest and the southern part into a desert . . .

That section would be kept short, at least in part because

5

he was mildly uncomfortable with scientific theories that tried to explain natural phenomena, but mostly because he knew he could not rely on his own instincts concerning science. He simply didn't have the feel for it that he had for poetry, or drama, or any literature. There he could point to the scene, the phrase, the word, even the syllable where the work failed, but in science he felt stymied. He could only guess at what was enough explanation. He would work hard to try to make that part interesting to a possible reader who had become immune to *any* science and actively rebelled at the idea of acquiring even the scantiest education in it now. And absolutely no mathematics, no equations or formulas. That part would require research, also, and he was not looking forward to it. He knew the Santa Ynez Fault lay to the south, not very far away, he believed, and the San Andreas Fault lay to the east somewhere . . . Well, the library was full of books about earthquakes and fault lines.

"Good morning," a voice called.

He looked over the railing of his balcony to see Miss Luisa waving to him. "Good morning," he said. "Another fine morning, isn't it?"

Miss Luisa had reached and passed the magic ninety, he felt certain, but there she was, straight, able, as weathered as any of the rocks hereabout, and as durable, apparently. Her voice was not the wavery voice of an old woman.

"For now," she said, nodding. "For now. I'm going to place my order for the weekend. Anything I can add for you?"

He smiled and shook his head. "In fact, I was going to offer the same service. Thought I might run down to Santa Barbara, pick up a few little things, some books, paper. Can I bring you anything?"

"No, no. Bobby will do for me. But, Mr. Ritchie, if I were you, I'd plan to get back by afternoon. I believe we might have a squall."

He looked out to sea and could not pick out anything different from yesterday or the day before. Still, he had faith in the ability of people to read the signs in places where they had lived a long time. The fact that he had never sharpened his own sensibilities in that direction he put down to inattention, a lack of interest. And, of course, a squall to Miss Luisa on foot was not at all the same thing that it would be to him in his rented Buick, which was almost like driving a tank. Actually he hoped she was right; part of his California experience, people had told him, must be to witness at the coast a real Pacific storm. Was that an oxymoron? he had wondered then, and wondered again now. The same people had also advised him to witness the miracle of an earthquake, and he had declined politely, at which they had laughed.

Now he smiled at the old woman and was taken aback by the stern expression that crossed her face. Had his smile been condescending, somehow frivolous? He had not intended it to be, but often people seemed to think he was . . . putting them down when he was trying to be friendly. He thought of the phrase "putting them down" and made a note to look up its antecedents. Shakespeare? Probably. Most phrases that apt seemed to derive from his works.

"Mr. Ritchie," she said then, "there's a time to be out in the weather, and a time to be indoors, and this afternoon's a time to be indoors. By two-thirty, three at the latest. There's a time to observe and a time to participate, a time to take heed and a time to dare. A time for things to stay the same. And a time for changes. When it's a time for changes you don't want to be a stranger in the wilderness."

He had risen at her words—what a wonderful paraphrase!—oddly excited, almost, he thought, frightened.

But that was from standing up too fast, a moment of vertigo, a slight spasm of muscles in his lower belly. Miss Luisa had turned away now. She raised her hands to put up her hood, and for a terrifying instant it seemed that she would take wing, fly into the gray morning light. A gust of wind had spread her voluminous cape, no more than that. He watched her start her brisk walk into town, the cape billowing out behind her.

He admired that cape quite a lot. It was dark, a deep purple that now looked black but in sunlight became violet. It had a sheen that suggested imperviousness to the elements, exactly the right garment for her daily walk to town and back. Often at sunset she wore the cape to the edge of the cliff where she stood facing the sea, the offshore breeze ballooning the cape until it seemed she might be carried aloft, blown like a cloud before the wind.

Slowly he regained his seat at the wrought-iron table and saw to his dismay that his breakfast was totally gone. He hated it when he was so preoccupied that he ate without conscious awareness of his food, which he believed should do more than merely satisfy the appetite of the body. Each bite should be considered, appreciated . . . A time of changes, he thought then, and again the tingle that could not possibly be fear touched him, this time prickling his skin, his scalp. Abruptly he decided to make a cup of real coffee. After all, he had a long drive, and he would plan to be back here, safely inside the mansion, no later than three.

2

▼ ▼ ▼ ▼

From a high enough vantage point the traffic on the Santa Barbara Freeway would look like a pair of snakes, one writhing north, one south, each vehicle a scale now reflecting sunlight, now fading as the creatures flowed easily over the path of least resistance, shedding scales now and again, accruing others with such regularity that each overall size changed little. As if sensing a goal within reach, the one aimed northward became elongated, narrower, and flowed faster; the ever-changing scales made new patterns without end.

One of the colorful scales, a yellow Toyota, gradually shifted its position, creating new patterns that sent ripples throughout much of the body, as it changed places with other vehicles and made its way to the right lane.

There were people who could turn frogs' legs and snails into good solid cash, Carolyn Engleman thought, behind the wheel of the Toyota, and there were those who ducked into the cellar if it rained diamonds, and waited until the storm blew over. She nodded in grim satisfaction at having classified the man she worked for. A cellar dweller. "How can you not make money in real estate in California, for chrissake?" her one-time lover and never friend Sal Doreli had asked, before she had stopped lending him money. "You name yourself Laurence Banning and open a realty company and chew your nails waiting for the earth to open up and flood you with gold," she had snapped. Today she would have added, "And you accept the most hopeless of the dirt-poor damned and their hardscrabble rock piles, and their ramshackle falling-down huts and pretend you've made a deal."

"Honey," Laurence Banning had said that morning, pretending an eagerness that, if it were real, would have qualified him as a certifiable nut case, "this guy has such a Texas accent, you wouldn't believe it! So he goes out there and makes himself a ranch, twenty acres! Practically overlooking the ocean. Spitting distance of being waterfront! And now he's homesick. I'd go, but I promised Madge . . ."

Laurence was six four and never had got used to the idea that his hands and feet were quite distant from his torso and his brain; he stumbled into things, forgot to duck at low overhangs, sprawled in such a way that hardly anyone else could move in the office when he was present. He had a long sad face, a woebegone expression of mild surprise most of the time, and no doubt counted bruises that he could not remember accumulating night after night. If Madge hadn't taken him in hand, Carolyn knew, he probably would have fallen headfirst off a boardwalk years ago, but on the other hand, protecting him meant abusing the other salesperson, and that person was Carolyn.

Friday night there had been a party at Grover Toomie's to celebrate something—his divorce? or engagement? both? Late, late night. Saturday night there had been a

dinner, movie, and gab session with her friend Linda No-
vak, and that had been a late night. Linda was trying to
decide among suicide, making up with her ex, having a
baby, and dyeing her hair red. Carolyn shook her own
head grimly. Until three in the morning the options had
been plumbed. Sunday, yesterday, Carolyn had shown a
couple from Toronto six different houses, spread out over
a hundred-mile radius, and they had decided at last not
to buy anything right now. You know how it is, he had
said, giving his new bride a loving and obscene caress.
And now it was Monday morning, and Carolyn should
have had the day off, should have slept in, should have
had her own hair cut later, should have stayed home long
enough at least to wash the damn dishes. She had not been
able to find a clean cup that morning. She cursed Laurence
Banning steadily as she drove.

Carolyn was thirty-six, with light hair that she used to
keep platinum, but had given up on because it was too
tiresome; now her hair was darkening, and that morning
it was too long, with too much friz. She was compactly
built, even muscular, and took care of her body with regular exercise, which she loathed. She had never married,
although there had been several someones in her past.
Significant others, she said to herself with a certain grim
self-mockery. And for nearly a year her feeling of frustration had grown. She was not a loser, she reassured
herself when the dissatisfaction grew oppressive, but neither was she winning much, she always added. She supported herself adequately; her Social Security was
mounting, as was her private pension fund. She owned
her two-bedroom house, without a mortgage. People in
real estate could count on finding a decent, affordable
house, or else what was the point? If at times she found
herself drinking a bit more than she used to, well, that
was middle-age privilege giving her a sneak preview.

If anyone had asked her what she wanted out of life,

where she was going, she would have answered—if at all—with a noncommittal shrug. Neither man nor woman was meant to know some things, she thought when the question occurred to her.

All these things were very much on her mind as she drove north that day, because of her mother. For at least a year now her mother had been sending her news items with patient regularity, clipped from the Des Moines newspaper, national magazines, church bulletins, God alone knew where else. The items all concerned AIDS, or herpes, or some other sexually transmitted horror, or the statistics on the risks to mother and child of a pregnancy started after the mid-thirties. Now and again the item concerned Walker Johns, the man Carolyn had nearly married a long time ago. Walker was doing very well these days, a partner in a car dealership . . . Last night her mother had called, catching Carolyn exhausted, her feet sore, her attitude surly, her checking account bottoming out faster than was comfortable, her throat parched, and her stomach empty. Her mother called to read the grim prediction that this was the year that the Big Earthquake would sink California. The calls were even more frustrating and futile than the letters, which could be put off unread until later, and then later again, but the calls were in real time, and she loved her mother very much, but neither of them ever had anything to say that the other wanted to hear.

"Dear," her mother had said piteously, "we worry so about you. If only we thought you were truly happy, it would make such a difference."

From there on Carolyn knew the script by heart. She had lied about someone at the door and had hung up, and sat regarding the phone with a seesaw mixture of guilt and rage. *No*, she had muttered at it, *I'm not happy. I'm miserable. Leave me alone!* And that was the truth, she had realized with a shock. Her appetite was gone, but her feet still hurt, and she went to soak them in a long fragrant bath, and then went to bed.

Okay, she told herself sourly as she drove north. Let the damn machine take the calls. And get back to work, make a buck. Rejoice, you're going to see a real Texas ranch. She leaned forward to peer at an approaching road sign. From here on she would have to follow directions that she had written in bold black print and placed on the passenger seat. She exited the freeway. There hadn't been anything since Santa Barbara except too much traffic to claim more than a fraction of her attention; even the ocean had been out of sight over the endless stream of cars and trucks. She knew from the road map she had consulted that it would be that way until she turned off the highway again, nearly twenty miles ahead, and in this stretch even the ocean was gone. From the next road she was to turn right onto Ridge Road. She gritted her teeth at the thought. She had been in California long enough to know what that name meant.

Most of the traffic continued on the freeway. Understandable, she decided, disgruntled with the scenery— scrub grass, low dispirited hills, deep erosion gullies, a lowering, gray sky that made her uneasy, and the mountains, sometimes close by, then more distant, like an uncertain wall. This was the transition zone, someone had told her—Laurence? Sal? Someone. And that was one of her problems, she thought glumly; her past was littered with "someones" she no longer remembered clearly. Transition zone, she reminded herself, the place where California was divided, a place neither this nor that, and it was impossible to tell if this area signaled decline into the sort of vast desert that bounded the Pacific shores of much of South America, or if the current phase was a pause in a grander scheme long underway, not yet finished. It looked like a piece of Georgia that had been lifted bodily and plumped down here. It must have been Cary who had labeled it transitional; he was from the East Coast.

She should move up north, she thought, not liking this zone of division. Up to Big Sur, Carmel, someplace where the desert was not, where it rained now and then, real rain, not the emptying of an infinite bucket. She realized that she had been glancing skyward again and again at the black-bellied clouds; the heaviness of the clouds made it seem as if the water were gathering behind a fabric already stretched to its limits. She drove faster.

When she finally found Ridge Road, she stopped on the shoulder of the state road and considered. The state road was narrow, but paved; Ridge Road was narrower and not paved, and it twisted out of sight altogether too soon. The hills were higher, trying to be mountains here; the canyons were steeper, and there were very deep, sharply etched erosion gullies. She hated her boss Laurence Banning passionately at that moment.

She consulted the directions again: five miles on Ridge Road to H.L. Jeffers's mailbox and turn left. And then how far? The directions did not go beyond the mailbox. Oh, what the hell, she decided finally; she would feel dumb, dumb, dumb having driven all this way and not finishing. With reluctance she started the Toyota and edged onto the dirt road. "How long can it possibly take to drive five miles?" she muttered.

It took half an hour. Scrub oak, manzanita, chaparral, and clumps of tough-looking grasses dotted the pale ground like afterthoughts. Some of the grass was even bright green, but there had been several deluges in the past few weeks. The green was quite temporary. More prevalent was a gritty black where the sparse growth had burned and then burned again many times over the years. Most of all, the land and everything on it was colored in tones of ocher, sienna, tan, brown, with the vivid green flashes occasionally, and outlines in black, the way a child might have drawn the scene. There were more rocks and boulders perched on the hillsides than plants; a ravine had determined the course of the road. Actually, she had to admit, the landscape was rather pretty in a desolate way. The landscape was one of the real reasons she stayed, she knew, even if she grumbled about it.

Having got on the road, there was nothing to do but keep going; the road was too narrow and the drop-off too steep to attempt a turnaround. She was cursing steadily under her breath by the time she reached the mailbox and saw a gray shack a few hundred yards away.

Walking out to meet her was a slouching man dressed in jeans, a dirty undershirt, and worn Western boots; he was over six feet tall, about forty, with large jutting bones and sinewy muscles. Hungry looking. He stared at her in disbelief when she got out of the car and approached him.

"They should have sent a man," he said, ignoring her outstretched hand.

"Sorry," she said. "This is my job, though. You are H. L. Jeffers, aren't you?"

"I thought that fella I talked to would come."

It was two-fifteen; Carolyn had eaten breakfast at seven that morning and nothing since, and she had a headache now. "So I'll leave," she snapped, and turned back toward her car.

"Shit," he muttered.

She opened the door and he yelled, "I'll show you." She reached into the car, got her camera from the glove box, and faced him again.

"What's that for?" he demanded.

"My boss will want pictures," she said coolly, and took a quick picture of the shack. It was gray, sagging at one corner, with a tin roof over a narrow porch in front, unscreened windows. When she again looked at Jeffers, he also seemed to be sagging in defeat.

Silently he led her to the house—three rooms, finished with rough boards, a mattress on the floor, no plumbing. There was a rustling sound from outside the back door, but no one else was in sight. They walked around the property for only a few minutes; it was clear that there was nothing to be seen but scrub sage and rocks. He had been digging, she realized with a sudden deep pity.

She took a few more snapshots, knowing it was for his benefit now, not because there was any point in it. Then they returned to the front of the house.

"They should have sent a man," he said again in a hopeless sullen tone.

This time she understood that he believed he might have sold his dream to a man. A man would look at the barren hills and see the gold foundation, the gold spine and bones, the gold flowing out of sight in the veins, heart of gold, mother lode, gold dust devils aswirl. It had to be here because the rainbow had ended here. In this ravine, that steep-sided canyon, beneath the rock ridges, in the shadow of that tortured oak tree, gold with the power of a magnet reached out to kindle the desire, the need, the lust for gold in a man's heart and loins. That was what he had to sell, a dream of gold; but to a man, not to her.

She saw a flutter of motion and turned to watch a crow take shape out of shadows as it flew from the oak tree; it threw itself into the air and rode a thermal as if caught in a whirlpool being drained into the sky. Finally it flapped its wings, once, twice, and then hung motionless facing seaward.

Gazing at the bird, Carolyn said, "Mr. Jeffers, go back home, back to Texas. We'll do what we can." She glanced at him but he was glaring past her. When she turned toward the house, it was to see an Indian woman on the crumbling steps, looking at the crow. She had on an ankle-length gray dress, as shapeless as a pillowcase, the color of the house. Jeffers muttered a curse and strode toward her. Carolyn glanced up; the crow was gone, and the clouds were crow-black and ominous.

Hurriedly she got her briefcase, took out the sales agreement pad, and approached the house with it. Meaningless, she knew, but they would go through the motions. She was anxious to get away before the clouds split apart; she was visualizing the awful five miles of dirt road, the erosion scars that crossed it, the boulder-ridden slopes.

The Indian woman watched without expression as Carolyn drew near and rushed through the explanation of the terms. Silently Jeffers signed the form; she separated the carbonless copy from the top sheet and handed it to him, and at last the Indian woman spoke.

"Go. Drive quickly. It is the time of changes." She turned and entered the house.

A thrill of fear shook Carolyn, as irrational as it was unexpected.

The deluge began ten minutes later. It came with a blinding black rain and screaming wind that entered the car at will and howled in her ears. Across the road brown water rushed, some spilling over the edge, cutting into it, crumbling it; more water ran down the roadway as if it were a riverbed. She had to drive slower and slower as the tires found less purchase. Around a curve the storm appeared to abate, the road became firmer; it was the southern exposure and the western that were taking the burden of the torrent. She prayed that most of the way down to the state road would be on the north. She could not remember how the winding road had been situated driving in.

There was a long downgrade ahead, with sheets of rain flashing across it, one after another moving down the slope; she had a vision of the boulders up there starting to roll, the avalanche of rocks and scrub plants. She pressed the accelerator harder, gripped the wheel harder. Think about insurance, she told herself, think about rates and how they will up your premium again if you wreck the car. She hit the brake too hard at the end of the downgrade and the beginning of a sharp curve, and felt a sickening lurch as her wheels spun. Go with it, she thought, and was in control again. Her long exhalation warbled out through her lips. Insurance, she reminded herself. Some kids had thrown rocks at her, chipped paint, and her rates had gone up, and now God was throwing everything at hand at her. What would they do to her rates if he hit?

She should have stayed at Jeffers's place until it blew over. It had not even occurred to her. For some stupid reason she had been frightened by the Indian woman, and now she could not remember why, unless it was because the woman had foreseen the storm, but so had she. Anyone with eyes must have seen it building. She should have . . . Another sharp curve brought the rain hard against the windshield, blinding her. The wipers were useless against buckets and buckets of water. She had to open the door an inch or so in order to see the edge of the river/road, the waterfall that was on her left. She crept downward, sometimes keeping the door open to align herself with the edge of the road, then driving a bit faster when a curve brought relief.

It had taken half an hour to drive up to Jeffers's house; it took nearly an hour to drive out, but finally she saw the state road only a few feet in front of her car, and she jammed on the brake again, and this time her car stalled out.

She leaned her forehead on the steering wheel and tried to relax a little. She knew she could not afford the relief of relaxing too much yet; these hills were too unstable, too often burned over, too often saturated. She started driving again, faster now on the blacktop road without the ravine at her left inviting disaster. The rain was coming down even harder, a thundering downpour; swift runoff waters made rivers on both sides of the road like parentheses, and where the road dipped, the rivers merged and swirled on the surface. She passed a tree caught in the churning water, half across the road, twisting and rolling. But it wasn't far to the real highway, she told herself. The real highway would be safe. Engineers had allowed for torrential rains, there were drainage ditches, catch basins, whatever was needed. The real highway would have other traffic, other people to help if anyone got stalled, or hit by a falling tree, or swallowed by an avalanche.

At the highway, she gave herself several minutes to try to ease the muscles in her shoulders, her thighs, her neck. She ached everywhere. A car passed, heading north, another, then two trucks going the other way. She took deep breaths until she felt some of the tension ebb away, and only then pulled out onto the real highway aiming south, to the freeway, to Santa Barbara, to safety. A motel. She would stop in a motel, let Laurence pay the bill for a room, a good dinner, a lot of wine, a stiff drink or two first.

The rain was hitting the car broadside now; visibility had not improved much, but the road felt firmer under her wheels, and ahead she could see the taillights of another car and a stretch of road. And even a bit of the hillside that rose to her left. She stifled a cry then because the hill was moving. Earthquake, she moaned, and was almost apathetic in her calm. She pumped the brake, trying to avoid a spinout, and she watched the car ahead of her rocking; it started to slide sideways in a curious motion that surely was not legal. Then she realized that she was moving sideways also, that ahead of her was the hill, the road now was at her right. She saw the other car spin out of control; the driver jumped out and came tearing toward her, and she was applying the brakes and shifting gears as if she knew exactly what must be done and how, but it was as if someone else had taken over her hands and feet and mind. She was not responsible any longer. She reached over to unlock the passenger door, a man clambered in, and she drove back the way she had just come, faster and faster, while behind them the road and the hill slid together to reform the land.

Her passenger's breathing was so labored he couldn't speak. He sucked in long gasping breaths and released them explosively, as if he could not get enough air, or, she thought, as if he was fighting hysteria, as she was also, but in a different way. She had removed herself curiously and felt almost like an observer, not a participant.

"Jesus!" He gasped finally. "Jesus."

Ahead, a brown river crossed the road, coming from the state road she had left minutes ago. Sagebrush was caught in the torrent. She slowed down and drove through the swirling water cautiously and then speeded up again. All these hills might start sliding, she thought, and wanted only to be away, far away.

"Slower," the man said then. "It gets curvy again."

She glanced at him. He was dripping, his hair plastered to his forehead, his clothes plastered to his body; he was shivering. She turned on the heat.

"Up ahead," he said, "a mountain. Rocky. It'll be safe there. Maybe you could stop a minute." His voice was shaky.

She nodded, navigated the new curves in the road, trying not to look at the hillside to her right, trying to keep her eyes on the road that had turned so treacherous even though it was a real highway. She felt the betrayal of the road was the ultimate betrayal. In California, she thought distantly, you couldn't trust the land, or the weather, or the hotshot producers, or buyers or sellers of real estate. You had to have faith in the roads with blacktop surfaces, or concrete, or what was left? And then the mountain rose at the right of the road, dark, massive, permanent, a rock mountain that would not slide. She slowed down and came to a stop, and sat unmoving, clutching the steering wheel in a hand-hurting grip.

"God," she said after a moment, "I wish I had a drink and a cigarette."

"Yeah. And I don't even smoke."

"Neither do I, not since last year anyway."

"Thanks," he said then. "You were swell."

She started to laugh and leaned her forehead down against the wheel and laughed helplessly. When she was able to raise her head again, he handed her a wad of tissues. He had wiped his face and arms, pushed his wet hair back. She remembered that he was cold and turned on the motor again.

"Let's decide what we're going to do before you start," he said. "You realize that not a single car has come this way since the slide?"

She had not realized it. Landslide, she thought, not earthquake. You were wrong, Mother, she also thought. The rain beat down, swept across the road. "I guess we could just sit tight and wait for help," she said. "I have a big beach towel in the trunk. You'd get soaked again, but then you could wrap up in it."

"Boise Wilkes," he said then. "Me. My name. Do you have a road map?"

"Carolyn Engleman. In the glove box. Why?"

"Not sure. I passed a sign for a town along here some-where, something Bay. If it's a bay carved out of the rocks, it could be our best bet. Otherwise we might be stuck here all night, maybe most of tomorrow." He found the map and studied it. "Here it is, a mile or two up the road, then a left turn. Cambio Bay."

"Toward the ocean? I don't think that's such a hot idea."

He shrugged. "We know what's south of here, and after we leave this mountain, it's the same kind of terrain north for about fifteen or twenty miles until we can reconnect with the freeway—unstable as hell, supersaturated, and

21

maybe already turned into chocolate tapioca where the road used to be. This map isn't too helpful, but it looks like the bay probably is rocky, and that means it's okay. I think. And there's a town there, food, a place to get dry and warm. Anyway, if you'll just drive forward a bit, we'll see. I don't want to leave the mountain either, remember. I know exactly what it's like to have your car disappear from under you."

Reluctantly she started to drive again, very slowly, wishing oncoming traffic would resume, wishing the rain would stop, wishing she were home, or even at Jeffers's place. But, she realized fatalistically when the sign appeared, she was going to Cambio Bay, three miles to the west.

3

At eleven in the morning on Sunday, the day before the storm, Iris Lathan looked at her daughter through squinting eyes and decided she was beautiful. Her blond hair was done up in a ponytail with a pink ribbon that matched exactly the color of her cheeks; her blue eyes gleamed with excitement. She was wearing light-blue denims with flowers and butterflies appliquéd down the side seams of both legs and a pink T-shirt. Bonnie shifted from foot to foot impatiently, enduring the scrutiny, and when Iris caught her up against her breast in a hug, she submitted without enthusiasm. She was five, Iris twenty-two.

Iris sighed and sat back on her heels, holding her daughter's hands. "Now, remember, you mind your father. Remember our game, shadow? You're going to be his shadow all day, never farther away from him than his own shadow, no matter what. Okay?"

Bonnie nodded, her gaze darting again to the door. A second later Iris heard the sound also; the outside door to the building had opened and closed. Bonnie had ears like a bat, she thought, as she often did. Now the child pulled loose and ran to the door to unlock it. Rick pounded up the last of the stairs and into the room.

"Hey! How's the princess? You look gorgeous, sweetheart." He swept her up and whirled her around a couple of times, grinning widely, and tucked her under his arm like a bag of potatoes. "How're things?" he asked Iris then, as Bonnie squirmed and swung her legs, and tried to tickle him under the chin.

Iris shrugged. "Okay. Look, make sure she gets a nap in the car, or she'll be worn out. And let her take her time eating, don't rush her, or she'll throw up later. And for God's sake, watch her around the animals!"

"Yeah, yeah."

"I'll leave her pajamas on the bed. Just stay with her until she's asleep, and then Mrs. Finzer said to knock on her door and she'll come across until I get home."

"You told me already. I know!"

"You have my number at work . . ."

Irritably he turned toward the door. "Jesus! Yeah. I've got it." He was leaving.

She thrust a small pink plastic gym bag toward him. "Here's some extra stuff for Bonnie. A sweater, some toys for in the car . . ."

He snatched it, and she ducked down and kissed Bonnie who was laughing silently, and now started to wave both hands; that, with her kicking feet, pink socks, and white shoes turned her into a pink and white flutter, a disturbance in the air. Rick left with her tucked under his arm, and as soon as they were out the door Iris hurried to the window to watch them emerge from the apartment complex. Rick was still carrying the child and she was still wriggling like a seaworm, anchored at the middle with both ends in a blur of motion. Rick was tall and slender, with beautiful longish hair that caught the slanting morn-

ing sunlight and gleamed with silver highlights black. Bonnie's blond hair and fair skin came from Rick strode to a silver car that looked very expensiv though Iris didn't know what kind it was, only that it big and silver and shiny-new looking. There was a flower on the antenna. She bit her lip, and then waved them as Rick opened the back door and buckled the chi in, walked around to get in behind the wheel, and the started down the street, turned out of sight. Neither had looked back at her.

Dully she faced the room again. It was small, with stained, colorless walls that needed paint; the furniture had come with it but it should have been tossed out to the junk man—a worn brown sofa, two chairs with worn cushions and wooden backs, a small black-and-white television. There were a few library books, children's books on a child's table, along with some coloring books, crayons. Beyond the room was an even smaller kitchen, and through a doorway was the bedroom with one bed that mother and daughter shared.

She would work two shifts that day, since Rick would have Bonnie until night, the first one at Sizzler from noon until six and then selling popcorn at the Ventura Mall theater complex until midnight. Iris had not yet moved from the window, but she was not looking at the street beyond it, or the apartment either now. She was seeing in her mind that long silver car that must have cost more than her two jobs would bring her if she put in a lifetime on them both. The car she drove was an eleven-year-old Dodge Dart, Rick's castoff, the car they had run away in when they were both sixteen. The tires were bald, and she never knew from hour to hour if it would start, or keep going once started, and she did not have enough money to fix anything if it stopped. Finally she left the window to get ready for work; she was already tired.

* * *

"Sweetheart," Rick was saying to Bonnie over his shoulder, "if you don't love the elephants most, I'll eat one." He glanced in the mirror and was rewarded by her wide grin, but he could not keep his chatter going. He knew Iris talked a lot to her, that she played games with her, read to her, that they did a lot of stuff together, but he didn't know how. "You see a bag on the backseat?" he asked. "Why don't you have a look inside."

He had gone to Schwartz's toy store and bought her a couple of dolls, and a picture book, and then, because he would have liked them as a kid, a bag of miniature animals—elephants, seals, rhinos . . . When he glanced at her again, she was playing with the animals. He put in a tape and nodded in time to the music. Now and then he checked the rearview mirror, keeping an eye on Bonnie, and also on the nondescript green car that was always within sight, an eighty-five Impala with a couple of guys in sport shirts. Although the Camarro he drove could have left them eating his dust, he did not try to shake them or make any sudden turns that might seem disturbing; he used the turn signal before changing lanes and kept well within the speed limit. The green Impala did the same.

They had lunch at a Wendy's, Bonnie's favorite, and by two they were in the south parking lot of the zoo. He drove very slowly now, turned into the D lane, following instructions, and shifted down. A Chevy pickup was backing out of a slot right on cue. He pulled into the space, and a moment later the Impala went past, neither man in it even glancing at him as he helped Bonnie from the backseat.

Rick suspected that one of the followers would check out the car and the other would keep right behind him.

He made it as easy as he could for that one to keep up, and after a few minutes he put them out of mind, and he and Bonnie covered the zoo until they were tired, hot, and hungry. Her hair was loose from the ponytail she had started with, and somehow she had smudged dirt on her face, and her hands were filthy, but she was smiling happily. It was time to leave, to find a quiet place to have some dinner, and then take her back home.

Bonnie spotted the car first, and tugged at his hand, pointing at the red flower. When they reached the Camarro he buckled her in, got behind the wheel again, and started driving. In the backseat Bonnie was gathering up her animals. Traffic leaving the zoo was bumper-to-bumper, stopping and starting under the direction of uniformed security people who were trying to keep it moving.

He stopped, started, shifted, and suddenly he looked at the rearview mirror again, not at the view, but the mirror itself; he looked at the glove-box door, at the steering wheel, the carved wooden knob on the stick shift, even the odometer, all exactly as he remembered them, but somehow wrong. Something was wrong. Suddenly he breathed, "Holy shit!" This was a different car. Every detail was exactly the same, and yet . . . This was not the same car he had been driving for the past four months.

He felt clammy all over; sweat broke out on his forehead, between his shoulder blades. He twisted around to look in the backseat; the pink plastic bag was on the window ledge; the dolls and books were there, animals lined up . . . Horns blared as traffic started to creep forward again. He shifted and followed, but he had to wipe one hand and then the other on his pants legs, and he rubbed his back against the seat to soak up the sweat that felt like ice water. Shit, he thought over and over, shit, shit shitshit-shit. . . .

He had gone to work for Mr. Wellington three years ago, as a messenger boy, an errand boy. Then the errands had become more important. No one told him that, but he knew from the way they watched him, timed him, and the increase in the pay. Four months ago Wellington had given him a new job. Caretaker, he had said. They had this house that visitors could use now and then instead of going to a hotel, important businessmen. But the house couldn't be left empty between guests. Rick could live there, take care of it, drive the Camarro, pick people up at the airport, take them back, be useful generally. A deal. A couple of times he had been told exactly where to go, where to park, how long to stay, and, he suspected, something had been put in the trunk of the Camarro. He asked no questions, did not open the trunk, but did exactly what he was told. Mr. Wellington liked that.

This time he had been told to go to the zoo, park in D lane, and return home no earlier than ten and no later than eleven. Period. And if he thought he was being followed to make it easy for the guys; after all, he had nothing to hide. That was true; he never had been picked up for anything, not even questions. He had figured it out. They wanted the house for something, a meeting maybe, and they wanted him to keep the cops away until night. Simple.

When he had to stop again, he became aware that Bonnie had slipped out of the seat belt; she was scrabbling around on the floor.

Jesus Christ, he said under his breath. "Get up and put the seat belt back on," he snapped. Her head appeared; she looked frightened at his tone. He tried to soften it. "Honey, it's not a good time to get stopped. They'll give Daddy a ticket if you don't buckle up. Can you do it yourself?"

For a moment he thought she was going to cry, but she climbed back to the seat and pulled at the seat belt, fumbled with it until she got it fastened, and by then he was moving. She twisted around and got her pink bag from the window ledge and started to put her animals inside. But a few minutes later she had undone the belt and was back on the floor.

"Bonnie, if I have to stop to fix that belt, I'm going to swat you. Do you understand me?"

She scurried back and did not move until he pulled up at a restaurant. When they returned to the car after dinner, he settled her in the front seat, which he lowered all the way, and almost as soon as they were on the highway, she fell asleep.

He glanced at her from time to time, and he reached over and brushed her hair back from her sweaty face. He felt a constriction in his throat. She was the first thing he had ever loved, the only person he had ever loved. He knew that what had happened with him and Iris back when they were kids had been just two kids hot to trot, but what he felt for Bonnie was like nothing he could talk about, explain, or understand. When Iris threw him out three years ago, he had wanted to kill her, not for her but for Bonnie. But he knew he couldn't keep the kid with him, not yet, not until she was a little older. Meanwhile he planned to get a stash together, get a good thing going for them for later when he would see to it that she had a good doctor who could do something for her. He would dress her like a doll, show her off . . .

She sighed in her sleep and he reached out and touched her cheek tenderly. He drove very carefully, taking no chances, not rushing the yellow lights, paying attention all the way. It was nearly ten by the time he got to the apartment, carried her inside, and put her to bed. She was so tired she hardly even roused. For a few minutes he stood over the bed watching her sleep. Then he crossed the hall and knocked on the door of the opposite apartment, Mrs. Finzer's apartment. She sometimes stayed with Bonnie when Iris had to work at night. He went back to the car and turned on the dome light to find all of Bonnie's toys, her pink bag, and took everything back upstairs to the third-floor apartment, handed them over to Mrs. Finzer, and left.

Forty-five minutes later he pulled into the underground garage at his house. He nodded to three men who did not speak, and went past them, upstairs, where he turned on several lights. The Impala had followed him all the way up the San Diego Freeway, into Van Nuys, onto Vanowen, and was now parked somewhere on the steep road outside.

In the basement garage the men were systematically stripping the seats out of the silver car, taking off the upholstery, removing packets and putting them in cartons.

"You're a little pig," Iris said to Bonnie the next morning, pulling off her T-shirt. "Little piggy, piggy, piggy."

Bonnie doubled over in silent laughter. She ducked away from her mother and stretched both arms up over her head, joined her hands, and opened and closed them.

"Okay. Not a pig. You're a giraffe, eating leaves from trees. Right?"

Bonnie became a lion, opening her mouth in a ferocious soundless roar, then she rolled over lazily, waved her legs in the air, rubbed her back on the floor.

Iris caught her and finished pulling off the clothes the child had slept in. "Dirty lion," she said. "Be an alligator, and get in the tub."

Iris scrubbed her and washed her sticky hair and toweled it, and managed to get enough clothes on the squirmy child for her to start eating her breakfast of Cheerios, which she liked to eat one by one. Iris went to shower and dress, and when she came out, Bonnie was at the little table lining up her miniature animals. She pantomimed an elephant, hands flapping for ears first, then one arm waving like a trunk, her fingers curling, uncurling delicately.

Iris put cereal into her own bowl, laughing at Bonnie. "Okay. You're really a monkey, you know."

Bonnie did not laugh; she did the elephant pantomime again and began to rearrange the animals on her table. Often Iris could follow her reasoning, make a conclusion about what the child was thinking, but it was getting late and she paid no more attention to Bonnie until it was time for them to leave. She had a basket of laundry to take to the Laundromat while Bonnie was in school. She planned out the day step by step. Take Bonnie to school all the way downtown, a special school for exceptional children, where she would stay until noon. By then the laundry would be done, and she would pick up Bonnie and bring her home. Her friend Charlotte and her daughter would come at twelve-thirty and take Bonnie home for the afternoon while Iris was at work, and Iris would collect her again at six. Back home, supper, read to Bonnie, or play a game or two, put her to bed, and then finally Iris would be able to relax. It would be another long day.

Rick got a call to bring the car around to Mr. Wellington's office by nine that morning. He felt groggy and stupid; he had slept very little in spite of being exhausted, or maybe, he thought, because of it. He put on cream-color slacks and a matching shirt, and a navy linen jacket. He knew he looked good in the outfit. He did not see the Impala that morning.

Wellington's business was on Santa Monica, a large showroom downstairs full of imports from South America, and offices upstairs. There was a parking structure behind the building. Rick had been inside the showroom only once and had not been impressed. He liked Chinese stuff, he had decided, jade and ivory, things with gleam or glitter, delicate-looking things; but all the stuff here was eerie, it gave him the creeps. The offices, on the other hand, were very fine. There was thick white carpeting, gold-framed pictures, golden statues, some big plants in brass pots. Mr. Wellington's desk was six feet by four, black with curved and carved legs, and leather tooling on top in a pattern that Rick had never been able to make out all the way. Pyramids and temples, and the weird flying snake.

Mr. Wellington did not get up from his desk when Rick entered. He was a thin-faced man of fifty or so, with gray hair. He was dressed in the only clothes Rick had ever seen him wear: gray silk suit, white silk shirt, maroon tie, polished black shoes. To Rick's eye he looked like an insurance salesman, or a mortician.

That morning Rick realized just how afraid of Wellington he truly was; he never had given it any real thought before, but he never had done anything out of line before either. He stood a few feet from the desk with his hands behind his back, the way he had seen Wellington's secretary Lerner stand, and he waited for Wellington to speak first, as Lerner had instructed him three years before.

"It went well yesterday?" Wellington's voice was almost without expression, like a computer voice.

"Yes, sir. No problems."

"And you took a child with you." His voice did not change at all, but Rick felt his hands go wet.

"Yes, sir. I thought, going to a zoo, it would seem natural to have a kid, not be there by myself."

"Whose child was it?"

Rick swallowed. "Just a kid." Quickly he added, "She doesn't know anything, sir. It was just a day at the zoo for her."

"What's there to know, Rick? As you say, it was just a day at the zoo."

"Nothing. There's nothing to know. I drove down to the zoo and back, that's all."

Wellington nodded; he opened the top desk drawer and brought out something Rick could not see. He looked at it, then opened his hand over the desk and two miniature elephants fell to the surface. One was a male with long tusks, the other was smaller, a female.

Both men stared at the animals. Wellington moved them apart with one long narrow finger. He kept his gaze on them.

"I'll give them back to her," Rick said fast. "She won't even know she left them behind."

"I'm afraid we have a little problem," Wellington said without a change of expression. "You see, the upholstery was loose on the back of the passenger seat. There's a space there. That's where these were found, in that space. I'm afraid that if she looked for them on the way home, she might have been puzzled by certain differences she encountered."

Rick shook his head. "She didn't. I put her up front with me. She slept."

"Perhaps. But what if she did notice? You do see the problem, don't you, Rick?"

"Look, Mr. Wellington, I'm sorry. That was a dumb thing for me to do, but I thought it would make it look legit if I took a kid to the zoo. You know what I mean? And the kid, she's a baby, and she's okay, I mean even if she noticed anything like that, and she didn't. But even if she did, she's okay. She can't talk. There's something wrong with her and she can't talk, not a word. She couldn't tell even if there was anything for her to tell, and there isn't. I mean, she slept in the front on the way home."

"Your child? You never mentioned a wife, a child."

"I'm sorry. It just never came up. We split a long time ago."

33

"No, of course it wouldn't have come up, would it? You are so young. What, twenty-one, twenty-two?"

"Twenty-three in June, sir."

"I see." He pressed a button on his phone and told Lerner to come, and then said to Rick, "Wait in the outer office."

Rick passed Lerner at the door. Lerner was over six feet, blond, movie-star handsome, in his thirties. He grinned affably at Rick as he entered and pulled the door closed after him. Rick nodded at the receptionist and kept walking.

His fear swelled and ebbed, swelled again. He walked fast, slowed down so he would not be conspicuous, then nearly ran. Maybe Wellington had counted on this, he thought, panicked, counted on his running, leading them to Bonnie. He caught a bus and left it, took a cab and left it, walked some more. Not to the apartment. No one could still be following him, but what if they were? He spotted a clothing store and entered, bought jeans, a sweatshirt, and changed clothes, carried his gorgeous linen jacket, his silk-wool slacks and polyester shirt in the bag. He made himself stop to think finally, outside an arcade that included a hot dog stand. He bought a Coke and sat at a small table with it, trying not to psych out everyone in his line of vision. Had that guy been behind him a couple blocks back? That one? He shut his eyes.

Bonnie went to that special school. Iris would pick her up around noon. It was vague, what Iris had said about it. He knew where the school was—Iris had bitched about having to drive so far—but he had no idea where he was now. Step one, he decided, meet Iris and tell her to run with Bonnie, give him time to straighten everything out. He would talk to Wellington again, explain. There was nothing to explain, he told himself, trying desperately to believe it. He had not done anything terrible, but he would play it cagey, buy some insurance, after all. Iris would need money. He found a phone book and looked up the address for a branch of his bank and took a cab to it, and then another one to the school where he walked back and forth until he became fearful that someone would report him to the cops: suspicious character loitering outside a school. He headed away from the school, and two blocks from it he saw the old Dodge outside a Laundromat.

Iris looked awfully white in there. The place was mostly full of Chicanos, and a few black women, and pale, blond Iris. There was a pile of stuff on a counter; she was folding clothes, laying them in the basket.

She blanched when she saw him. "What happened? What's wrong?"

"Come on." He swept the stuff off the counter into the basket and grabbed it up, hurried to the door.

She was clutching his arm. "What happened? Where's Bonnie?"

"Still in school. Listen, there's a problem." He reached the Dodge and jerked the back door open, shoved the basket inside and swung around to face her. She looked terrified.

"What did you do?" she asked hoarsely.

"Never mind. Look, here's some money, it's all I've got. Take it! Get Bonnie and take off for a couple of weeks. Take a little vacation."

"What have you done?" she whispered, ignoring the bills he thrust at her. "God, what have you done?"

He grabbed her purse and shoved the wad of bills into it. "Damn you, listen to me! You've got to get Bonnie away for a while. Don't come back until—" He realized there was no way to know what *until* might mean. "Call my sister first. I'll be in touch with her when it's okay for you to come back. Stay out of sight, keep Bonnie out of sight. Go as far as you can. Now. Don't go back to your place first. Just go!"

She stood as if paralyzed, her eyes enormous, her face

a ghastly, dead white. Abruptly she wheeled and ran around the car and pulled the door open.

"Tell Bonnie . . ."

"Go to hell!" she cried, and started the car, making it jerk and backfire.

A very large black woman laughed raucously and yelled, "Good for you, honey! Good for you! Lordy, Lordy, it's a time of changes!"

Iris had never been so frightened in her twenty-two years as that moment when the car surged ahead, leaving Rick open-mouthed, yelling something at her. Ten minutes later she had Bonnie in the car and was heading toward the coast highway, the only road she trusted her old car on. North; she had to go north. South was Mexico, east the desert; she had to go north.

4

▼ ▼ ▼ ▼

Iris had stopped in a supermarket in Santa Barbara to buy peanut butter and grape jelly, bread, apples, milk and cookies. At a 7-Eleven she got a large container of coffee for herself, and they picnicked at a beach, but the wind was blowing in hard and the sky had become threatening. Neither felt like exploring the beach, or lingering any longer than it took to eat and use the rest room. Although Iris knew her terror had communicated itself to Bonnie, she was powerless to hide it. When she tried to talk, to voice reassurances, the words stalled in her throat; she felt as if a tight band had been wrapped around her neck. Even breathing was difficult.

She tried to plan, but her brain had gone mushy, and instead of the future, she kept thinking of the past, remembering when she had run away with Rick. He had been the best-looking boy in high school, and she had been an honors student, and somehow they had blown it all. She could no longer remember why. Her mother? Too easy, she thought with dissatisfaction. A lot of mothers became born again and their daughters did not run away at sixteen. Her optometrist father who was never around for his child? Again, too easy. Too many fathers were that shortsighted. She could blame no one, finally, just Tucson and the desert and her own misery and boredom and the demands of a surging sexuality that had overwhelmed her.

She had been so afraid that time, also. They left school together in his car, this car, newly waxed, polished, with a new tune-up, good tires, and they had started driving, up past Phoenix, north and west to Nevada, to Las Vegas where they both lied about their ages and played the slots and lost sixty dollars, exactly half of what they had left by then. They had gotten married in a tiny, stifling room that had peach-colored, fat cupids suspended by fishing lines from the ceiling.

It would be okay, Rick had said again and again, and now she knew that he had been as frightened as she, but at the time she had not realized that, and had believed it would be okay. On to Los Angeles, to great jobs, probably in the movies or on television, or modeling. Either of them could have been a model in those days. Now she just felt old and skinny and tired all the time. Mostly tired all the time. Then Rick had joined a gang that did something awful. She suspected drugs, but she had not asked, and in fact had refused to let him tell her anything three years ago, the first time he had come home to their two rooms with any real money. Hundreds of dollars in cash. Laid out on the wobbly table it had seemed a fortune. Bonnie had been asleep in the next room, their silent daughter who was heart-stoppingly beautiful. That night she had realized that she was afraid of him, afraid he would bring home AIDS, or drugs, or gang members, or something worse, even though she could not define what might be worse. They did not talk, they never had talked; she had screamed at him to get out, and in relief he had gone. Now she knew what could be worse—a threat to their daughter. This morning Rick had been as afraid as she, and that was terrifying. What had he done? How could he have done anything to expose Bonnie to those people? She knew he adored the child as much as she did; yet he had done something to put her at risk. Finally she could identify one of the emotions that was tightening her throat, constricting her chest: It was hatred. She hated him with more passion than her love for him had ever aroused.

Bonnie was fidgeting restlessly, and she had to stop again to let the child get in the backseat. "We'll make you a nest of towels and your blanket, and let's see what else . . ." She arranged the clean laundry, trying to make Bonnie comfortable. Before she could settle herself behind the wheel, the storm hit with a dismaying ferocity, and she sat clutching the steering wheel wanting to weep. She did not trust her tires enough to drive an unknown road in a blinding rainstorm.

Bonnie had jumped to her feet and now rested her chin on the back of the seat, staring out the windshield at the torrent. Iris patted her hand and eased in the clutch. "Tell you what," she said, trying to sound cheerful and reassuring, "we'll stop at the very next town we see and go to a motel and watch television until the rain stops. Okay?"

She knew no one was following her. Somewhere back there she had missed her turn and was on a state road, not 101, but that was all right. This road had less traffic than 101, and everything that appeared in her rearview mirror caught up, passed her, and vanished. It would be all right to stop as soon as she could, and get some rest, and maybe tonight her head would not be filled with cotton, maybe while Bonnie slept she would be able to think of something she could do.

She did not notice when the features of the landscape changed, when the mountain rose to her right. It seemed that the rain had eased slightly, and for a moment she was tempted to keep driving, then she saw the sign: CAMBIO BAY, 3 MILES. She read it as Cameo Bay; the name conjured up an image carved in ivory, ageless and serene, non-threatening. She made the turn.

She stopped at a small grocery store that had a café attached, intending to buy Bonnie something to drink, a treat, ice cream, just something. But the café seemed full of young people in roisterous good spirits, yelling back and forth, playing with each other while a balding man in an apron moved among them unhurriedly with orders. The students appeared to Iris as foreign as aliens from another world.

Clutching Bonnie's hand tightly, she veered and entered the grocery instead. There was a frozen-food chest. She found ice cream bars and took two to the checkout. A middle-age woman rang up the purchase.

"Is there a motel here?" Iris asked.

The woman looked at her, then at Bonnie, and nodded. "But I doubt you'd want to be there with them." She motioned toward the shouting young people in the café. "I'd say Miss Luisa's place would be a better bet. House-keeping rooms. By the day, or week, or month, I guess. Anyway, she wouldn't let that crowd in her place, so it'll be quiet, let the little girl sleep."

And expensive, Iris added silently, but if she bought food here, they would save on dinner and breakfast, she could make a lunch to carry tomorrow . . . She nodded. "Thanks. Where is it?"

The woman gave instructions; Iris bought hot dogs and soup and cereal, milk and juice, and the smallest jar of instant coffee she could find, and they were ready to go out again into the driving rain, to find Miss Luisa's house.

The town was so small, it would have been impossible

to miss the way. Down a few blocks to the end of Main Street, a left turn, follow the street to the end where the driveway wound up to the big gray house on the point. She paused when the house came into view; it was much bigger than she had been prepared for, monstrous, with balconies and turrets and gables. The rain came down more fiercely, hiding the house now. They would stay one night, even if she couldn't afford it. One night of peace and rest and warmth. She was shivering; among the clean clothes in the basket had been a hooded cotton jacket for Bonnie, but she had nothing comparable, and she was wet and cold. She drove up the winding street, up the curving driveway, and stopped at the front of the house, still far enough to get soaked again walking from the car to the porch.

Then she saw a tall figure on the porch, waving to her, motioning to her. She leaned over Bonnie and opened the window. The person was waving for her to drive around the house. She nodded and followed the driveway around the side to a wide covered area, a second entrance, out of the rain, sheltered by the house from the wind coming in off the ocean.

"Come in, dear," a voice called from the porch, which apparently wrapped around the entire ground floor of the building.

Iris got out of the car, hurried to open Bonnie's door and then hesitated. "I'm looking for Miss Luisa's Guest House," she said to the woman on the porch.

"I know. Come in. Come in. This way." She held open a wide door, and Iris and Bonnie followed her inside.

The woman at the store must have called, Iris thought, shivering hard, grateful for the warmth of the house. As soon as the door closed behind them, the sounds of the wind and rain vanished; inside, it was warm and the air was heady with the fragrance of baking bread.

"This way," the woman said, leading them through a

hall, into another one, on into a kitchen. Iris blinked. She had assumed they were going to the front entrance, a registration desk. She looked hard at the woman who had ushered them into the kitchen: tall and lean, middle-aged, with kind dark eyes. Her hair was gray, with wispy tendrils about her face, and a large, old-fashioned bun in the back. Her dress was mid-calf length, with long sleeves, the kind of dress Iris remembered her grandmother wearing.

Everything had become dreamlike. There was a large round table, a checked yellow-and-white cloth on it, laid with cups and small plates; there was a fireplace with a small, crackling fire; there was a little round woman at an oversized stove removing bread, clucking to it softly, pleased with the golden-brown loaves. She brought one to the table and placed it on a cutting board; the tall woman poured hot chocolate, as the round woman cut into the bread, passed it hot and steaming to Iris, who found herself seated, with a light blanket around her shoulders. Bonnie was seated also, in a chair that was exactly the right size, the right height; she had already begun to eat a piece of the hot bread dripping with butter.

"This is Martica," the woman was saying. "And, of course, I'm Luisa." The plump woman nodded, smiling broadly. "And he's Julio. He'll bring in your things and put the car around back."

Iris had not seen Julio enter, but when he held out his hand for the car keys, she brought them from her pocket and handed them to him. He was smiling, a brown man with downy white hair, almost as round as Martica. Iris swallowed chocolate and suddenly set her cup down.

"Wait," she called to Julio, who grinned at her and kept going. She turned to Miss Luisa. "Tell him to wait. We have to discuss the room. That is, I'm looking for a room for me and my daughter."

Miss Luisa nodded. "Of course. They are actually little

apartments, housekeeping rooms, I believe they're called. I don't let out single rooms, you see."

"But how much are they? And all this? The food, the hot chocolate? I don't have a lot of money, and I just want a room for tonight. The storm . . ."

"Yes, the storm. Isn't it a wonderful storm!" She left her seat at the round table, crossed the kitchen, and opened drapes at wide windows overlooking the ocean. Bonnie jumped up and joined her at the window; she leaned forward with her hands on a low sill, her nose against the glass almost.

Iris stood up, both hands pressing hard on the tabletop. "Bonnie, come back here! Miss Luisa, please, just tell me how much the rooms are. I think we will probably have to go to the motel."

"Come, my child," Luisa said to Bonnie. "I'll move your chair so you can see out. And then maybe a little strawberry jam on your bread." She smiled gently at Iris as she moved Bonnie's chair. "Is one twenty-five too much, dear?"

Iris took a deep breath and nodded. "I'm sorry," she said. "I should have brought up the price before we accepted your food. How much for the bread and chocolate?"

"I could come down a bit, you know. One hundred. How is that? And, of course, our hospitality has no price attached. How ridiculous! Martica is offended."

Martica had gone to a cabinet and now returned with a little blue pot of jam. She cut another piece of bread for Bonnie, buttered it, and added jam this time. She smiled at the child and patted her on the head as she started to eat again.

"And as far as staying just one night is concerned," Miss Luisa went on, "we'll just have to wait and see, won't we? You know the roads have washed out. It might take a few days for maintenance people to get here and put in temporary roads. It might be the end of the week. Anyway, when you get ready to leave, we'll prorate the bill and charge only for the days you actually stay with us. Really, my dear child, you can't do better at the motel. I believe the least expensive room they have, and it's a single room, mind you, is twenty-five a night."

Iris sat down weakly. "Prorate? One hundred dollars? That isn't daily?"

Miss Luisa looked horrified. "Oh my no! Monthly. I charge monthly rates only and adjust them according to the length of your stay."

"I didn't know the roads washed out," Iris said slowly. "We just came in from Los . . . from the south."

"Both directions," Miss Luisa said.

"But we just drove in," Iris said again. "How do you know?"

Miss Luisa waved vaguely. "Oh well, people tell me things. Now, about the rooms, you'll want television, naturally, for the child to watch now and then. They all do like the cartoons, don't they? And an ocean view. It won't keep on storming, you know."

Iris looked at her, then at Martica, the warm and cheerful kitchen with the blazing fire, the storm beyond the windows. Dreaming, she told herself, and soon she would wake up and be cold and tired again, and afraid again. But for the moment, the dream was irresistible. She drew in a long breath and felt her eyes burning.

"My dear child," Miss Luisa said, "you can rest now. You are perfectly safe here."

Safe from what? Iris thought. The storm? Roads washing away? A car with bald tires? Rick and whatever danger he threatened?

But if the roads had really washed out, then no one could come after her and Bonnie yet. For a day or two, maybe she really was safe, Bonnie was safe.

When they finished the hot chocolate and could eat no

more bread, Miss Luisa guided Iris and Bonnie to their rooms. Bonnie skipped at her side, even took her hand, and Iris followed, trying to make sense of the many halls and stairs and doors, both open and closed. One room was a library.

"It's simple to find," Miss Luisa said over her shoulder to Iris who had slowed at the doorway. "Just come down the front stairs and turn right. The door is always open, the light always on. You can't miss it."

Then she opened another door and ushered Bonnie through, and motioned to Iris. "I hope you like these rooms. I'm fond of them myself, such a nice view from here. But the second bedroom is rather small, I'm afraid."

Iris gave her a searching look; she had started to think Miss Luisa was mocking her, but the other woman's expression was one of concern. "We're not used to a second bedroom," Iris said. "Bonnie is used to sleeping with me."

"Well, if she wants to, then of course you will continue that way. Perhaps she will like her own room for a time. It's through there."

There was a living room with a folding door that opened to reveal a small kitchen. One door from the living room led to a child's bedroom with a twin-sized bed covered by a quilt in gay colors. The walls were pink and creamy white, the curtains pink, a bookcase with many books, a chest of drawers painted white with animal decals behind knobs on the drawers . . . Bonnie stopped in her tracks just inside the room, then spun around and hugged Miss Luisa, hugged Iris.

"Well," Iris said faintly. "That seems to be settled."

"I thought she might like it," Miss Luisa said, a touch smugly.

The other bedroom had another quilt on a larger bed, comfortable furniture that included a rocking chair before wide windows overlooking the ocean. There were a few magazines on a table, a few books on another one. The basket of laundry was at the foot of the bed. Neither woman mentioned it.

Miss Luisa glanced about, nodded in satisfaction, and said, "I'll leave you alone now, dear. You get some rest. You look very tired." She walked back through the living room, to the door, and turned, smiling at Iris. "Please feel free to use everything in here that you want. Everything, dear. Have a good rest."

"Thank you," Iris said. "You're so kind—" Miss Luisa left, pulling the door closed behind her. Slowly Iris went to it and turned the lock. Los Angeles, Rick, her jobs at Sizzler and the movie theater all seemed very far away, unreal. She took a deep breath, another. Bonnie came to her, took her hand, wanting to lead her somewhere, to the bathroom, the kitchen. Laughing, Iris followed, and they began to explore the apartment together.

At that moment Rick was in a dark bar nursing a beer. He did not especially like beer, but he needed to be in out of the pounding rain, someplace dark, where he could try to plan, where no one would bother him for a while. He would give Iris another day to hole up. She would make it to San Francisco sometime tomorrow early. He felt certain she would head north, try to lose herself and Bonnie in a big city. They used to talk about moving up to Frisco, or Berkeley, or Oakland, back when they still had dreams that included both of them. So late tomorrow he'd go back to Wellington and make him understand that taking the kid to the zoo had made real sense. He had shown initiative, that was all. And Bonnie couldn't be a threat to anyone. He'd explain about her talking, how she couldn't, how the doctors said to give her time, wait, but that waiting hadn't helped yet. And besides, she had been in the front seat, sleeping. He gnawed his lip, remembering how she had kept scrabbling around on the floor, looking for the damn elephants. She had been searching for them, she knew they should have been where she had left them. She was smart, with a good memory, she just couldn't talk. But Wellington didn't have to know that. Let him think she was a dummy, the way they thought in school. Special school for exceptional children! Retards, that's what they meant, but she was smart, all right. Iris knew it and so did he.

As far as Wellington was concerned, the kid was a retard, deaf and dumb. Hadn't been able to learn to sign even. They told Iris they wanted to start her in a school for sign language, and Iris said no, not yet. The doctors said to wait. Rick shook his head hard, trying to clear it of Iris, doctors, just keep in mind what he had to tell Wellington, convince Wellington. He could stay out of sight for another day, and by tomorrow night he would have a good story ready, he told himself, and gnawed his lip.

Stuart Wellington stood in his rich office facing out, watching the wind-driven rain march across the street as if in platoons, one following another with uncanny regularity. Behind him Lerner was finishing the report: no Rick, no Iris, no child. Not yet. But they would find them within twenty-four hours, if they were still in the city. Wellington nodded. And if they had left the city? They would still find them; it might take a little longer.

He had made a mistake, Wellington admitted silently, aware that Lerner was waiting for new instructions. He had underestimated Rick, or at least misjudged him. A gust of wind drove rain against the window, inches from his face, and he backed away fretfully. He hated the wind and the low-pressure troughs that roared through the city now and then, filling the streets with swirling, filthy water. He sat behind his desk and regarded Lerner with as little expression as he usually displayed. He motioned for Lerner to be seated also, and thought another few seconds, to finish the scenario he was forming in his mind.

"There are several alternatives," he said finally, in his precise way. "They have all run together, or he has sent the woman and child away, or she has independently left. If you find them together, they can be handled together, but if they have separated, he must be dealt with before anyone approaches the child."

For a second there was a flicker on Lerner's face. It vanished swiftly and he nodded. Sometimes Wellington solicited an opinion from Lerner; he had few secrets from him. He almost asked for a second opinion now; the reason he did not do so was his certainty that Lerner would not approve. The child was only five, barely five, and she was mute. As Rick had protested, she was no threat, even if she knew anything. She couldn't understand what she knew, and she could not communicate it. He was fascinated by the thought of having information locked up in one's head, exactly as the information on the Rosetta Stone had been locked up for centuries. Would anyone ever find the key to that child's information? Probably not. Why would anyone bother? He could see the plausibility of this one face of reason; the other side was more complicated. He did not explain it to Lerner because he did not believe in explanations to subordinates.

Rick had made a mistake. Taking the child with him had been a mistake for which he would have been forgiven after proper chastisement. After his punishment he would have been a better employee, in fact. His real error had been that he had disobeyed a direct order, and he had lied. Neither of those could be forgiven. The fact that Rick had withdrawn money from his account, the fact that his wife and child had gone somewhere without returning home to pack, made it certain that he had warned them away. And that meant that the child had noticed the difference in the car. He had underestimated Rick in that he had not understood his devotion to his daughter. A man who loved his child enough to put his own life at risk was dangerous, especially if that man knew as much as Rick knew. He was too dangerous to live.

"If Rick sent them away," he said then, "he probably will wait until he thinks they are safely hidden and then he will come back to try to bargain. If that is the case and he calls or shows up, find out what you can about his wife and child, especially if he has told the wife anything about his work. I doubt it, considering the kinds of jobs she has held, the fact that they have been apart for three years. But find out. And then kill him. We will take the next step after that, when we have more information."

This time no flicker crossed Lerner's face.

5

▼ ▼ ▼ ▼

Carolyn drove up to the general store in Cambio Bay and said, "I don't know about you, but if I'm going to be stuck here, there are a few necessities." She gave Boise Wilkes a sidelong glance and asked more diffidently, "You fixed okay for money?"

"My wallet's as wet as everything else about me, but plastic doesn't melt. And thanks."

She glanced out the windshield at the driving rain and shrugged. "It's not getting any better. Might as well do it, I guess." They both made a dash for the store. Not exactly a boutique, but good enough, she decided, surveying the interior. A few tables of clothes and a rack of women's wear on the left, men's department on the right, children in the rear. Jeans, a sweatshirt, a top or two, underwear . . .

She was finished and chatting with the clerk when Boise joined her, dressed in jeans and boots and a plaid shirt.

Now that his hair was drying, it was starting to curl. Brown hair, brown eyes, and he wasn't wearing any rings. She always noticed that and then chided herself for it. She grinned at him.

"Two choices. Motel with a bar, or Miss Luisa's Guest House, with housekeeping rooms or apartments. I'm for the motel."

"First the bar," he said. "I'm buying. Join me?"

"You betcha."

Now the clerk shook her head. She was gray-haired, with thick glasses. "You won't like the motel, not with all them college kids whooping it up like it was Mardi Gras or something."

"A pack of them got stranded too," Carolyn said in explanation.

Boise paid for his purchases with a credit card, and he and Carolyn stood outside the store under the overhang considering their next move. Neither of them suggested that they separate now that they were safe in a town. The rain drove in from the sea; rivulets ran down the gutter of the street; no other person was outside.

In the end they went to the grocery store and bought a few things, including bourbon and wine, and then headed for Miss Luisa's Guest House.

"My God, look at it!" Carolyn breathed when she drew up before the house on the point. There were gables and cupolas and balconies, steep roofs of red tile awash with the rain, a broad porch that ran out of sight around both sides, double doors with stained-glass panes. Four floors, maybe five, she thought, at least twenty-five rooms, maybe thirty, or even more. She could not see how far back the house extended.

The front door opened, and a short stout man stepped out carrying an oversize black umbrella. He hurried to the car and held the umbrella for Carolyn, escorted her to the

51

porch. Boise was right at their heels. The man opened the door and motioned for them to enter as he shook the umbrella before following them inside.

The lobby was small, with a desk and two potted orange trees. A neat little stand-up sign said LUISA'S GUEST HOUSE, LUISA RAVEL, PROPRIETOR. "Oh dear, oh dear," a woman exclaimed, coming from behind the desk. "You are both so wet. Oh dear, are you stranded too?"

She was tall and straight, with black hair drawn back almost too severely at first glance, but then it seemed just right for her. Her facial bones were fine, her skin unblemished, without makeup. Her eyes were beautiful, very dark with thick straight lashes. She could have been any age from thirty to fifty. Her clothes did not help determine her age—a simple black skirt that came midway down her calves and a long-sleeved white shirt that looked like silk.

Carolyn's appraisal was swift, but before she finished and was prepared to answer the question, Boise was talking.

"My car got caught in a slide and this kind lady rescued me. So, yes, we're stranded, all right."

Shit, Carolyn thought with resignation, as he cleared up their arriving together with almost indecent speed. If this woman was his type, she, Carolyn, obviously didn't have a chance. She nodded. "We have no idea how long we'll be staying. All I need is a simple room with a shower."

"How awful!" the woman breathed, her eyes wide. "You must have been terrified. I'd guess what you really need is a drink first, and then inspect the rooms." She looked from Carolyn to Boise. "If you have things you want brought in, Julio will get them for you and move your car around to the side, out of the weather. If you want him to, I mean."

Without hesitation Carolyn handed over her car keys. Julio ducked his head, opened the front door, and vanished out to the porch.

"Please, come this way. I'm Luisa Ravel." She pronounced it to rhyme with gavel.

They introduced themselves and followed her through another doorway into a spacious corridor lighted by two chandeliers glowing softly. Carolyn caught her breath again, as she had done outside the house. The corridor had a long rug runner in a pattern she was not familiar with, vaguely Kerman, vaguely Navajo. Pale paneling that looked like pecan rose about four feet; above it the walls were covered with flocked paper in a soft peach color with traceries of violet and green. The ceiling was fifteen feet high at least, finished with creamy carved wood in leaf and flower designs. Carolyn felt her hand being tugged by Boise and moved again. They went past doors on both sides of the corridor, some open, some closed, all carved, with faceted, tear-shaped crystal knobs that reflected the chandelier lights in prismatic radiance. Some of the rooms were lighted, others dark—parlors, a library, a music room, a television room . . .

There had been stairs, two staircases, she thought dazedly, and they had left the main corridor for a narrower one, and then left it . . . Now they were in a room overlooking the sea and the storm turning it to froth. This room had half a dozen small tables with chairs, a massive bar finished in dark wood with matching stools, and a spinet piano.

Carolyn sank down into one of the chairs and gazed at the rain streaking past the window, suddenly immersed in a sharp childhood memory. She played weird games, she had been told repeatedly by her mother and her sister and two brothers. For years she had collected pictures of furniture, cut from magazines, from newspaper advertisements, circulars. She had shoe boxes filled with paper furniture, all carefully matched for scale and a style that suited her. Sometimes she laid out rooms—bedrooms, dining rooms, living rooms, playrooms—all exquisitely fur-

53

nished, in harmony to a mysterious inner system she felt and could not explain. She covered her bedroom floor with her furniture, but in her mind's eye houses rose, mansions grew, castles towered; in her mind's eye her furniture occupied three-dimensional space more real to her than any dollhouse. In fact, she had never played with dolls or dollhouses. Her constructions were much more elaborate than any physical building could have been.

And this house, she suddenly thought, was what she had been attempting to build thirty years ago. She had thought, *When I grow up, this is the kind of house I want.* And Luisa's Guest House was the house she had built in her head. Even the furnishings were what she had ordered, searched page after page for, tried to draw when her magazines failed. She remembered the goose bumpy sensation she had felt the day she finally found a spinet piano . . .

"Carolyn?"

She snapped back at the sound of her name. Boise touched her hand on the tabletop.

"Are you okay?"

"Fine," she said quickly, aware that she had heard nothing from the time they had entered the bar. A mixed drink was on the table in front of her. She tasted it—vodka and bitter lemon. She must have ordered it; she could think of nothing she wanted more at that moment.

"Well, I'll leave you to decide," Luisa said. "If you want another drink, please help yourself. Julio will show you to your rooms when you're ready. Just touch the bell on the bar here. See you later."

She left without a sound. Boise's gaze followed her, then dwelled on the open doorway.

"Decide what?" Carolyn asked.

Boise turned and regarded her thoughtfully. "You've been gone somewhere, haven't you? Did you hear anything we said?"

She hesitated, then shook her head and lifted her drink again.

He looked puzzled. "Well, there aren't any single rooms, just apartments, some bigger than others. Price one hundred twenty-five a month. I said we'd both take one. And she invited us to join her for dinner, to celebrate our safe landing in the storm." He finished off his own drink and shook his head. "If we can find the dining room. This is the damnedest house I've ever seen."

Again Carolyn felt the disorientation she had felt only moments before. She heard her older brother's voice asking sarcastically, "How can you find your way to the dining room when there aren't any walls or anything?" "You just think yourself there," she had said. And that was right for this house, too. She felt certain that she could find the dining room, or her own apartment, or the wine cellar in the basement, or the highest turret room, any room. She knew how to do it, if only she could remember.

She did not protest when Boise summoned Julio to guide them to their apartments. She wanted a shower, and a few minutes of quiet, time to think, maybe even take a short nap before dinner. Julio led them through halls they had not seen previously, up short flights of stairs, down a few steps, twisting and turning in a maze-like way. He finally stopped at a door, opened it, and bowed to Carolyn.

"Your room, miss," he said politely as he moved aside for her to enter.

"Where is his room?" she asked.

Julio nodded down the hallway. "Up the steps on the left, first door after."

Boise grinned. "See you in a while." He and Julio continued on down the hallway, and she entered her room and closed the door.

The living room had a sofa in a muted teal-blue brocade,

cherry coffee table, end tables, crystal lamps with Tiffany shades . . . In the bedroom was a four-poster bed, also cherry, with fluted posts that gleamed in a rich patina. The rugs were Chinese. She touched the one in the bedroom—silk. Dazed, she went into the tiny kitchen to find it fully equipped down to a copper hood over an electric stove and a copper carousel from which hung an assortment of gleaming pots, pans, skillets . . . On a counter was her bag of groceries. She drew out the bourbon she had bought earlier and found a glass in a cabinet, opened the refrigerator for ice cubes, and was drawn up short again. The refrigerator was stocked: butter, eggs, jam, fruit in a crisper drawer, cheeses, bacon in the meat drawer, and two bottles of white wine.

Finally she poured her drink, added an ice cube and a splash of water, and returned to the living room where she sat in a cherry rocking chair at the window overlooking the sea. The rain obscured the vista, sheeting in hard in horizontal waves. No sound of the storm disturbed the silence.

She did not turn to look at the room again, but she knew there would be a desk—an escritoire, she corrected herself—with spindly legs and three drawers that would no doubt hold writing materials. And at the high poster bed, a little stool covered with real needlepoint . . . She drank deeply, suddenly chilled.

Iris jerked awake when Bonnie touched her arm. Iris was stretched out on the couch in the living room, although she had not intended to fall asleep. She could not even remember the last time she had slept while Bonnie was up and active. She sat up blinking and then heard a tap on the door. The child had already gone to open it.

"My dear, I'm sorry. Were you resting? And I disturbed

you. I'm so sorry." Miss Luisa stood in the doorway. Bonnie took her hand and drew her into the room.

"I wasn't really sleeping," Iris said quickly. "Well, I must have dozed a bit. It's so quiet after all the storm and the drive . . ."

"It is a quiet house, isn't it? I just wanted to make sure you have everything you need, everything Bonnie needs. And," she went on without waiting for a response, "I wanted to invite you to dine with a few of us tonight. We have several guests who have been stranded by the storm."

Iris had already started to shake her head before Miss Luisa finished speaking. Miss Luisa smiled at her and turned her gaze to Bonnie. "Actually, I'm an emissary for Martica. She asked if it would be too impertinent if she invited Bonnie to have dinner with her and Julio. She misses her grandchildren, you see."

Bonnie was nodding; she looked imploringly at Iris, nodding harder, her eyes very big, the way they could get, and very bright blue.

"But that's too generous . . ." Iris started.

Miss Luisa held up her hand. "I believe she's making gingerbread for dessert already, and she's planning chicken and dumplings. Of course, she'll spoil the child no end, if you'll let her." She laughed and added, "Actually, I think what she hopes is that you'll let her read to Bonnie down in the kitchen after dinner. Would you like that, dear?" she asked Bonnie.

The child nodded again and took Miss Luisa's hand as if it had been settled. Two grandmothers, Iris thought weakly, after years of having none at all. She felt tears hot in her eyes and said, "You're both very kind."

Miss Luisa shook her head, suddenly grave. Iris felt a wrench of yearning, as if she never had been looked at with more warmth and even love than in that moment. If only her mother had ever looked at her like that. "My dear," Miss Luisa said after a pause, "you have brought us this delightful child and you are willing to share her. It is you who are kind. We both thank you." Then very briskly she said, "Now, our dinner will be at seven in the main dining room. Bottom of the stairs, two doors left. And since our other guests have been stranded without luggage, the dress will be completely informal. Shall we go down to the kitchen and keep Martica company, Bonnie?"

Iris watched them out of sight, listening to Miss Luisa's voice until it faded: "Now, darling, if Martica doesn't always speak English, we just pretend we understand anyway. Just nod and smile and she'll remember and speak your language again presently. She used to sing to her granddaughters. I suspect she'll sing to you, too. I believe one of them was a dancer at a very young age, about your age . . ."

Slowly Iris closed the door. The tears that had stung before now rolled down her cheeks as relief melted the core of ice that had been holding her upright. Relief from a tension that had been more unbearable than she had realized. Safe, she thought, taking a shuddering breath as the tears stopped. She had brought Bonnie to safety.

His mother had named him Tyler Carrington (her maiden name) Wilkes, but his father had called him Boise from the first day. All through school he had been T. C. Wilkes. He stood at the window watching the lashing rain until darkness hid it the way the rain had hidden the ocean. He opened his window a crack in order to hear the storm that seemed intent on raging through the night. The wind screamed through the small opening, and that was better than the quiet it displaced.

He held a drink, but the glass was hardly touched. He

was going over and over his own panic reaction to the mudslide, marveling that he had fought death like a madman, that he had shaken like a schoolgirl after the danger had passed. And without hesitation he had told Carolyn that his name was Boise. He had not used that name since childhood, had never used it, in fact; his father had used it for him. He should call his father, he thought almost absently. But why the hell had he dragged out that nickname now?

He was also considering Luisa Ravel; who was she? What was she? For an instant he had seen Elaine in her, but it had been fleeting and when gone left no trace. But there had been something, something. A blurring around the edges, he thought bleakly, and knew that was wrong. Elaine had been mad, had seen the world through a strange blur that was unfathomable to him, but her edges had been hard and sharp until the end. For four months he had been moving on, moving on, leaving the past, always leaving the past, and it had been working. But now, with this woman, Luisa Ravel, this screwball house, the mudslide, everything had come undone. He felt his frustration mount because that was wrong, too. His near death was responsible for his black mood; it was that simple. His panic, the shame he felt because of it, that was responsible.

He had been stupid, a fool, to believe that the past was already fading to acceptability. He rubbed his eyes, trying to remember the months he had been driving, the places he had been, what he had seen, where he had slept, anything. The four-month interlude was like a memory so far removed that the knowledge of having had such a memory was the only trace he could find now. What he remembered was the last night he had seen Elaine.

"I believe I'm pregnant, darling," she had drawled. She had become stick-thin on a kooky diet. That night she had worn a body stocking with purple-and-green blotches randomly spaced; her pale hair was cut short and spiky. (Pale hair, he said under his breath; bottle-platinum, nothing like Luisa's black hair.) That night he had watched Elaine silently, on guard.

"Unfortunately, the child isn't yours."

"Have you talked to Malik about it?" Malik was her psychiatrist.

"No. I won't. What we'll do is go to France. I'd like to live in France, wouldn't you? For a few years." Her eyes were lovely: hazel, large, luminous.

"We'll go to the doctor tomorrow," he had said. "Maybe you're mistaken."

She smiled, moving about the room languidly. She had decorated it in mauve and orange, with a lot of brass. It was very ugly. "No doctors. A midwife. A French midwife."

Once he had loved her, he reminded himself that night. He said, "We probably should tell the prospective father, don't you think?"

She shook her head. "He says I can't have it." She pressed both hands against her flat stomach. Her hip bones jutted out like sails. "But I won't let him near me again. I'll tell him I was joking, that it's your child. Your son." Her eyes became vague, and she looked about the hideous room as if searching for something. "Where is he, Tyler? Where is he?"

"I have to go now, Elaine. I'll see you tomorrow."

She drifted toward him. "So soon? But we have plans to make. I think I'd like to go by ship this time. A long cruise would be such fun."

She reached out to him. Her hand was skeletal; she was wearing an emerald ring and half a dozen jangly bracelets. Her nails were mandarin-long, painted purple, pointed. That was the last time he ever saw her. He went from her apartment to a pay phone and called Malik, and when the doctor tried to soothe him, he hung up and called Elaine's father.

At three in the morning, with her father sleeping on her sofa, Elaine Wilkes either fell or jumped out of the seventh-floor window. The next day Boise had started to drive. And this was as good a place as any to bury the car for a while. He lifted his glass and drank.

Harold Ritchie was humming happily as he brushed his hair and then leaned closer to the mirror to inspect his teeth. Satisfied, he turned off the bathroom light and entered his little living room. It was looking more and more like home, he thought, at first with contentment and then with near dismay. All this stuff to be packed up when he moved on. Today alone he had bought half a dozen books, and there was a stack by the leather chair that he favored, and yet another by the desk that held his computer and printer.

And what a day it had been, he mused, humming. The old lady had been exactly right in her prediction: storm before three. Roads washed out and everything, a real Pacific storm, and he had experienced it, just as his friends had advised. He would have to write to Herman and Betsy first thing tomorrow and tell them about it. He often told himself he had to write to someone or other, to share an experience, to rave about a new book or a play he had attended, but he seldom did so. He suspected none of them would care, that, in fact, they were bored, or too amused, by his enthusiasms. This day of the great storm he had been as excited as a boy, running from window to window to look at the rain, the wind, almost hoping for a tidal wave or something, and then learning that the roads had washed out! He felt it was almost his fault because his wish had been so fervent for something big to happen. Just like a boy. He could think of no one who would truly understand and appreciate what this meant to him.

And now Miss Luisa had invited him to dinner. This was a first, he felt certain. She probably did not entertain her guests often. Again, it was special, because of the storm, the mudslide. It was all too much, he thought, nearly manic with joy. He had found a lovely used-book store that had yielded two very old books about the myths of the West Coast. He had had a beautiful lunch of crab and avocado salad, more than his daily quota for cholesterol, no doubt, and tonight a dinner party. He felt like skipping as he left his apartment to go find the dining room. His only regret was that he had no one he could tell.

At the head of the main stairs was a young woman, just starting to descend. She noticed him and nodded pleasantly, then looked beyond him and stifled a scream; her hand flew to her mouth and clapped against it.

He turned to see what had startled her so; there was only Martica hurrying along on one of her never-ending chores. Her plump little body moved faster than he would have thought possible. He looked again at the woman on the stairs. She was very pale, hysterical, he thought with disquiet. Possibly even ill.

"Are you all right?" he asked as he approached her. "I'm Harold Ritchie, a guest here. That's just Martica, you know. She works around the place."

Carolyn looked at him finally. "I thought . . . she was someone else," she said slowly. "I'm Carolyn Engleman," she added. The Indian woman she had just seen was dressed in a nice shirtwaist dress, tan, with long sleeves. She wore sensible low-heeled shoes. And she was round, plump, with a round plump face; the other Indian woman had worn a shapeless gray sack down to her ankles, and she had appeared more angular, perhaps a bit younger. The differences were real and they were vast, but the instant that this Indian woman, Martica, had looked at her directly, there had been a shock of recognition, and Carolyn had known that the last time she had seen her had been up the mountain at Jeffers's joke of a ranch.

6

▼ ▼ ▼ ▼

Dinner started with a clear soup enlivened by shreds of smoky black mushrooms, tiny rings of brilliant green scallions, and cut-up pink Pacific shrimp. The tureen was a deep crystal bowl that was flawless; the soup swirled in shifting traceries of black, green, and pink when Miss Luisa stirred it before ladling it into crystal bowls. She crowned the first serving with a dollop of whipped sour cream and a sprig of parsley, and surveyed it with narrowed eyes.

"Pretty, isn't it? I like food to be pretty."

Already the steaming soup was melting the cream; streamers that looked like smoke spiraled gently in the bowl. She set it down before Iris and started to ladle a second bowl.

Iris and Harold Ritchie were to her left, Carolyn and Boise to her right. They sat at one end of a dining table that could have served a dozen more. At the far end of the table was a mammoth arrangement of flowers in every

hue and texture, and at this end the decoration was simpler: a shallow dish of bronze chrysanthemums flanked by
two candles, a cut-glass decanter of pale wine, gleaming
silver . . . It looked like a page out of *House Beautiful*,
Carolyn thought, keeping a watchful silence. When they
had all been served, the cream making constantly changing
designs in five small bowls now drew and held the gazes
of all. Carolyn finally tasted the soup and very nearly
nodded. Food out of *Gourmet*.

Across the table from Carolyn, Harold Ritchie was saying to Iris "The stories are absolutely fascinating! I had
no idea the mythology of the West was so rich. It's as
many-layered as the Greek or Roman mythos, or the
Egyptian, as any on earth, I am certain. The story of
Coyote as Firebringer is a variation of Prometheus, but
without the punishment. That's what makes it so en-
thralling. Western civilization created such vengeful gods,
so full of wrath, but the Amerinds had no need for all
that, apparently. Of course, I am a newcomer to the subject, but it is so exciting. Do you know where Coyote
stored the fire he stole? In trees. It's still there today waiting to be released. Isn't that lovely!"

Iris looked confused by his enthusiasm. Carolyn grinned
at her helplessly, and at the head of the table Miss Luisa
smiled.

"Would anyone like more soup?" She glanced at them
and nodded. "While we wait for our fish, let me tell you
one of the stories you won't find in any of your books,
Mr. Ritchie. There are many such stories, remembered
by fewer and fewer of the people, I'm afraid. Julio and
Martica know many of them, of course. This is one that
I heard as a child."

God, Harold Ritchie thought in dismay, he would need
a tape recorder, too. If only he had thought of it before.
Julio entered the dining room and began to clear the table
efficiently and silently.

"When the world was new," Miss Luisa said, "Great Chief and Squaw lived in their longhouse on a high point overlooking Cambio Bay. While Great Chief was ordering the heavens, Squaw strode through the valleys and over the mountains and plains scattering bundles of sticks and mud. Where she paused, tepees rose, longhouses sprang up, adobes grew and the people roamed the lands. Then Great Chief said, Why are there so many people, and yet we have no child of our own?"

Julio rolled a serving cart to the table. Harold Ritchie could have cursed at the interruption, but Miss Luisa paid no heed to the business going on at her side as Julio uncovered a silver platter on which lay a baked salmon adorned with half slices of lime so thinly cut they were transparent, overlapped like scales. He placed the platter before Miss Luisa, added serving bowls of vegetables, and plates, and withdrew again, all without making a sound. Miss Luisa began to put servings of the fish and vegetables on plates stacked before her. She continued her story throughout.

"Squaw agreed with Great Chief that they also should have a child, and she brought forth a daughter. The girl grew up as swift as the hare, as gentle as a doe, as playful as the otter, with a voice sweeter than the sweetest bird . . . and so on," Miss Luisa said with a smile. She had served them all and they began to eat again.

"As time went by, the girl grew to be the loveliest maiden of all. Squaw said, We must find her a husband soon. But Great Chief said, Not yet. There is time enough. And the year passed, and again Squaw said, We must find a husband for our daughter, and once more Great Chief said no. Now Squaw called Crow and said, Fly to the farthest tepees and the highest adobes and the greatest longhouses and tell the people that the maiden is the loveliest of all. Soon the braves and warriors began to arrive to see the maiden and bid for her hand."

Miss Luisa laughed suddenly and shook her head. "Look at you! You're not eating your dinner."

With a start, Boise realized that was true. He and Carolyn exchanged glances, his puzzled again, hers warier than ever. Across the table Iris looked guilty and began to eat as a scolded child might, and Harold expelled a breath as if he had been holding it too long. He laughed also and took a bite.

"This is the best dinner I've had on the coast yet," he said, and then blushed because it sounded like the obligatory praise that he detested.

Miss Luisa ate quietly for a minute or so, poured more wine for Carolyn and asked her to pass the decanter on to Boise. They were enchanted, Iris thought suddenly, all of them were enchanted. She ducked her head swiftly, afraid her eyes might be sparkling too much with the wonder of the idea of enchantment. When she glanced at Miss Luisa a moment later, she was met with a soft smile, a secret smile as if the woman understood her thought exactly. Again Iris saw her as the mother she never knew, the warm and understanding and accepting mother she had yearned for without being able to name what it was she was lacking, what her need meant to her.

Boise watched the shared moment between the painfully thin girl and the beautiful, sophisticated woman who was their hostess, and he wondered what Luisa Ravel saw in the girl, what it was that had been communicated between them, why the girl was even there. When Iris had been introduced, there had been mention of a child, but that was ridiculous; she was a child herself. She looked to him to be no more than seventeen, maybe sixteen. He felt irritated, even annoyed that those two had a secret, Luisa Ravel and Iris. No last name, he remembered. Just Iris. Maybe that was the secret, her last name. He continued to eat his dinner, which was superb.

Harold Ritchie was in an agony of indecision. The food

was too good not to keep eating, and it would be boorish to ask Miss Luisa to interrupt her dinner in order to finish the story. But what if she forgot she was in the middle of it? What if she fell asleep at the table? God, he thought then, what if she had actually forgotten the rest of the story? She must have heard it eighty years ago; she said as a child. What happened next? he wanted to scream at her. Go on with it. Instead, he served himself more fish when she turned the platter toward him with a slight smile.

To Carolyn it seemed that the atmosphere at the table had changed drastically from near somnolence to a rising tension that had no cause. No one had said or done anything awful or even rude, but the tension was there, and the fact that she could not account for it made her more uneasy than ever. Luisa knew what had brought it about, she realized, gazing at the woman at the head of the table. Who are you? she wanted to demand. What she saw no longer was enough: forty, handsome, articulate, and perfectly comfortable in spite of the charge in the air. Carolyn sipped her wine and watched and waited.

Luisa raised her glass and regarded it thoughtfully, and took a sip. "Well," she said, "when Great Chief saw the young men arriving in droves, he began to criticize them. One was too short, one too fat, or too tall, or had crooked legs, or a weak back, on and on. Each one was sent away until only two warriors remained. During the night, as they slept wrapped in their blankets, Squaw slipped out of the longhouse and went to them and with her own hands molded each of them to perfection. The next morning she sent the maiden to awaken the two last suitors. The maiden fell in love with both of them instantly. This time, when Great Chief said one was too short, the girl laughed; when he said the other had crooked legs, she laughed even harder.

"Great Chief was perplexed. Then he said he would have to test the young men. They had to bring a deer before dusk. Squaw sent them both a deer. He said they had to have a large salmon before dawn. Squaw sent them salmon. And so on. All right he said finally, without good grace. Let them catch her. He knew the maiden was as swift as the wind, but he did not know that Squaw had molded the braves with her own hands. Let them go to the beach, he said, grumbling. She will start first, and if one of them catches her before she reaches the stony arm of the mountain where it curls around the shore, that one will marry her."

Luisa must have signaled with a foot button, Boise thought, when Julio appeared to clear the table again. As before, Luisa paid no attention to him, issued no orders. She continued the story as he moved around the table.

"No sooner had the race started when Great Chief realized he had been tricked, and that one of the young men would actually catch the maiden as she flew across the sand. With a howl of rage he called Wind and ordered it to carry the girl across the bay and leave her there unharmed. And then he cried in a voice like thunder, Return and scour this side of the beach. Hurl both these bozos into the ocean."

Boise laughed and even Carolyn smiled now. Harold looked at them, shocked.

"Well, Wind had already taken the maiden across the bay before Great Chief finished speaking, but now, as quick as thought, Squaw waved her hand, and the young men were turned into stone pillars that Wind could not budge, and across the bay the maiden was also turned into stone. Squaw raised both hands and said in a voice like an earthquake, There they will all stand until her shadow falls on one of them, and him will she marry. And as for you, out of my longhouse!"

Luisa poured herself more wine now and drank thirstily. "I didn't remember how long this story was," she said. "But it's nearly over, thank heaven. Anyway, Great Chief stormed around and tried to undo the spell, but the earth and the creatures thereof belonged to Squaw, and there was nothing he could do about that. What he could do finally was shift the moon and sun just a little so that her shadow never quite reaches either young brave. It wanders south in summer and north in winter and never reaches her lover." She nodded gravely, then laughed. "Tomorrow there will be sunshine, and you can see Tres Indios and the shadow for yourselves. Now, for dessert, we have walnut mousse. And coffee." Magically, Julio was there to serve it.

Iris left to put Bonnie to bed; Harold jabbered excitedly about the story—the first Amerind story he had heard, he went on and on, that indicated a sharing of powers by a female and male deity. He was urging Luisa to agree to tell it again for a tape recorder, to tell any others that she remembered before they were all lost. Boise finished his coffee, still studying Luisa every time he thought she might not notice. Carolyn was thinking about the Indian woman who presumably was Martica, and presumably lived here and had not been at Jeffers's ranch. There was nothing else she could think. The woman couldn't have gotten from there to here ahead of Carolyn and Boise. But she could have, she contradicted herself instantly. There had been a decrepit truck up there. She could have driven straight down to Cambio Bay. But why? Why not? She tried to stem the dialogue in her head, but it continued with unanswerable questions and ridiculous answers. Iris returned, holding the hand of a beautiful child whom she introduced.

"Bonnie wanted to say good night. And I . . . It was a lovely dinner," she said shyly. "Thank you very much." Bonnie ran to Luisa who leaned down to her; she threw her arms around Luisa's neck and kissed her cheek, and Iris flushed when Luisa stood up and kissed her on the forehead.

"Good night," Iris whispered, and fled. At the doorway, Bonnie looked back and waved; her eyes were dancing, brilliant blue lights.

Boise was riveted; seeing that tiny, perfect creature had brought back his sense of wonder at another child, his son, whose hands had been so tiny, each finger perfect, each toe. Each fingernail a marvel of perfection in such an impossibly small scale. His smile had been brilliant, his eyes gleaming, just as Bonnie's eyes had gleamed and flashed. He started at the sound of Harold's voice.

"I'll go, too," Harold said. "I'll write down your story before I forget any of it. Maybe I'll be able to buy a tape recorder in Cambio Bay tomorrow. The store must have one. I wonder if the roads will be cleared yet, just in case I have to go to Santa Barbara again. But that's silly. That store has just about everything . . ." He left the small group, talking.

"Isn't it nice that he's found such excitement again," Luisa said, smiling after him. "I'm sure he had that kind of excitement as a young man starting his first big research project, and now he has recaptured it. I'll walk you to your rooms, if you like."

Or even if we don't, that contrary part of Carolyn's mind said. It had been less invitation than order. It was time to go to their rooms.

They left the dining room by a different door from the one Carolyn and Boise had entered by; they went up different stairs, narrower and steeper, and, Carolyn thought with distrust, they rose higher. Then they were at her door saying good night, and she went inside. She waited only a few seconds to open the door and peer out; already the hallway was empty.

What she wanted was to talk to Boise. There was something screwball about this house, about Luisa, Martica, everything. The way Luisa treated Iris. She narrowed her eyes and began to pace. Iris was little more than a kid,

71

naive, pretty. Carolyn realized where her thoughts were taking her and came to a stop in the middle of the room. Iris had a child, she reminded herself; she wasn't that naive. And it wasn't any of her goddamn business, she finished angrily. She glanced at her watch. Boise would be in his room by now.

She opened her door and looked both ways, then slipped out and headed up the hall. Julio had said up the stairs on the left, first door after that. She walked slower, passing closed doors, in absolute silence. The whole house was silent, holding its breath, watching her. The grim thought made her shiver; she resisted the urge to whistle or hum, anything to make a sound. She came to a staircase, but it led downward.

Down there was the wide corridor with the beautiful rug and the chandeliers. Library, dining room, other general-use rooms, no bedrooms. She turned around and looked at the hall with its closed doors. No stairs leading up. Deliberately she began to walk the opposite way and continued the length of the hallway. No stairs leading up. She came to a different staircase that went down, this time into darkness, possibly the stairs Luisa had used in guiding them back to their rooms.

Julio must have lied about Boise's room. But why? He had said up the stairs on the left, had even pointed, and there were no stairs on the left. Behind one of the closed doors? She knew that was possible, but she did not believe it. Slowly she retraced her steps to her own door, and she realized that she could not have said how she knew it was hers. It was identical to all the others, carved, polished, with a lovely crystal knob that reflected available light with kaleidoscopic effect. Although she had not counted doors at any time, she knew this was hers as surely as if it had her name on a plaque on it. She stood before it in indecision, but there was nothing to do except enter. She couldn't go around trying doors to locate the stairs. She went inside, closed the door, and turned the lock.

She surveyed her apartment with disquiet. It was her dream apartment, an idealized apartment, the realization of a childhood fantasy, and it frightened her more than she could comprehend.

7

▼ ▼ ▼ ▼

Cambio Bay has a reduced population this night. People who went to work up in San Luis Obispo, or down in Santa Barbara, or points even farther away could not return; children cheered the news that the school buses would not make the trip home. The youngest ones are in private homes, teachers' homes, homes of parents of their classmates; some of the older high school boys and girls are at the YMCA, determined not to close their eyes all night, to savor this adventure.

In Cambio Bay the lights start going out early; it has been a day of stress for the adults. In the Cronin house there is a lot of giggling; the Cronins have not been separated from their two children a single night in eleven years. Spenser (Speedy) Tydall is still trying to figure out the best way to haul that car out of the mud. It will be a good job for him if he can get a handle on the best way to manage it. Of course, the insurance company will pay, not that poor guy. Hell of a thing, he broods, standing on

74

his porch listening to the wind. Hell of a note when the road sucks your car out from under you. He glances up at the house and thinks that he has never seen it entirely dark, not once in his sixty years. Well, maybe back during the blackouts, but this train of thought takes him down a different path, away from the house. The war and fire-bomb threats, blackouts, and now reparations. Concentration camps, for God's sake! The wind is dying down finally; tomorrow will be fair. Satisfied, he goes back inside. Might as well go on to bed, can't make any plans about that car until he sees it. Tomorrow he'll take the dude out in the truck and have a look, then decide.

In Luisa's house a light goes off and a different one comes on. Iris looks at Bonnie, who is sleeping so peacefully that Iris cannot carry out her intention of taking the child into the other bedroom so they can share a bed as they have been doing nightly for three years. When she finally goes to bed, she feels lonesome, abandoned even, but the feeling passes swiftly. She stretches out both hands; her fingertips come exactly to the sides of the bed. She stretches her legs one way, then the other, and now she is smiling. She has not had such a large bed all to herself since she left home at sixteen. The last time she was this relaxed was when she was under dope in the hospital having Bonnie. She knows the moment she starts to drift away, and the moment is intoxicating, delicious. She falls asleep smiling.

Carolyn read until the words blurred, and the book wobbled, and settled first on her stomach, and then to one side when she turned over away from the light. Now she is dreaming. She is laughing softly in her dream, watching the wavelets race to her toes, break up in confusion, and race in again. Down the beach the two handsome braves are regarding her surreptitiously, and she is pretending to be unaware of them. Her own glances in their direction are as surreptitious as theirs. Without transition, the way it happens in dreams, she is running as fast as the wind, and they are running after her, and still she is laughing with delight. She is the speeding figure on the beach, and also she is above her and looking from somewhere else. Then the dream changes and she runs even faster, desperate now not to be caught; the pursuers are monstrous, evil. The sand is too deep to continue running; it draws her down into it, each foot sinking, sinking. She is near exhaustion, and still the monsters behind her keep coming. She can hear their harsh breathing as she struggles to free one foot, the other. She cannot turn and look at them; to look at them is to die. She is mired now and cannot free herself from the sand that is as treacherous as quicksand. With a despairing cry she stretches out both arms as if in prayer, and the arms become wings that bear her up higher and higher, into the wind, facing seaward. The cry she makes this time is a scream of exultation.

Boise sat at his window, listening to the wind whistling through the narrow opening he had provided, and relived that night four months ago, and then on into the next day, the day he had started driving away. The police had called him at four in the morning. When he arrived at the ugly apartment, a doctor was there ministering to Elaine's father, who had been tranquilized to a zombielike state.

A police officer, a woman with red hair and hard eyes and a gentle voice, told him what happened. "We got the call from a patrol car. The window in her room was the only wide-open window on this side of the building, so we came up here to check first. Her father was asleep on the couch. No note."

Boise looked past her at his father-in-law, Jimmy Kamisky, who was the color of putty, with heavy stubble on his cheeks and chin. Jimmy Kamisky had been a state representative, mayor, alderman, and even a federal judge.

Now he was a seventy-year-old defeated man, his only daughter dead, his wife dead.

"The father says," the officer went on, "she was pregnant and afraid you'd make her abort the child. He says she told him you killed her other child."

He brought his gaze back to her with an effort, puzzled by the incongruity of her gentle voice and hard eyes.

"Talk to Rudolf Malik," he said. "Her psychiatrist. Can I go now?"

"Were you divorced, legally separated?"

"No."

"Then I'm afraid there will be some formalities, papers to sign. Can you come down to the office later this morning? Around ten?"

She told him an address, her name, and he started to leave, but paused at the door to look one more time at Elaine's father. *We killed her*, he said silently. *It took both of us, but we did it, old man.*

He went back to his apartment, stood under the shower for half an hour without thinking, and then called his lawyer, Terry Bruno. At nine he went to his lawyer's office.

"I talked to Malik," Terry said without any time wasted on small talk or condolences. "She wasn't pregnant. She belonged in an institution. You want me to handle everything?"

Boise nodded silently and Terry exploded in a red-faced rage. "Jesus Christ! Why didn't you divorce her like I told you to! Jesus H. Christ, what a goddamn mess!"

The next few hours were a blur. Boise sat around, drank coffee, and later drank bourbon. He signed some papers and talked to the red-haired officer with Terry at his side, and signed some more papers, and at three he was in his car, supposedly on his way home. The next time he noticed his surroundings, he was on a county road, floorboarding the Mazda, tears blinding him. It was getting dark.

He found a place where he could pull over, and sat there until his tears stopped, his shaking stopped. "You're out of it," Terry had said. "Beat it. Take off a few days, get away. Get drunk. I'll handle everything."

Boise sat in his Mazda and stared at the road, one he never had seen before, and he turned the key, shifted, and started to drive.

He had stopped now and then to buy things he needed, underwear, a razor, once a sweater, a couple of shirts, just things. He had decided he needed a suitcase when he realized he was carrying things in tattered paper bags. And he had no idea of where he had driven, where he had stayed, what he had seen along the way.

He had hiked in some mountains somewhere, had bought a sleeping bag and slept under the stars somewhere, had stayed in motels and hotels, had eaten meals, even read books, but he had not picked up a map or a newspaper, had not turned on a television.

Now in Cambio Bay, in Luisa Ravel's guest house, he sits at the window and sees Jimmy Kamisky's gray face, sees Elaine in her body stocking with great splotches of the wrong colors. Journey's end, he is thinking, shouldn't bring with it the journey's beginning images, but his thoughts are becoming disconnected, incoherent, and he is drifting finally into sleep, sitting in the rocking chair, legs sprawled out, hand dangling over one arm of the chair.

His sleep is dreamless, the deathlike coma of utter exhaustion until a hand strokes his cheek in a fairy touch, as light as a whisper of air stirred into motion by butterfly wings.

He cannot move, his body is caught in the paralysis of deep sleep. "Sh." The voice is so soft the sound is like a sigh, not a spoken word. A finger traces his lips, and then warm lips cover his own for just a moment, an innocent kiss, a promise only. The gentle hands are on his chest, move down his body, to his thighs. They find his hands and draw him up from the chair and he can now respond. He catches her to him in an embrace and feels the warm soft breath on his neck, feels her back with his hands, strong and firm and pliant. Her breasts against his chest are firm. She pulls away and leads him to the other room, where she stops at the side of the bed and begins to unbutton his shirt.

He can see nothing. The blackness is total; it is more like being blind than being in the dark. He smells a fragrance of cloves, flowers from an old-fashioned garden. Her hair is silky and long, her skin more satiny than he knew skin could be.

Now with hands and lips and tongues they explore each other until he can stand it no longer and she guides him into herself. He comes quickly with an explosive intensity that makes him cry out.

"Sh," she murmurs. "It's been so long. Sh."

They rest; he strokes her body that is warm and moist all over. He pulls damp tendrils of hair from her cheek and kisses her temples, breathing in her fragrance, the spiciness of cloves, the musky scent of love. The next time he enters her, he controls his excitement better even as he is drawn into her deeper and deeper and this time it is she who gives in to near frenzy. The shared orgasm is like none he has ever experienced before. They fuse, they melt into each other, they become one; he feels her convulsive opening as his own, her responsive flood of release is his, and he knows that she is one with his heart-wrenching ejaculation. They cry out together and hold each other hard.

He feels her heart racing and his own thudding heavily. Where her body and his are joined from shoulders to thighs sweat has formed; when he shifts to avoid crushing her, there is a popping sound. She laughs in a low voice, and helps him roll over in such a way that they are not untangled. She draws her arm out from under his side; there seems to be no room for it at first. Again she laughs quietly and finally the arm is positioned between his chest and hers, her head rests in the hollow of his throat, and she sighs.

He opens his mouth to speak finally and she presses her finger against his lips, then removes it and touches his eyelids tenderly. "Sleep now," she murmurs.

In Cambio Bay the wind has become no more than a fitful breeze, as if out of petulance it is not yet willing to stop. The town is dark except for night-lights left burning here and there: a wavery light in the grocery store, the sputtering motel sign, a weak fluorescent blue flicker in Speedy's garage. In Miss Luisa's Guest House one light goes off, another comes on, the way they always do. Her guests are all sleeping now; their dreams are pleasant.

In the east the sky is showing streaks of paleness. There are still too many clouds for a proper dawn to break, but gradually the pale areas start to merge and grow and march across the sky. The bay the town is named after looks like a silver mirror in the pale morning light. The mirror has minor flaws, a very slight rising and falling motion that distorts the reflected image of the Indian maiden as she continues to gaze toward her suitors.

8

▼ ▼ ▼ ▼

Carolyn stood on the cliff overlooking the bay that sparkled in the sunlight and that was nearly as calm as a farm
pond. The college kids were down there already tossing
a Frisbee, chasing each other, not quite daring the water
yet. It was still cool. She saw Iris and Bonnie with Luisa.
Bonnie was a whirlwind of motion, darting this way and
that, picking up something, dashing back to her mother
to show her, running away again. She seemed to make up
with motion what she lacked in speech, and, in fact, her
flashing movements were eloquent, a spontaneous expression of delight and joy.

The stone arm of the mountain curled about the bay in
a protective attitude, warding off the north wind, taming
the westerlies. To the south the headland made another
barrier. The entrance to the bay from the sea was narrow,
no more than twenty feet, and obviously not navigable;
water foamed and sent up a spray where the sea encoun-

tered concealed rocks there. The tumult of the sea was barred; the bay was serene.

From the top of the cliff Carolyn could see the stone columns sharply defined, the maiden across the bay, and on this side, rising from the sand, the two warriors. Carolyn remembered her dream and smiled in self-derision.

Then she turned to walk around the guest house to the sheltered drive where her car was parked, in order to get film from her glove box. She paused long enough to finish the film already in her camera, getting the magnificent house from the side facing the sea, then the northern exposure. She knew those two shots were too hasty, but she wanted to use up this roll and start some serious photography. The house, the pillars, the town, everything. In the back of her mind an idea was forming that this could become a wonderful resort, a grand playground for those weary of L.A. and nearby beaches. The bay even looked swimmable, she had decided, studying it from above. Later she would go down to have a better look. Luisa Ravel was myopic; evidently she had no business sense, or else she simply had not considered the value of what she had here. She could charge over a hundred dollars a night and keep a full house. If there was space for horses, a tennis court, a heated pool . . . Carolyn hummed as she circled the house.

She was still taking pictures of the house when she saw Boise stride down the drive on his way to town. Earlier she had seen Harold leave. She wandered again to the back of the grounds and studied the garden there. It was a kitchen garden, protected by a high fence from the sea wind, apparently providing vegetables enough for a small army. Vegetables grew in neat raised beds, interplanted with beds of flowers and sprawling herbs. Carolyn knew little about gardening and recognized hardly anything that she saw. Beyond the garden were vines, berries of some sort, and farther back rhododendrons, and finally trees.

Plenty of room for a stable, she decided, getting more pictures, and she continued her stroll.

She wandered, snapping pictures now and then, and eventually followed a trail down to the beach where she stopped to take more snapshots. She spoke briefly to Iris and watched Bonnie playing in the sand, digging a moat, filling it with water, digging again seriously and happily. Carolyn took some pictures of Bonnie, and would have taken Iris's picture, but Iris shook her head and even put her hand up to her face. Carolyn shrugged and moved on.

Eventually her meanders took her into town, where she decided to have coffee. Before entering the café, she saw Boise coming down the street, and she raised the camera and snapped him, too. He seemed of a piece with the town, dressed in his jeans and boots, his plaid shirt. He waved and joined her.

"I'm having coffee," she said. "Want some?"

"Sure do." He looked disgusted. "It's going to take three or four days before they even start on clearing that piece of road that swallowed my car."

"Has anyone been up there yet to see how bad it all is?"

They ordered coffee before he answered. "Just got back. Speedy Tydall," he said with a slight grin, "took me in his pickup. Can't get close enough to spot the car, though. It's a whole new landscape. Might need a helicopter to haul it out of the muck."

"Well, Luisa probably can use company for a few days," Carolyn said lightly, and was surprised at the expression that crossed his face. Embarrassed? Troubled? She did not know him well enough to interpret that look.

He was thinking: It had not been Luisa. He was sure of that. And not Carolyn. Her hair was too short, too crinkly, Luisa's too long. Someone younger than either of them. Not Iris. She was too thin. A phantom lover, conjured out of some boyhood fantasy without a match in the real world? Even though he knew the phantom lover had not been Luisa, he was uneasy at the prospect of seeing her again today, and he was irritated at his unease.

The same balding man who had served the college crowd the day before now brought their coffee.

"Is there any news about a way out of here?" Carolyn asked him. "Will they work on the road heading north, do you know?"

"Hear they'll take a convoy out over the mountain," he said. "Logging road."

"Well," Carolyn said in satisfaction to Boise, "you can ride out with me, if you want." She called after the departing waiter, "Are the phones working yet?"

He shook his head. "Nope."

"How do they know about the convoy?" she muttered. Then, more decisively: "Boise, do you think there's something odd about this place, Luisa and her house, this town?"

"Like what?" he asked carefully. "Look, there are probably half a dozen short-wave radios in a town this size. No mystery."

But there was a mystery, he added to himself under his breath. Carolyn sensed it, and so did he. He finished his coffee and stood up. "I'll see if I can find out something about that convoy. My friendly garage man, Speedy, might know something. See you up at the house. I'll decide later if I want to trust a logging road up and over the mountain."

She nodded and watched him walk away. She knew she would not wait for him to collect information for her. She had planned on buying a few things at the grocery store adjoining the café, but she wouldn't have to if she could leave. Up and over the mountain and home, she had no doubt about her decision.

By the time she arrived back at the guest house, she had been assured by three different townspeople that the road maintenance crews were out putting up detour signs, making sure the roads were safe, and that she would be notified when the convoy was made up. It was those college kids, the motel owner had confided. Their mamas and daddies were having fits, and they had money, you know. If it was just the rest of them in town, they could stay for months before anyone would get around to doing anything.

She paused on the sidewalk to the guest house and raised her camera again. Luisa and Harold Ritchie were having a conversation before the wide porch. Luisa looked up and smiled as Carolyn advanced the film and aimed again. Perfect, Carolyn thought, perfect.

She entered the house and started to snap pictures of the interior, but it was unsatisfactory. Many of the doors that had been open were now closed, and she couldn't even find the spacious dining room without appearing to snoop. She went up to her room instead to collect the few things she had scattered about. And in the upper hallway, she stopped. There were the stairs Julio had said would lead to Boise's room.

She stood for a long time at the staircase leading upward. No door could conceal it; there was no door. Just an ordinary staircase, not ornate like the main one, not narrow and steep like the one Luisa had used to guide them to their rooms. A short, normal staircase, six steps up. She photographed it and then climbed the six stairs. At the top was one of the fancy doors, closed, and another short corridor with two other closed doors.

Without warning she was twisted by terror, and she ran back down the stairs, back to her own room, which she entered, and where she then stood with her back pressed hard against the door. "It can't be," she whispered. "It can't be!"

When her ragged breathing became more normal she moved again, this time to the desk with three drawers. She opened the middle one and found paper, pens, and pencils. Abruptly she drew back and pushed the drawer shut again. Not paper from this house. She went instead to the table where Julio had placed her briefcase and took out a notebook. The notebook had pages and pages of sketched house plans. She could draw any house she had ever entered, and often drew houses after strolling through. Her hurried sketches were accurate, in scale.

She sat at the desk and started to draw the ground floor of the guest house; after a minute she flipped to a clean page and started over. Too much space not accounted for, she thought savagely a moment later, and started over yet again. This time there were too many rooms, and they were too big.

She was still at the desk, frustrated and angry, when there was a knock on her door. Hastily she closed the notebook and stuffed it back into the briefcase, and then went to open the door.

"Hi," Boise said. "I'm playing Western Union. A bunch of people are going to leave from the motel in a couple of minutes. They want to know if you intend to tag along."

"God, yes! You?"

He shook his head, taken aback at her vehemence. "Guess not. I got hold of my insurance company. Phones are working again. Anyway, they think I should stick it out until an adjustor gets in from San Francisco, tomorrow or the next day." He shrugged. "They need to see the slide, personally, visually, the guy I talked to said. There are worse places to wait for an insurance company to move."

"I doubt it," she snapped. "I'll be ready in five minutes." She started to close the door, then asked, "Do you know if Iris is leaving?"

He shook his head. "Her tires are too bad to tackle a dirt road. She'll wait for repairs."

"Is Luisa around? I have to settle my bill. And will the convoy wait for me?"

"I'm sure they'll wait. I'll see if I can find Luisa. See you downstairs."

When she got to the small lobby a few minutes later, Boise was leaning against the front desk. "Luisa said to forget it, catch up next time. She's busy cutting flowers with Bonnie."

Angrily Carolyn rummaged in her oversized bag searching for her wallet. In it she had a twenty-dollar bill, a five, and two ones. She pulled out the twenty and slapped it down to the desk. "Tell her there won't be a next time, will you? See you around, Boise."

He picked up her grocery bag and walked out with her. "What happened, Carolyn? Why are you so . . . sore?" He had started to say frightened, and changed the word at the last second.

They had reached her Toyota. She yanked open the door on the passenger side and dumped her briefcase on the seat, took the bag from him and put it on the floor, then walked around the car and jerked the other door open.

"Take a look around, Boise. A good look. If I were you, I'd move to the motel. So long." She jerked the car when she started, and her wheels screamed when she got to the end of the driveway and made the turn to the street.

The students were in three cars; Carolyn followed them, and was followed by a salesman who had been in the motel when the storm hit. They were led by a state trooper. The road they used was a forest service road, kept in decent repair for the fire fighters. She drove with furious concentration, her gaze riveted on the car in front, on the gravelly surface of the road itself. She saw almost nothing else until she was once again on a real road heading home.

Back in west Los Angeles she detoured to Beverly Boulevard to drop off her film to be processed; she stopped at a grocery store for milk, cream, a steak. And then she went home. It was dark by then. She switched on lights as she moved through her house. It was a two-bedroom house, with a den, a fireplace in the living room, dinette space, a patio, a utility room with pantry space. A steal when she bought it, and worth nearly two hundred thousand now. But more important than that; she liked it. The rooms were spacious, with intelligently placed windows, and good acoustics throughout. An architect had designed it for himself and his bride, but she had shacked up with a film producer instead, and he had gone back to Boston. He would have given the house away to be rid of it. He almost did give it away.

Carolyn had furnished the house with sleek modern pieces, low and long pieces, with good wood and very good fabrics, all in grayed blues and greens and rust. Once, when it occurred to her that it was too contemporary, too expected somehow, she had brought in some things that were not expected—two pieces of silvered driftwood, a geode as big as a grapefruit, cut and polished to reveal sapphire spirals against a milky blue background, and some pottery pieces. One held a barrel cactus, bought because it could take the neglect she subjected houseplants to, and another held wilted and browning mixed flowers. She glowered at that one as she passed it, turning on lights, turning on her answering machine on her way to the kitchen.

She listened to the messages as she unloaded the various bags she had brought in with her, and prepared her steak on the stove-top broiler. There was nothing on the machine that she had to attend to right away. She sipped a fine dry burgundy as she tossed the salad, and then she sat down to eat. Already the mudslide, Luisa's house, Cambio Bay seemed very distant, not something that had happened to her. And she was dead tired.

When she finished eating, she contemplated the sink, full of dirty dishes from at least a week. The dishwasher would not cope, she thought with disgust, but she loaded them all anyway and decided to face those that had to have a hand scrub another time. Then she went back to the dinette table to have coffee, and finally to open and examine the notebook of sketches that had been such a bitch. A bitch, she repeated, and got up again to bring a pad of graph paper to the table. Soon she was cursing under her breath.

"All right," she muttered. "We'll try it piecemeal." She sketched in the entrance to the guest house, added the hallway beyond the door. Ten feet wide, two chandeliers, a music room, sitting room or something, closed door, dining room, closed door, wide staircase . . . She put down her pencil carefully, left the desk, and poured herself a glass of wine and sipped it standing over the drawing. All wrong.

She had been studying houses all her life. As a child she had built a thousand imaginary houses, had drawn houses again and again, floor plans, elevations, everything. She had studied architecture for more than a year before deciding that it was not for her. She had sold real estate for eight years; she had sold dozens of houses on the basis of her quick sketches; her observations about square feet of closet space, kitchen counters, window placement had helped her sell many others. Clients failed to notice things like that, but she always did. Always.

But she couldn't draw Miss Luisa's Guest House.

The next morning she picked up her snapshots at Wally Gilman's shop on her way to the office. She snubbed Laurence Banning for not being alarmed about her absence. He didn't notice the snub. And she showed the Wylie place to Greta and Herman Meyers. They all stood in frozen silence when two roaches scurried down the drain in the bathtub. The Wylie house was Pepto Bismol pink, with the two obligatory palms flanking the front entrance, and a sickly jade hedge, ten inches high, separating the property from its next-door neighbor, an arsenic-green two-story house that was identical to this one except for the color.

On the sidewalk in front of the house, Greta Meyers, very pink, corseted, and proper, said it wasn't what they had in mind. She did not meet Carolyn's gaze, seemed embarrassed by the whole thing, in fact. Maybe, she said timidly, not looking at her husband, they wouldn't find the right sort of place, maybe they should go back to Chicago.

"Shut your face," Herman growled. "What else you got?" he asked Carolyn.

He wanted a two-car garage, she wanted one floor. Under a hundred thousand, he snapped at Carolyn. Four bedrooms, upstairs, garage. One floor, his wife moaned.

Carolyn got rid of them at two. She suspected Herman would belt Greta as soon as they were alone. They were screaming at each other in front of their motel when she left them. She returned to the Banning Realty Company office on Beverly Boulevard. Rita Starr was at the front desk in the office. Rita was perhaps twenty, impeccably made up, her luxurious black hair a wonder of accidental styling that would not shift an inch in a hurricane.

"Wally Gilman said call him," she said when Carolyn passed her; she did not look up from *Variety*.

Carolyn sank into the chair behind her own desk and brought out the packet of snapshots Wally had developed overnight for her. She separated out the ones of the Jeffers house and ranch and scowled at them, then shrugged and put them aside for Laurence to see. Then she began to study the others, the pictures of Miss Luisa's Guest House and Cambio Bay.

After a minute or so her hands began to shake; she gripped the edge of her desk and looked about her familiar office as if to reassure herself that it was there, that it was real. A small space, two clients' chairs, a wall of pictures of Choice Properties, a window with vertical blinds, everything beige, walls, carpet, blind, furniture, picture frames. She closed her eyes hard, then opened them and looked again at the snapshots. All the Jeffers pictures were fine, sharp and clear. Good photography. There wasn't a single picture of the guest house that was in focus.

She found the two pictures of Bonnie; there was the beach, sharp, in focus, the bay, sparkling blue, the rocky arm of land beyond the bay, the black pillar of the maiden against the cloudless blue sky. That was the wide-angle shot. In it Bonnie was simply another blond little girl. The next shot, a closeup, had her against the blue of the bay waters. In it her hair shone like silver, her blue eyes gleamed. There were several freckles on her nose, all clear, unmistakable.

But not a picture of Luisa had come out. Not a picture of the guest house had come out. Smudges, blurs, indistinct figures, indistinct shadows, blotches of darkness against the sky, looming shadows . . .

Her hands were still shaking when she began to sort the pictures again, this time putting together those that were clear. The mission ruins, sharp, ocher-colored against the hill that rose behind them. Main Street in the village. Spencer Tydall's garage, the grocery store, the café sign, all clear and sharp. A good picture of Harold, looking at, speaking to shadows, backed up by shadows. That one went into the stack of dubious photographs. She stared for a long time at a snapshot of Boise, approaching her at the café entrance. Next to him was a little boy, four, five years old. She bit her lip. She added it to the stack that included Harold and the shadowy form.

She closed her eyes and visualized the garden, remembered how she had focused on a vibrant green broccoli head, then on a clump of flowers, carnations, pinks, something like that. There were no garden pictures.

She searched for and failed to find any snapshots of the

interior of the house—the corridor with the chandeliers, her own apartment with its fairy-tale furnishings, the stairs that led to Boise's door . . .

The shots from outside were of a large, gray structure, no details visible, no definition, just big and gray.

Her hands were shaking too hard to keep picking up and putting down the glossy photographs. She pushed her chair back from her desk and stood up and went to the one window with vertical blinds. She separated the slats and stared at the street beyond. Unending traffic, white concrete, straggly palm trees in containers before entrances of businesses—several other realty offices, a law firm, a school of some sort, Swedish massage. She let the blind fall back into place, suddenly aware of voices in the office.

Laurence had returned with clients. His voice was too loud, too cheerful—no sale yet. She swept the flawed photographs together and put them in her purse, and left, only vaguely aware that Rita was speaking to her, that Laurence might have called out her name.

She drove home without noticing traffic lights, other traffic, pedestrians, or anything else. Her house was on the side of a canyon in a subdivision called The Pines, developed more than twenty years ago, replanted with pine trees to justify the name. Her lawn faithfully turned brown every summer although at the moment it was green; there was a hedge with red trumpet flowers that were supposed to lure hummingbirds. She had never seen a hummingbird around. There were twin bayonet plants in her front lawn; they had been called century plants in the listing. If they bloomed, they died, she had read, and hoped they never bloomed.

She had a driveway, but no garage; she parked and entered her house, which was dim and cool, and built for people, on a human scale. She found herself standing inside the living room almost wanting to pat the walls, touch the woodwork. Angrily she went straight through to the kitchen where she got bourbon from a cabinet, ice and a glass, and poured several fingers and drank down most of it. She poured again, and this time took the glass to the patio. There was another ten feet of yard beyond the patio; then the canyon dropped down several hundred feet.

The view from her patio was spectacular, more so at night when the lights came on below her house, but very nice even in midafternoon. She narrowed her eyes, not seeing the scene before her. Whom did she know in Santa Barbara County who owed her a favor? she was thinking, going down a list of names. Finally she nodded to herself and went back inside, leaving the bourbon on the patio. She looked up the number for the Santa Barbara Courthouse and called Virginia Hazelip.

After telling Virginia what she needed, she made coffee and a sandwich, remembering now that she had not eaten lunch that day, that she had been out with those creeps all morning, and . . . When the phone rang she snatched it up before it sounded a second time.

"Are you sure?" she asked after listening a few minutes. "Did you double-check?"

Virginia said testily that she was sure, she had even checked the Cambio Bay plat, and they hung up, Carolyn feeling more frightened than ever. There was no listing in the tax files for Luisa Ravel or Miss Luisa's Guest House. According to the official records it simply did not exist.

9

▼ ▼ ▼ ▼

Maybe there was another Cambio Bay farther up the coast, up in San Luis Obispo County, she said to herself, but she did not even bother to check her map. She knew where she had been. Maybe it was a tax scam of some sort, she thought then; Luisa might have paid someone off to erase her. Could that be done? Carolyn moved to the table in her tiny dinette space and spread out the snap-shots. No picture of Luisa, no picture of her house or garden. She stood at the table and fought the trembling in her hands, in her legs. The photographs swam in and out of focus until she finally turned away from them.

She walked to the patio, feeling stiff-legged, jerky; she retrieved her drink, sipped, finally focusing her eyes on the the vista below that stretched out into a hazy distance. She knew that if she went inside to sketch the view out there, she would capture it. Not fine art, she never even pretended to be an artist, but faithful, in scale, with the proper depth. That was the kind of memory she had, good memory for details and an ability to reproduce them later. She had not learned the names of most of the trees and shrubs, the ornamentals imported from distant tropical lands, the native plants, but her fingers knew nothing of language; they could render a good facsimile of everything out there.

She told herself that she had been too tired the day before to sketch the guest house, that she had been too preoccupied with the mudslide, too shocked by the danger she had escaped, too everything, she finished irritably. She could close her eyes and see exactly how the driveway turned off the street up from the village. A second shallow curve, the wide porch that surrounded the whole house, double front doors with stained-glass panels. She knew the images in her head were true; the camera of her mind was more faithful than the expensive Olympus she had used.

She returned to the dinette table and pushed the snap-shots aside to make room for her pad of graph paper and tried once more to re-create Miss Luisa's Guest House. Very soon she was biting her lip in vexation and cursing under her breath.

After a few minutes she had to give up on the first floor, just as she had done before, she remembered with a chill. All right, she told herself firmly, and started on the second floor. Up the stairs to a hallway that stretched right and left. A few doors to her room, on the left. How many doors? She did not know. She sketched in her own apart-ment in rough rectangles, blocks of space that could be filled in later. Out the door to the hall again, turn right, three doors down, stairs on the left. Six steps. Boise's apartment at the top, on the right. She dropped the pencil and stared; she shook her head in denial of the rendering of the image in her mind.

The telephone rang, startling her. Normally she let her machine take calls, but she wanted to get away from the table, away from the insane house plans she was drawing. She hurried to the living room and snatched up the phone on the second ring.

"Hey, Carolyn! Wally here. Mind if I drop in? Got something to show you."

"Busy, Wally—" she started.

"Ten minutes, babe." He hung up.

She scowled at the phone and cradled it. Maybe he had messed up the photographs, she thought then, and was nearly overwhelmed with a feeling of relief. Something he had done had blurred them, the wrong chemicals, wrong timing, something. She went back to the table and sorted the pictures one more time. She put the good ones in her purse and left the blurred ones out to confront him with the evidence of his carelessness. Damn him, she was muttering by then, giving her the willies over nothing, making her act like a goddamn idiot. By the time the door chime sounded she was furious.

Wally Gilman was five three, fifty pounds overweight, with Harpo Marx ringlets. None of that would have mattered if he had not thought he was cute. He invariably wore a white T-shirt over chino pants, always rumpled, never ironed, and sneakers without socks. When it was cool weather he wore a plaid tan-and-green sports coat. He had the coat on that afternoon. He was a very good photography technician, the one Carolyn always used.

As he entered her house, he asked breathlessly, "Where are the pictures?" at the same time that she was saying "That's a shitty job you did."

He shoved his way past her. "Where are they? Let me see them. Get Packer to check out your damn camera."

She pointed toward the table and he rushed into the dinette and began to paw through the photographs. He looked up at her. "Not these. The ones with the kid. Where are they?"

She thought he meant the very good picture of Boise

with the child at his side, stowed away in her purse; she shook her head. "At the office, maybe. I left some there. These are the ones I'm sore about."

"Jesus," Wally said. "Listen, babe, you're a lousy photographer, but you've caught yourself a little gold mine. Where's the television?" He was gleaming with sweat, his eyes almost glassy with excitement.

"Hold it, Wally," she said, blocking him at the doorway to the den. "What's happening?"

"Want you to catch the local news," he said. "Come on, it's already started. Explain while we wait for the big story."

She led him into the den where he pounced at the television and tuned it to a local all-news station in the middle of a summary about the progress on repairing the washed-out roads. He turned the sound down and backed a step away from the set, wiping the sweat from his forehead with the back of his sleeve.

"I caught it on the noon 'Eyewitness News.' Left messages all over town for you to call. Even on your machine. Don't you play back the messages? What's the point in having it if you don't play them back? Anyway, it'll be on all the local news shows. They said it would be."

She crossed her arms and drew in a sharp breath. "For God's sake, what will be on?"

"Wait. You know who Stuart Wellington is?" When she shook her head, he said impatiently, "Sure you do. Wellington's South American Imports, and that's just what shows. One of his guys got knocked off this morning, and he's green-bile mad about it. Tell you, babe, I sure wouldn't want to be the one that cooled his boy. Wait, here it comes."

The bland announcer, with his improbable hair styled in such a way that he had to half turn his head in order to use both eyes, was talking about yet more gang killings. "And this morning, in order to protest these senseless killings, Stuart Wellington made the following announcement."

The camera made a sweep of the opulent office before it settled on Wellington at his desk. He appeared sober, sad. A prissy, gray man, Carolyn thought; his hands were tightly folded on his gorgeous desk as if he were in Sunday School waiting for his gold star. Carolyn watched, mystified, unable to make a connection between the citizens' council that Wellington was proposing and the picture she had taken of Boise. Wellington went on to offer a reward of ten thousand dollars for information leading to the arrest of those responsible for the death of his employee, Rick Lathan.

"Furthermore," Wellington continued, looking gravely into the camera, full face, "I will offer a reward of five thousand dollars to anyone who can furnish information concerning Mrs. Lathan and her daughter. Rick was a good man, a young man, conscientious and hard-working, devoted to his lovely wife and beautiful daughter. Have they also been slain? Have they fled in terror? Have you seen this mute little girl?" Now he turned over a picture that had been flat on his desk.

Carolyn had already steeled herself, as she realized he was talking about Iris and Bonnie, not Boise at all. Wellington was holding a picture of Bonnie.

The camera returned to the studio; in a hushed, breathless voice the newsman gave details of the drive-by shooting of Rick Lathan and the disappearance of his wife and child. There were a few more details about Bonnie collected from her special school and then a recapitulation of the council Wellington proposed to form and the rewards he was offering. Carolyn heard little of this.

"See, babe?" Wally said with a grin. "Not a big gold mine, not the mother lode, but good enough for a day's work. Figure you can cut me in for twenty-five percent, seems fair to me. Where are the pictures?"

She shook her head. "Maybe at the office with the others that turned out okay. I don't even remember her. You sure about this?"

"Babe, I processed that film, remember? Am I sure! Let's go get them."

"Just wait a minute!" she snapped. "Tell me what you meant, what you said about Wellington. Who is he?"

Wally looked murderous, but he said, "I don't know from nothing, Carolyn. Just rumors, talk. You know how it is. There's talk that he brings in stuff that he doesn't bother to register with the import office, that's all. And it's just talk."

"A crook," she murmured. "Why does he want the little girl?"

"Jeez, you heard him. He wants to see that she gets a doctor, education, stuff like that. It's a gesture, that's all. So it won't mean much in the long run, but in the short run it means five thousand. But you're not the only one who's seen the kid, you better believe. I mean, a kid who can't make a sound? People remember something like that. Someone else will pop in and collect. Now let's go get those damn photos. Where'd you snap them? Where are the negatives? They'll probably want them, too."

She shook her head. "Damned if I know. Usually they go in the file at the office. Probably I left them with the others. I told you, I wasn't paying that much attention to the good ones. I just brought the duds home."

Wally pushed past her and went to the table again, shuffled through the pictures. She was thinking furiously, uncertain why she was lying to him. If Rick Lathan had been killed today, Iris had already left him. Was she on the run? Had she been threatened? Aware that he had been threatened? No answers, just questions; she joined Wally at the table.

"I'll find the stuff tomorrow," she said.

"You crazy or something? Look, Carolyn, five thou

might not be a lot for you, but I can use a piece of it. You know what I mean? By tomorrow there could be a dozen reports about the kid. We get there first."

She shook her head. "That didn't even look like the same kid. Just a little kid with blond hair. There are a million like her on every beach in the state."

He gave her a scathing look, then motioned to the ruined photographs scattered across the table. "Look at them. Jesus, what a mess. I worked over them, Carolyn, trying to save what I could for you. Get that lousy camera checked out. But the point is, I worked over them, really studied them trying to see why some are so rotten and others pretty sharp. The kid's the same one. Believe me, I know."

She looked at her watch and said, "Not now. Tomorrow. I've got a date. I'll find the prints and the negatives in the morning and give you a call."

For a second she thought he might actually try to hit her, he looked so furious. His hands clenched, sweat beaded on his upper lip, made a film across his nose. A thousand lousy dollars, she thought in disgust. He backed off, stomped to the door, and paused to glare at her.

"Where'd you spot her?" he asked meanly.

She shrugged. "On my way to Santa Barbara. Just on a beach somewhere. How the hell do I know where I was? I stopped for a walk."

He yanked the door open and left, slammed it after him. She followed and locked it, then went to the living room where she pulled the drapes closed, locked the patio door.

When she returned to the table to pick up the photographs again, she suddenly wondered why Wellington hadn't shown a picture of Iris.

She sat down at the table in thought. He must not have had one. Bonnie's picture had looked like a school picture;

probably it had been in her father's wallet. But no picture of Iris? She frowned at the table, not seeing it, remembering how Iris had avoided having her picture taken on the beach. But she had left days before Rick was killed, Carolyn reminded herself; she couldn't be involved in his death. She shook her head and stood up briskly, started for the kitchen to make coffee and scrounge for dinner, then stopped again.

Wally might not wait until morning. If he had the pictures and the negatives, he could have all the money himself, not just one thousand. She had known Wally for seven years; she knew he would be thinking that way, as angry as he was with her. He would think he had given her a chance to split it, and now he would cut her out. She glanced again at her watch, then at the phone. No one would be in the office now. Would he break in? She nodded slowly. Probably. And he wouldn't find what he was looking for. Then what? She had said she had a date. Would he watch her house, make sure it was empty, and break in here, too? Again she nodded, more slowly, but with as much certainty.

She picked up everything from the table then and put it all in her purse, where she already had the small glassine envelope that held the negatives. She had intended to study them for a clue about why so many had failed. She stood without motion for a moment, trying to reason out what Wally would do if he failed to find the pictures anywhere. He wanted that money, and he was certain about what he had seen. Would that be enough for him to go to Wellington with?

She bit her lip and drew in a deep breath. Maybe, she admitted. Maybe it would be enough because Wally knew he had seen that child. Wellington was a complete unknown to her, beyond outguessing. Why did he want Bonnie and Iris? Why the reward? It was such a reasonable amount. Higher than that would seem suspicious, but five thousand was enough to make someone like Wally behave like a goon. A smart number, she conceded, and she wished she had never seen Iris and Bonnie, that she had refused to go out to Jeffers's ranch that day, wished she had not had the wild idea of turning the guest house into a real resort and taken so many pictures to fortify her idea. All she wanted was to be left alone, out of whatever trouble Iris was in.

But what she might get, she admitted with a shiver, was company: Wally, or Wally and others. And they would be able to take the pictures, or anything else they wanted, she also admitted, and now she ran through her house to her bedroom.

She began to pack hurriedly, just enough for a few days, to give things time to settle, to get in touch with Iris and warn her about the reward. What Iris did after that was her own business, but that was the least she could do. She would call her from a motel room, just repeat what had been on television, and she would get rid of the pictures of Bonnie, and the negatives, everything, and deny they had ever existed. If Wally made an ass out of himself, let him take the heat. Her anger mounted as she threw clothes into a suitcase, made a sweep of the bathroom, and then stopped once more at the table to pick up her graph-paper pad. Before she shoved it down into her briefcase, she ripped out a sheet and scrawled: *I lost what you were looking for. If you mess up my house I'll cut off your balls with nail clippers.* She weighted it down with her glass that still was a quarter full, and that reminded her to make a detour through the kitchen where she picked up the bottle, and wine, and forced them into the bulging briefcase, and the sandwich she had made earlier and had not yet tasted. She kept that in her hand. Then she left without turning off a single light. If he burgled her house, let him feel conspicuous, she thought bitterly.

It was six-thirty, and only a fool heads out for a freeway at that time, she thought, driving. As a realtor she had learned every back street, every ground street for a hundred miles, and she used that knowledge for the next hour, always heading north until it no longer seemed an act of insanity to merge into the Santa Barbara Freeway traffic. She thought of driving as flying on the freeways, or creeping on the ground; in her mind the two were practically unrelated. Now she hit seventy-five and held it there until she came to the Santa Barbara exit.

There had been no actual decision to head north, to Santa Barbara. She could have gone to Burbank, or to San Diego, or almost anywhere in the southern part of the state. She knew most of the areas well, and knew people in most areas, but she had turned north, as if, by retracing her trail, she stood a better chance of getting in touch with Iris, being done with this whole affair sooner.

She crawled through the motel cluster until she spotted a VACANCY sign and headed in, nodding in satisfaction; there was a seafood restaurant attached to the place. She checked in and called the realty office to tell the answering machine that she would be gone a few days. Next she called information for the number of Miss Luisa's Guest House, and nodded when the operator said they had no listing under that name. She hung up gently.

She had a shower and went to dinner; she bought a newspaper and found no mention of Rick Lathan's death, or Wellington's announcement; she watched television until the news came on, and there it was again, edited more than before, with Bonnie's picture. She studied her own pictures, and tried to draw the guest house again, and finally went to bed feeling dissatisfied, as if aware that every action she took, every move she made was being done without real thought now, mechanically. Going through the motions of being in charge, she told herself severely, and ordered herself to stop behaving like an idiot. She and her circle of friends took turns being sympathetic listeners; they understood the rules they played by; no one got really involved. It was not expected, would have been looked on with suspicion, in fact, as numbers flashed, wheels turned, debts and favors were weighed and measured against each other. Tacitly they agreed it wasn't worth it. And by damn, she grumbled in the stale-smelling motel room, she did not intend to get involved with a perfect stranger and her mess. Then she could fall asleep.

She dreamed she was approaching Luisa who waited on the porch, a friendly smile of welcome on her face. Carolyn came wide awake, and she knew she was going back, just not why.

10

▼　▼　▼　▼

When the Spanish priest left the trail on his mule to follow a faint path over the rocky projection that delivered him to the bay of sparkling waters, there were no more than a dozen Indians living near the shoreline. The priest had a moment of doubt that this was indeed the destination the Holy Father had intended, but on consulting his orders, he had to accept that his mission was to build a church here, convert natives here, live here until directed otherwise.

Through his guide, he spoke with the strange Indians who were tall and straight and much harder-looking than the three Indians who made up his entourage. "I shall build a church there," he said, indicating the point. Up there was nothing but rocks; the site's only attraction was its view of the sea. It would serve as a signaling place for the great Spanish fleet exploring the waters northward. The natives shook their heads.

Perhaps the guide did not understand; perhaps he chose

not to understand. The priest climbed up to the point, where he knelt clasping his breviary, and gave thanks to God for delivering him safely to this spot where he was to build a church. The native Indians watched him for a short time, then returned to their pursuits of fishing and gathering the abundant shellfish of the shallow bay.

He sent his guide to them to offer employment, wages for builders of God's church. The natives had lost the ability to comprehend or make themselves understood even minimally. Finally the priest had to bring in additional Indians from the south. The chief architect among them had built forts and temples on mountains so high that the air failed to support the eagle in flight. He had overseen the terracing of peaks so steep that even the llamas could not tread there. He had built channels for rivers so swift that even the fish dared not swim in them.

On arriving at the sheltered bay, he examined the headland, the point the priest had claimed, and he shook his head.

"Not here," he said.

"Here," the priest insisted.

The master architect shook his head again and now turned to survey the surrounding landscape, less barren here than most places along the coast, no doubt with springs of fresh water that nurtured the trees, that supplied those who lived on the shores of the bay.

Finally he said, "Here is the spirit house of my ancestors, and theirs, back to the time when the world was new. We build there." He pointed to the hillside opposite the point.

"Get out," the priest said in a cold fury. He would exorcise any spirits here, banish them back to hell and their master the Devil. If there were invisible spirits here in an invisible spirit house, he would cleanse the earth of them for all time.

The new Indians withdrew and joined the natives at a distance that permitted them all to watch the priest do battle with the spirits of the spirit house. They watched him chant his magic spells and cast his magic water on the ground as he called on his Great Spirit to come to his aid. They watched the woman spirit approach him and take his hand to lead him away out of sight. Then the Indians, natives and strangers alike, returned to the fires where fish were being baked and oysters were steaming in sea water heated to boiling with hot rocks.

In the morning the priest awakened at the mission site. He arose, uncertain of his surroundings, of the events of the previous night; when he looked at the point, he saw the spirit house. He fell to his knees in prayer. When his architect began to step off the ground for the mission on the hillside, he did not protest.

Harold Ritchie sat on the back porch and gazed at the ruins across the way on the hillside, clearly visible above the housetops between the guest house and the mission site. He closed his eyes hard and looked again. The late-afternoon sun lighted the adobe and rocks in sharp detail, with exquisite contrast. The air was still, and he could hear the pipes.

He looked at the book he had laid down only a moment ago. The story about building the mission had gone on to say that the builders, far from their own homes, had played their pipes in the evenings, to ease their pain and loneliness and to placate the spirits in the spirit house.

Harold knew it was a coincidence, a trick of a wind so slight that it did not even stir the trees, or else Julio or someone in the house was playing a strange instrument. He gazed at the ruins and moistened his lips. The music was hauntingly beautiful. At first he thought it had almost a childlike simplicity; but he realized gradually that it had the complexity of a Bach fugue, with a scale he did not know and combinations he never had heard before, and it

107

trembled with poignancy. Sad and sweet, he thought, and found himself leaving his chair, leaving the porch, going down the wide steps; he turned to leave the grounds on a path he had not noticed before as he began to walk toward the mission ruins.

Iris and Bonnie had brought a basket of shells up from the beach, most of them intact. They were on the lawn not far from the back porch. Bonnie was washing the shells in a bucket of water and arranging them on the grass in a pattern that probably made sense to her, but seemed random to Iris. Iris had learned not to try to help Bonnie arrange things. The child had a sense of order that was incomprehensible to her mother. Iris gazed past the child at the lovely garden. So many blooming flowers, butterflies, bees. The afternoon sun slanted down in tilted columns of ever-changing motes. A rising and falling insect dance caught the sunlight and gleamed, vanished, gleamed again. Paths wound through the garden, over there to the vegetables, another to vines in bloom, another to . . . She had no idea where most of them went. They vanished in the rampant growth too quickly, and none of them continued straight for more than a few feet.

Bonnie caught her attention then because of a new stillness in her posture. She was listening to something. Iris envied her keen hearing. Whatever it was, Iris could not hear it.

Bonnie glanced at the pattern of shells before her, added one more that she had been holding, and then picked up the bucket of water and walked with it to one of the many paths. Assuming she intended to empty it among the flowers, Iris waited, considering the design of pale shells against the lawn. It almost made sense, she thought after a minute or two, and abruptly realized that Bonnie had been gone too long. She stood up and looked around, then

called her. She called again, louder, and now she started
down the path the child had taken. "Bonnie, come on out.
Don't hide on me."

She wanted to keep her voice light, wanted it to sound
as if she were laughing, playing the game, but she heard
a stridency, a note of fear. She looked behind her. Already
the house was out of sight, hidden by shrubbery and trees,
and the paths branched and branched. "Bonnie!" she
yelled, and started to run.

Harold Ritchie was breathing hard by the time he
reached the hillside where the ruins began. The area was
almost barren, rubble-filled. In spite of the drenching rain
of the recent storm, it was dust-dry here. Old bricks poked
up from the pale ground, a foundation stood, part of a
wall with blank windows, no roof. A rotten timber was
at a slant, supported by cut rocks that were two feet by
three. The music had stopped.

Harold had been up here already, had found nothing of
interest among the mean little foundations of mean little
buildings. There was a garden area marked by a rock
boundary, weed-choked and ugly, and the main building,
a church presumably; several other buildings had been
erected, had fallen down again. Suddenly he uttered a cry
of surprise.

"Bonnie! What are you doing up here? Where's your
mother?"

The child stood at the corner of one of the buildings.
And the music had come back, louder, clearer than before.
He hurried to Bonnie and looked beyond her for Iris. The
child took his hand and tugged; he followed her several
steps, expecting to see Iris hurt, unconscious, something.
Then Bonnie stopped and pointed back the way he had
come.

The music was everywhere now, in his head, vibrating

in his bones, causing a shimmer before his eyes, as if he were inside a mirage gazing out through dancing molecules in the air. He looked across the village to the point and he saw the spirit house. The house was a stone structure against the blaze of sky filled with the afternoon sun. It was a longhouse built of monstrous timbers. It was a skin-covered great house. It was the mansion he knew with cupolas and balconies. It was a white unadorned building that looked like marble. The point was bare, with a straggly pine tree and many rocks. There was a brick building . . . Everything was vibrating, scintillating, flashing sparks . . .

He fell to his knees and pressed his hands hard against his eyes. When he took his hands away and opened his eyes again, the music was gone. Across the way was Miss Luisa's Guest House, looming dark against the bright sky.

"Bonnie," he whispered as soon as he could get the word out. "Bonnie?"

He was alone. He searched through the ruins, but he knew he was alone.

Iris fought the panic that weakened her knees and seized her diaphragm in a spasm that made breathing hurt. She took a step, then another, peering among the plants, not calling now. Another step, and she was back on the lawn. Bonnie was sitting where she had been before, rearranging her shells. When Iris whispered her name, she looked up as if preoccupied, and then she smiled her beautiful, radiant smile. Iris sank down to the grass beside her.

They were still in the sunlit patch of lawn when Julio appeared with a basket.

"Look," he said with a wide smile. "I show the little girl my whistles. Okay?" He waited before Iris with only a sidelong grin at Bonnie who was already on her feet trying to peer into the basket. It was about two feet across, hand-made, with an intricate design of dark and light strips, and little shells worked in here and there.

"Whistles?" Iris repeated helplessly.

"Yeah. In the forests the people don't see each other too good, you know? So they take the whistles, tie on belts, and when they want to talk, they blow the whistles. Look, jaguar whistle."

He held up an object that looked like a tiny clay cat, put it to his lips, and blew through it, a sweet, low sound. "Everybody got a different sound," he said, handing the jaguar to Bonnie to look at. "When they all talk together, it's like symphony, you know?"

Iris looked at the cat also, chocolate brown, with a high shine, beautifully worked in clay and fired. It looked priceless, she thought, suddenly nervous as Bonnie turned it over and over to study every inch.

Martica came into sight carrying another basket, this one filled with vegetables from the garden. She paused, then shook her head. "All afternoon. That's how long it takes to show the whistles and try them." With an exaggerated sigh she turned to Iris. "All right if he keeps her busy all afternoon?"

"I don't want her to be a bother—"

Martica snorted and moved toward the house, calling over her shoulder to Julio, "Come on. Come on. You can spread them out on the table on the porch." They all followed her to the porch.

Julio put his basket on the table and pulled a chair in closer for Bonnie. "This one a condor," he said. "Big bird, loud mouth." He blew it, a piercing cry, like a piccolo. Bonnie clapped her hands and he passed it over to her, leaning in to point to the wings.

Iris watched, smiling slightly. As Bonnie studied the condor, Julio pulled up a second chair and sat down. A few feet away was a wicker chair and footstool. Iris stretched out on it and watched her daughter handle the whistles. Her smile deepened when Bonnie put one of them to her lips and blew tentatively, then again. She looked so delighted with the sweet call, Iris felt her eyes start to burn, and she closed them hard.

When she looked again, the table seemed covered with the clay whistles, animals, birds, alligators, snakes, jaunty little people. As Julio identified each one, he blew a different sound, soft and melodious, piercing, shrill, throbbing . . . Iris realized that he was telling Bonnie a story, using the whistles for sound effects.

"Now Hawk could see farther than anyone else in the village, and she could hear better than anyone else in the whole forest, so her father sent her to the mountaintop to keep watch for the enemy." Hawk's sound was sharp and high; her father's very low. "Hawk's brother was jealous of the little girl, and he said, 'Why can't I keep watch?' " His whistle sound was somehow whiny.

The story continued, but suddenly Iris sat upright. The girl in the story was mute, she realized; she swung her legs off the stool, prepared to take Bonnie upstairs in protest. But the child was watching Julio with rapt attention, and the whistles seemed now to mingle and blend as he picked up and put down one after another, all the time keeping up the narrative. Iris leaned back again, not listening to the actual words, but absorbing the story and the sound effects of the whistles.

The boy thought of a plan to discredit his sister, to fool her into thinking she had seen the enemy so she would blow her whistle. He called on various animals to help him, but one after another they refused—the hummingbird, butterfly, alligator, snake, monkey . . . Finally he called to Wind to help him, and Wind made a cloud in the form of a sail, and another in the form of a boat, and he sailed them close to shore. When Hawk saw the sail and the boat, she blew her whistle and the people fled into the forest to hide. The chickens did not get fed; the corn did not get harvested; the beans dried on the vines as the people waited for the attack. At last the father sent the brother to the mountaintop to see if the enemy was still approaching, and the boy reported that he could see nothing but a cloud on the water.

Iris could no longer keep track of the various sounds of whistles; it was like being in the middle of a concert, a symphony orchestra with dozens, even hundreds of instruments playing at once. Still, the story went on.

The father sent the girl back to watch again, and this time he told her to blow the whistle only if she saw and heard the enemy. This time Wind gathered leaves and formed them in shapes like men and whirled them about in the forest so that she saw first one, then another, and she heard the cracking and snapping of many footsteps. She blew her whistle a second time, and again the people fled in terror. When the boy was sent to report on the progress of the enemy, he could see nothing but leaves blowing in the wind.

Now the father was so angry with the girl that he sent her deep into the forest and told her not to return until she had gathered enough feathers to make him a bed, and the brother was sent to keep watch for the enemy. The boy could not see as far or hear as well as his sister, and the enemy sneaked into the village unseen and unheard.

Eventually the girl called Hawk had gathered enough feathers to make a bed, and she returned to find the village deserted, with nothing left but ruined gardens and destroyed houses, and broken whistles trampled into the ground. She gathered up the whistles and tried to mend them, to call back her family, but even if she could hold the pieces together, the sounds they made were ugly, distorted, harsh. The whistles Julio blew in this part sounded discordant, the music in them gone.

Hawk then began to carve a new kind of whistle, one that would not break if dropped, one that would make the

113

sweet music of all the broken whistles. And when she finished, she played music never before heard in the forest.

Iris thought she must have been dozing. Now the air throbbed with music that was poignant, sweet and sad, melodious beyond any sound Julio had made before. She ached from the beauty of the music, and felt it in her blood, in her head, on her skin.

"Hawk closed her eyes and played as she never had played before. She walked a circle around the destroyed village, and below her feet the ground stirred, but she did not look. She played and walked another circle, and on all sides she could hear rustlings and stirring, but she did not look."

Iris heard his voice telling the story, and the sweet, sad music of the pipes now drowned out by his words, now overwhelming them, all together. She listened to Julio's voice again, and realized that she had not heard any of the words for a long time.

"Hawk made yet another circle, playing the new music, and suddenly there was the whistle of the father"—the deep bass whistle sounded—"and that of her brother—" The whine of his whistle was mingling with the pipes and the bass. One by one Julio brought them all back, all led by the melody of the pipes. "So, when all the people were restored, and all the animals, and the garden, and the fires in the firepits were blazing, they had a feast and danced and sang until the sun rose in the morning."

The music stopped all at once. The silence was so complete, so unexpected that Iris caught her breath and held it, as if afraid of being the one to bring sound back. Then Julio laughed.

"You like my story, little one?" he asked Bonnie.

She sat as if transfixed, her eyes wide, high color on her cheeks. She smiled then and nodded, and Iris released the breath she had been holding.

"So. Okay. Now we see which one you like best. Okay?"

Iris heard a clatter behind her and turned to see Harold Ritchie sinking into a chair. He was washed of all color, down to his lips.

"Are you sick?" she asked, and hurried to him. His face was shiny, his hands shaking.

"I'm all right," he said hoarsely. "I was listening. I'm all right now." He was staring at Julio.

"I'll get you a drink of water or something," Iris said uncertainly. He was already looking better, his color returning. She took a step backward. "Just sit still a minute. I'll be right back."

She realized in confusion that it was dusk; the sun had set, and the evening was cooling off fast. She began to hurry toward the door to the house just as it opened and Luisa walked out.

"Don't you people know it's getting dark?" she said, mock-scolding them all. "While you've been out here playing games and blowing whistles Martica has cooked up a huge pot of stew, and she insists that you all come in and eat it immediately. Dear, are you getting chilled?" she asked Bonnie, and rested her hand on the child's head. "Is that the whistle you like best? I do, too. Bring it in out of the cold now."

She herded them inside to the kitchen, where the table was already set for six, the table where Iris and Bonnie had had hot chocolate and steaming bread on their arrival. Iris felt as if that had been a long time ago, another lifetime.

"You can wash in the bathroom through there," Luisa said, surveying the table, motioning with her hand toward an open door. "Harold, would you like a glass of wine while we wait?"

Bonnie stood her little whistle by the sink as she washed her hands. A hummingbird whistle. Suddenly Iris felt a chill course through her. Harold had been in shock, she realized; his symptoms had been those of shock. And she should have been just as shocked, just as disbelieving, as bewildered as he. All that music out on the porch, she thought, couldn't have happened, not with clay whistles, not with just one round little man telling a story, creating all the sound effects. All that music, she repeated silently. She watched Bonnie drying her hands. The child had accepted it without question, and so had she, Iris thought in fear. All that music.

11

▼ ▼ ▼ ▼

Late that afternoon Boise sat in the café chatting with Bobby Shehan, who owned it and the grocery store. Bobby was the balding, aproned man who had served Boise coffee yesterday.

"Born here," he said, exactly as if Boise had asked. "Went off to school, took a look around, and hightailed it back. Suits me here, I guess. Where you from, Boise?"

"Pennsylvania."

"Didn't think it was Idaho. Not with that accent."

Apparently everyone in town knew about the Mazda, Boise had come to realize. Many people had expressed sympathy; some had even offered a ride to San Luis Obispo, or down to Santa Barbara as soon as they could get through.

"Wonder how the road crew's making out," Boise said after a moment.

Bobby glanced at the wall clock. "Be here before six,

betcha. Old Doc Carmody doesn't like overtime. He's the crew boss out this way."

Boise sipped his coffee. "Guess I'll hang out until he shows up."

Bobby had a customer or two in the next few minutes, and Boise gazed out the window at the street. It was quiet. The town was too small for people to drive around much; everyone he saw was on foot. The kids had been brought home over the mountain detour; now a couple of preteen boys flew by on ten-speeds. Two women met across the street and stopped to chat, then continued together out of sight. It was five minutes to six when he heard a motor sound. He expected to see a road maintenance truck; what he did not expect was to see Carolyn Engleman's Toyota roll past the window.

He jumped up and ran to the door to wave her to stop. Although she was already to the intersection, she must have seen him in her rearview mirror. She made a U-turn and came back and parked. A second later the road crew truck came into sight at the end of Main Street. The truck stopped at the café and two men in heavy work clothes climbed down and went inside.

"What the hell are you doing back here?" Boise asked Carolyn, surprised at how glad to see her he was.

She hesitated, then said in a rush, "I have to see Iris. And I have to talk to you. Someplace quiet. The bar at the motel? I'm going to check in there for the night."

"How did you get in? Are the roads open?"

"There are detour signs everywhere. The south is still closed off, and it's about fifty miles out of the way to go up and around through the north. But the road's okay. They shoved the mud off with bulldozers, I guess. Can we talk?"

He studied her a moment, then nodded. "Give me a minute with the crew chief and I'll go over to the motel with you. Okay?"

"Take ten," she said. "I'll have a word with Iris and meet you in the bar."

He remembered that when she had raced off, she had looked badly frightened. She looked frightened now, but also determined, maybe even angry.

"Ten minutes," he said, and trotted back to the café to speak with Doc Carmody, who was a wiry, red-faced man in his sixties.

"It's a goner, Mr. Wilkes," Carmody said. There was no doubt in his voice or manner. "I've flown over that southern stretch half a dozen times today. Not a trace of a car, or a road. Write it off." Bobby brought coffee and Boise said something inane and left to meet Carolyn in the bar. And, by God, he thought morosely, he deserved a drink or two.

The Cambio Bay Motel was L-shaped, with a dozen rooms, a small office, and a bar that looked too big for such a modest establishment. Probably local people made up most of the clientele, Boise thought, as he entered the dim room. No one was in sight. The bar top was weathered, smooth oak, highly polished, but pale in spots from many years of scrubbing, many alcoholic washes. High stools without casters were evenly spaced along the bar. There were several tables, and three booths. He waited on a bar stool until Carolyn appeared in the doorway.

Boise stood up. "Did you see Iris?"

She shook her head. "Martica said Iris and Bonnie are off somewhere. I asked her to tell Iris I'll be back in a while." She did not add that she had looked all over the beach for them, or that they should have been home because it was dinnertime, or that she thought Martica had been lying. She especially did not tell him that when she started to enter the house, to call Iris, she had become panic-stricken, because here in the bar with Boise she no longer believed it herself.

"Well, pick a booth," he said. "I'll see if I can find someone to take an order. What do you want?"

She hesitated, then said gin and tonic. Nothing too strong; something she could sip slowly, linger over. She watched him leave in search of help. Then she dug out the photographs and her graph-paper pad from her bag and put them on the table, facedown.

She had rehearsed exactly what she planned to say, keeping it all objective, straightforward. Clean, she had thought. Keep it clean and if he doesn't believe any of it, that's okay. When Boise returned and sat opposite her again, and a man appeared behind the bar and began to mix drinks, she forgot everything she had intended to say. Everything odd that she had noticed, everything she had feared now seemed impossible, even silly. Even the reward for information about Bonnie now seemed reasonable, not the conspiracy she had let herself believe in yesterday. She frowned at the table, her fingers tapping lightly.

"Heard your car's a goner," the bartender said suddenly, drinks in his hands, no tray. He put the glasses down, and added, "Good thing you got a friend to haul you out of here. It's a long walk to anywhere." He laughed and walked away shaking his head.

"Here's to you," Boise said, raising his glass, "friend."

She smiled slightly and took a sip, then put her glass down. "Do you want a ride? After I see Iris I could leave. We could be down in L.A. tonight."

"You said you had something to talk about. What is it?"

She felt awkward. Had that sounded like a come-on? She looked at her fingertips, then at the graph pad, and finally pulled it toward her and found the pages where she had tried to sketch Luisa's house. Her attempts looked inept, amateurish. Impatiently she opened the pad at an earlier page and turned it so that he could see.

"This is what I do," she said slowly in a low voice, pointing at some floor plans she had drawn. The sketch was well done, accurate. "I sell real estate, draw houses for clients, make sketches. I can be pretty good." She waited for him to examine the sketch and then nod before she flipped through the pages to the last few, and again turned the pad toward him.

"Look at them, Boise. I tried over and over again to sketch Luisa's house. I can't do it. It's as if the rooms slide away from me when I try to visualize them enough to reproduce them."

He was not smiling at her, she told herself, but she knew that a smile lay behind his eyes, that he was suppressing it. She flipped to the last sketch.

"Look. This is how we went up the first time, when Julio took us. Remember? Here's my room. He said your room was down the hall, up the stairs on the left, first door. Didn't he?"

Boise was studying her, not the sketch she had made. Her intensity was unsettling, almost fanatical. He had known a few fanatics and feared them. They were unpredictable, unswerving.

"Look at it," Carolyn demanded in the insistent way he had feared she would adopt. He looked at the sketch. "The main stairs," she said coldly, furious with him, making little effort to hide it. "And here's my apartment. These are all outside windows with an ocean view." She pointed as she spoke in her hard cold voice. "On up the corridor to the stairs on the left. Up the stairs to your apartment. Do you have an ocean view?"

"Sure," he said, but then he realized what she had drawn and he pulled the pad all the way across the table to study it. "You made a mistake. The stairs must be on the right."

"You know they aren't."

He did know it, but the way it was drawn, his apartment could not have an ocean view. He studied the floor plan, scowling at it. Only six steps, he remembered; his room couldn't be on the floor above the hall and the other rooms on Carolyn's floor. And the stairs leading left would take it back into the interior of the house, not to an outside wall. Finally he looked up to see her watching him with a remote expression.

He picked up his scotch and drank, but found that it was not what he wanted after all. "We've both made a mistake," he said finally. "Or it's an Escher house." She did not return his smile.

"There's more," she said, and turned over a photograph. They were in no particular order. This was of Harold Ritchie and the shadows that should have been Luisa, against the shadow that should have been the guest house. She pushed it across the table. "I'm a decent photographer," she said coolly. "This is how I earn my living, remember. I was out looking over another property that day; all those pictures are fine. Harold's fine in that one. There are a couple of Bonnie, one of you, all good pictures unless they include Luisa or her house, or the grounds."

He wanted to bring back the smile he had felt twitching his mouth a few minutes ago, but it was as if he had forgotten how to do that. He studied her, then said, "You're talking as if you believe the house is haunted or something. You must know that's insane." His voice lacked conviction because he suddenly remembered with a startling sensation of sexual pleasure the phantom lover he had possessed his first night in the house.

The memory was intact, complete; his hands remembered the firmness of her breasts, the downy moist skin; his body remembered her body heat, the moment they had become one explosively, the intensity of her desire, and his own. He remembered her fragrance, the cadence of her murmuring voice, the fairy touch of her fingers on his lips, his eyelids. He remembered the sweat, the weight of her body, the shifting of her body, then his so that bone did not rub bone. The memory was of a flesh-and-blood woman whose desire equaled his, whose release was as intense as his. Not a phantom lover, not a dream, or hallucination, or fantasy. His body knew and remembered; the memory was in his blood, on his skin, in his mind, in his penis that he had thought dead. She had restored him to life, not by stripping away his defenses, but with a touch, and she was real. He knew this once more, as he had known it then. She was a real woman. Yet, until this moment, he had forgotten; when he had thought of her at all, it was as the phantom lover, a wistful reverie that he yearned to relive, that he recalled only with effort as if from a great distance, revived from a distant past. Luisa had sent her to him, he realized bitterly, and then spirited her away again. The thought that he had been used, manipulated, sent a wash of fury through him.

"You know as well as I do that there's nothing really spooky about that house, or Luisa." His voice was harsh; his sudden anger was too intense, it seemed coiled, hunting for a target that would bring release. He picked up his scotch and water and drank most of it.

"Something happened to you, too, didn't it?" Carolyn asked, almost in a whisper.

"No," he snapped. "Look, you had a terrific shock that day. I know, because I did, too. The house is confusing as hell, probably added to half a dozen times by half a dozen different builders who paid no attention to what had been done before. That happens with those old places. And you somehow ruined a photo or two."

"Every single one that should have her or her house in it," Carolyn said with icy calm. She pushed the whole stack across the table and watched him turn over the next one and examine it.

He glanced at the next few, all blurred, impossible to say what she had tried to photograph, and then found the first one of Bonnie, a long shot with the bay behind her, and the Indian maiden pillar, all sharp, in good focus, clear true color. He paused over it and turned another one over, nothing but murk. And the next one of Bonnie, again sharp, good color; a good view of Main Street, Tydall's Garage halfway down the street, the sign legible. Suddenly he froze.

His hands began to tremble, and before he could control himself, he lunged halfway across the table and grabbed her shoulders, began to shake her.

"How did you do that? Why? My God, what kind of a monster are you?"

All color drained from her face. She was holding her glass; with a reflexive twist of her hand she splashed the drink and ice in his face. He dropped his hands, stared at her a moment, and then lurched away from the booth and ran from the bar.

Hastily she snatched up the pictures from the advancing flood of gin and tonic and jammed them all into her bag. She found a ten-dollar bill in her purse and flung it down on the table, and hurried out. Boise was vanishing down the trail to the beach.

Elaine's father had called him at the office. A terrible accident. Meet me at the hospital. His memory leap-frogged over the rest of the day, parts of it as clear as today, parts of it irretrievable. He had no memory of driving to the hospital. At first he had thought it was Elaine who had an accident. He remembered with sharp details the look on her father's face when he said it was Jaime. He was dead. An accident. He fell down the stairs. And Elaine's father had not been able to look at him directly. Elaine was under heavy sedation. She had called her father and he had called her psychiatrist and then the ambulance for the child, and then Boise.

Elaine's father had taken command, arranged the funeral, arranged for Elaine's hospital treatment for the next two months, arranged Boise's compliance in the lie that insisted it had been an accident.

"What good will it do to punish her? For God's sake, what will that accomplish? Don't you think she's punishing herself enough? Let Malik decide. Leave it alone."

Then Elaine had come home and he found that he couldn't speak to her; his throat tightened, the words froze. She smiled and chatted about inconsequential things. She started her diet and said one night that she would redecorate, would he like the spare room for a study? It was silly to have a whole extra room going to waste, wasn't it? He left her that night.

After that he could talk to her just as long as he didn't try to say anything real. And then she had left him more permanently than he had ever dared hope for, and he had started his long drive. Jaime had lived four years, two months, eleven days.

Boise walked blindly, unaware when others came down to the beach in time for sunset, unaware when they left. When he became aware again, it was too dark to see the stairs that led to the trail.

"Over here, Boise," Carolyn said quietly. She stood at the bottom step, a pale figure against the cliff.

He did not know how long she had been there waiting for him, or even if that was what she had been doing. He walked through the crunching dry sand toward her. Now he was chilled.

"Here," she said when he got close. "I have a bottle."

He took it and drank. Bourbon. He handed it back.

"Boise, I don't know what you think I did. Whatever it was, it was unintentional. Will you tell me?"

He could see her in the faint light, pale, quiet, her arms folded across her breast, probably as chilled as he was. He reached out and took the bottle again and drank more deeply. This time when he returned it, she took a drink, too.

"I'm sorry," he said wearily. He could see the photograph in his mind's eye, taken here in Cambio Bay; he was wearing these clothes, striding toward her, and at his side a child who, for one insane moment, he had thought was Jaime. "I thought I saw someone who wasn't there."

She touched his arm, her hand warm and firm on his cold skin. "He's there," she said almost without expression. "But Boise, when I took that picture of you, you were alone on the sidewalk. I swear it."

A dozen stairs climbed the steepest part of the ascent to the top of the cliff. Where the stairs ended, a trail with a solid handrail continued up to a parking area dimly lighted with a single old-fashioned lamp that cast a pale glow. Carolyn had moved her car to the area, and they headed for it in silence. She fished the key from her pocket and opened the door.

"I have to talk to you," Boise said. "I want to see all those pictures again. You know there must be an answer."

"Sure," she said. "Get in. I'll take you back to the motel. I want to check in. We can talk in my room."

He started to say she was being silly, that there was nothing wrong with the guest house, but he bit the words back and got in. Something was wrong, he accepted; it simply didn't fit any preconceived pattern, didn't make any sense.

She drove slowly through the empty parking area, on toward the motel, and slowed even more. There was a NO VACANCY sign on, and nowhere else was there even a glimmer of light. She stopped at the curb.

"Shit," she muttered.

"I guess with the detour there aren't any customers passing by," Boise said. "Café?"

She shook her head. "You can't look at the pictures in

there. Half a dozen people would be at the table looking with you. If it's open, that is."

She tapped her fingers on the steering wheel and thought. "I'll take you back to Luisa's and go in long enough to speak to Iris while you look over that stuff again. Then I'll take off. I'll come back tomorrow."

"Carolyn, for Pete's sake! You're acting like a heroine in a grade-B movie. Look, I've been there most of the week, and so have Iris and the kid, and Harold's been there for several weeks, and until tonight we've all been pretty content." He slouched in the seat, looking straight ahead in an angry attitude. "Have you been threatened? See bloodstains, hear noises in the night?" He stopped because that was getting too close.

But she was thinking of Iris and the newscast. "Is television working around here yet?" she asked, and he turned to give her a puzzled look. "Up at the house? In town? Anywhere?"

He shrugged. "Not at the house. I don't know about in town. The telephones in town are okay now, but not at the house."

She thought, by tomorrow probably it would all be restored, television, newspaper deliveries, people coming and leaving. By tomorrow Iris probably would see the announcement about her husband, the reward for information about her whereabouts. By tomorrow Boise would find out about it anyway, why not tonight? She said slowly, "Will you tell Iris something for me? In case I miss her tonight." Her hands were gripping the steering wheel hard because she had suddenly realized that *they* would not let her see Iris tonight. She didn't even try to make sense of the thought, but relaxed her hands and then turned off the key, turned off the headlights. They were parked on the street in front of the motel, as good a place as any to talk, she decided.

Boise agreed reluctantly and she told him about the newscast, and then had to back up and fill him in on Wally who had processed the film.

"Jesus Christ," he said when she finished. She started to speak again and he put his hand on hers on the steering wheel. "Wait a minute. Let me think about it." He remembered his hand on hers after only a moment and hastily withdrew it.

Finally he sighed and looked at her. "Okay. You could be right about the scenario. She left Los Angeles in a hurry in a car that shouldn't be driven farther than the nearest car cemetery. I don't think she has any clothes except what she's been wearing since she got here. She's afraid of something, that's for sure. And you probably know your pal Wally enough to know if that's what he would do, go try to collect the reward even without the picture. Carolyn, have you considered that you might have given them a lead to where Iris is now?"

"What do you mean? I told Wally the picture came from below Santa Barbara."

"Okay, but he has eyes, and he's used to really looking at pictures, I take it. Is there a formation anything like the three Indians down there? Will someone recognize that section of beach? And, Carolyn, that state trooper who led the convoy out of here will remember you and your car. Believe me, that's the sort of thing they remember. If your friend links you to the kid through the photograph, they'll also link you to Cambio Bay eventually, if they really want to."

"Are you police?" she asked, sorry that she had told him anything.

"Lawyer. State attorney general's office, Pennsylvania. We study the legality of pending legislature, things like that. But you don't have to be a cop to know some things. What exactly did Wally say about Wellington?"

She repeated it; not enough, she was thinking now. She

should have asked questions, should have asked someone else. For the first time she thought she should have given Wally the pictures and negatives. She would be out of it and eventually might even have collected a piece of the reward. She could not think of any good reason why she had not done that, or why she was sitting in the car in this little town talking about it to Boise.

He said briskly, "Look, you're getting chilled, and I sure am cold. Let's go to the house. You don't have to see Luisa. We'll go straight to my rooms and get something to eat and decide what to do about Iris."

"You decide," she said. "I really want to get out of here. I've told you what I know. I'll give you the pictures and even the negatives. Burn them, or give them to her, I don't care. I can't do anything else."

"Carolyn," he said softly. "She's stuck here as much as I am. Her rear tires are too bald to go out on the highway again, and her spare's worse than they are. Julio was looking over her car today, and I helped. I know. How far do you think she'd get, a woman named Iris, a mute child named Bonnie? Even if they didn't show her picture, how about her driver's license, the plates on the car? They'll probably pick her up the first day she starts driving again."

"You think she's really in danger?"

"Don't you?"

After a long pause she said, "What I think is that I should tell her about Wellington and the reward and leave the rest of it up to her. If she goes to the police, or to reporters, anything like that, she should be safe unless she's done something herself."

"Why did you come back?" Boise asked abruptly.

"To warn her. Give her and Bonnie a chance to decide before decisions are made for them."

He made a snorting sound, then said mockingly, "So, this kid you never saw until a few days ago has such a claim on you that you drove more than two hundred miles just to repeat a newscast that she'll probably hear anyway by tomorrow."

"It's crazy," she said after a moment in a voice that was almost inaudible.

"Yeah. Crazy." He sounded as troubled as she was.

She turned the key, pulled on the headlights.

"Now what?"

"I'll take you back to the house."

"And come up with me?"

"Yes," she whispered.

She felt as if she had been kidding herself all along, lying to herself, pretending this and the other, when all the time she had known she had to return to the house. There were a dozen friends she could have crashed with for a few days, weeks, however long she needed, until she was sure that Wally had crept back behind his baseboard again. She thought of all the things she could have done: check into a motel anywhere. Or she could have driven up to San Francisco. Could have flown out to Des Moines to visit her family. She could have called the police if Wally showed up in a mean mood. She could have ended it all by simply handing over the stuff, telling Wally what she knew about Iris, and then gone on about her business without a backward glance. None of her affair.

In theory, all that was true; she could add to the list of alternatives, make it much longer, but in reality nothing on that list had been possible. What she had to do was return to Miss Luisa's Guest House.

12

▼ ▼ ▼ ▼

Boise's apartment was as spacious as the one that Carolyn had occupied before, and the windows overlooked the ocean, although they had made a left turn to reach the stairs. In this apartment, the furnishings were dark, mahogany with no frills, a dark-green bedspread, tan glove-leather chairs and sofa. Carolyn nodded, as if in confirmation, and then, at Boise's insistence, sat down out of the way.

"You drove all day. I'll cook. I have steaks and some fruit and not much else. It'll do. Good wine, though." He opened the refrigerator and frowned. Salad greens, tomatoes, a casserole with a cover. Silently he removed the cover: potatoes and cheese and green onions in a cream sauce.

Carolyn was watching without expression. When he glanced at her, she pointed at the counter where a loaf of bread was on a cutting board. A little note was propped up by it: *Martica always makes too much of everything. Enjoy it, if you want it. If not, leave it all and we'll clear it away tomorrow.*

His voice was strained when he began to talk as he unwrapped steaks. "Tell me something about you. Who are you? Where are you from? You know."

She nodded. She knew. No talk about any of the pictures, not now. Not about Iris and Bonnie, not now. Not about the house, about Luisa and Martica who cooked too much and wanted to share it with paying guests. She bit her lip enough to keep it from trembling and said lightly, "Carolyn Rose Engleman. Isn't that silly? Third child in a family of four kids, two brothers, one sister, Dad and Mom. He's a salesman, business equipment, and she's an elementary school teacher. My brothers and sister are all Successes, capital *S*, you understand."

He looked at her briefly with a grin. He understood.

"I was in college for six years and never came within sniffing distance of a degree. Six years, six majors. Psychology, English, Science, Architecture, Gym—" She scowled when he laughed. "I intended to become a coach of a girls' soccer team at one time. Have you ever looked at my muscles?" She made a muscle in her arm and he nodded gravely, with respect. She slumped again and said, "And let's see, what else? Oh, Ancient History. Greece and Rome and the Babylonians and Egyptians." She sighed dramatically. "Facts, facts, facts. Shovel them in and watch them drip out. Nothing took. After about the fourth year, Dad said, Let's have a talk. After that I was sort of on my own, but still determined for another two years."

Boise had put the casserole in the oven and had the steaks ready for the broiler. The salad greens already had been washed and dried and needed nothing but a toss with oil and vinegar. He poured more wine for them both and leaned against the counter. "Go on. And then?"

"Work. Career. Money. All the usual."

He shook his head. "Men, affairs, marriage. All the usual."

Carolyn shrugged. "Good wine, you were right about that. Yours? Or the house wine?"

He looked at her sharply and for a moment her face was pinched. The moment passed; she looked amused again.

"So I got a job with a studio, dyed my hair platinum, and waited to be discovered. I was in research. All those textbooks, you see. You want to know about the pyramids? Ask Carolyn. What did Babylonians eat for breakfast? Ask Carolyn. What sort of scribbles should a scientist have on his blackboard? All that kind of thing. My kind of thing. And no one noticed my gorgeous platinum hair, or my lovely muscles. Oh, my gluteus maximus and my pectorals might have gotten more than a passing glance, but only from the nerd of a supervisor." She sighed.

Boise was grinning as he slid the broiler pan under the flame and sipped his wine. He took plates from a cabinet and found silverware and napkins. Carolyn pulled the leaf of a table into place and took the plates from him, set the table, and then seated herself at the chair that allowed her to see into the kitchen. Only one person at a time could be in that space, but it was enough. Boise was an efficient cook, unflustered, in control. She looked at the wine in her glass and drew in a deep breath. In control, that was the key. He was right in not wanting anything except bantering nonsense right now. She suspected that he was timing the steaks to the second. When he turned them a few moments later, she knew he was.

"So," she said pensively, "after a while, I realized that no one discovers researchers, and I saw the writing on the wall, budget cuts, less research. Don't let facts clutter up the script, and so on, and I went back to school, real estate classes, got my license, and started the next adventure." She shrugged and added, "Believe me, I've been in places that no one should have gone in before. Too many."

He glanced at her with sympathy. He had worked for the legal department of the housing agency back in Pennsylvania for a time; he had seen some of those places where no one should ever have to go. Back home those buildings were older, dirtier, probably the only difference. He tossed the salad expertly, placed it and the casserole on the table, and brought out the steaks—everything ready at exactly the same time. They ate in silence for several minutes.

"Good," she said then. "Didn't know how hungry I was. Light-headed from starvation."

He nodded. "Me, too." Then he said, "Thanks, Carolyn. You're a good cooking companion."

"Next time I'll have to start reading to you from the encyclopedia or something. I just ran out of anything to talk about."

His cue, he understood, and thought how strange it was that he and this woman who had known each other for only a day or two could speak in such cryptic nonreferential sentences, and derive meaning, catch nuances. Possibly nuances that weren't even there, he added.

"My story is much less interesting than yours," he said. "School, law school. Marriage. In-law influence got me a job, which I probably quit a few months ago."

"You don't know if you quit?"

He shrugged. "I quit." He realized only then that he had quit the job, quit Pennsylvania, maybe quit law. He knew suddenly that everything he had thought he had was gone: his son, wife, job, car. Even his name. He grinned at Carolyn. "When I was born my mother named me Tyler, and that's been my name, that or initials, ever since. But Dad called me Boise. I think because I was conceived on a trip that took them to Boise. Anyway, that was his name for me. And now I'm Boise again."

"Oh, dear. I don't think I could learn to call you Tyler.

You know, Little Toby Tyler, the circus, the big evil ringmaster . . ."

He looked blank, then abruptly laughed. "I haven't thought of that damn book in thirty years! That's why I went to initials!"

"Well, of course."

He made coffee and while they waited for it, she washed their few dishes. Boise spread the pictures on the table and studied them intently in silence. He rearranged them, as she had done before, separating the clear, good ones from the others with shadows. He included his own with the child in that group.

He did not linger over the picture of Jaime, nor did he doubt that it was Jaime. The picture had been taken in Cambio Bay, of him wearing the only clothes he had possessed then, and Jaime had been dead for over a year. He knew there were a number of tricks that photographers could play with prints, adding figures, removing them, airbrushing out unwanted anything. And he knew that Carolyn had done none of those things. The picture was impossible and it existed. There was no point in lingering over it. Looking at it would not explain the impossible; he studied instead the picture of Harold and the shadows that should have been Luisa.

Something was niggling at the edge of his memory, he realized, and frowned into space trying to tempt it out into the open. Something about Harold? Something Harold had said? Or done? He narrowed his eyes as he tried to recapture the various meetings he had had with Harold, and suddenly he had the elusive memory.

"Carolyn," he asked then slowly, "how old would you say Luisa is?"

Startled, she said, "Forty maybe. Why?"

"I would have thought even younger than that. But Harold seems to think she's ancient."

He remembered exactly now. He had met Harold Ritchie down on the beach. Harold was looking forlorn and upset and they had talked briefly. Then Luisa, Iris, and Bonnie had appeared from the far end and had gone up the stairs, Harold watching them broodingly.

"She won't talk into a tape recorder," he had grumbled. "Old people get like that, afraid of new things, I guess. But a tape recorder! It's not like stealing her soul or anything."

After Boise told Carolyn this, she shook her head doubtfully. "Some people are terrible about guessing ages. And Harold is so . . . out of it. You know what I mean."

"Then he said his grandmother had been like that, active right up to the day she sat down and went to sleep and died. At ninety-four." Boise pulled his gaze back from the remembered scene with Harold and regarded Carolyn thoughtfully. "I don't think we see the same woman Harold sees. Or even that you and I see the same woman."

Carolyn hugged her arms about herself, shivering. "Okay, okay. There's a mystery about her and about the house. We walk inside and become enchanted or something. I mean, obviously the house itself doesn't change, and I don't think Luisa does either." She looked pinched again. "Enchanted. Like tonight. I intended to go find Iris first thing. I know they're in at this hour. Bonnie is in bed sleeping by now, and Iris must be nearby. And I forgot. That's what I came here for, and I forgot, and now it's after ten, and too late to go scouting." She bit her lip, then said, "I'll write myself a note. First thing in the morning, let's talk to her and see if she has any plans of her own. If she doesn't, maybe I can take her somewhere, to friends, or relatives not too far away. Almost anywhere. I'm a free agent. For heaven's sake, she might even want to go back home and collect the reward herself. Maybe she was running away from her husband, nothing more than that."

"Maybe. In the morning I'll make a few calls, people I know back east who know people in Los Angeles. If there's anything to those rumors about Wellington, the information's available, if we just find the right people to ask."

He got up and began turning off lights in the kitchen, most of them in the living room. He went into the bedroom and returned with a blanket, a sheet, and pillow. "I'll take the couch. I expect it's every bit as comfortable as the bed."

She nodded, not doubting it. As he began to arrange his bedding, she asked, "Why are you getting involved? I don't know why I am. Do you?"

He straightened up and shook his head, then sat down hard. "That picture of me with the little boy. He . . . he looks exactly like my son. He died when he was four. Bonnie's the age he would be now. Maybe for her, not for Iris. I don't know."

Not now, Carolyn wanted to whisper. She wanted to walk past him, go into the other room and close the door, go to bed, and sleep without dreaming. He looked like a blind man, under sentence of punishment too familiar and too tormenting to bear. He wouldn't try to stop her, she knew, if she simply walked past him, into the other room, closed the door. She doubted that he would even be aware that she had left. Presently he would get up and pour himself a drink and maybe another, and eventually he would sleep, and not hold it against her in the morning if she walked past him now. It might even be more awkward for both of them if she tried to get him to talk about it tonight. She knew that people often resented it when sympathy broke through their defenses and left them helpless. Helpless and blind, she said to herself, gazing at his face, his eyes staring blindly into something she could not see.

She felt removed from the scene, like a director in a play, or simply an observer, as she watched the woman who was Carolyn Engleman walk to the couch and sit by the man who was Boise Wilkes, a man in despair, utterly dejected, beyond reach. The character who was Carolyn could see only his lowered head, the vague attitude of his profile, hard and rigid and uninformative; she could not tell the depth of his misery, but the observer who was Carolyn understood it and ached for him. Observer and actor merged again; she took his hand in hers and said, "Tell me about it. About your wife. About your child."

Harold paced in his apartment, ignoring now the many books that were piled here and there, ignoring the pages of computer printout he had meant to correct. The scene at the ruins and the scene on the porch were twining about each other out of control, first one, then the other demanding explanation. How on earth had the man done that? he kept asking himself. There must be a tape recorder, he thought then. Concealed in the basket, or in his pocket. Special effects, special music to accompany his storytelling. Master storyteller, of course, just as Luisa was. And Martica. Earlier, at the ruins, that must have been Julio playing the pipes. Maybe he was taping it up there, out of sight, to play back on the porch. He paced and tried to reconstruct the scene, and in his mind he saw Julio manipulating the whistles with unbelievable speed, and he heard the pipes in his mind now just as clearly as he had heard them in the afternoon at the ruins, then again on the porch. A tape recorder, he reminded himself, and he didn't believe it this time any more than he had before.

Persephone, he thought then. The same story, but told from her viewpoint, with variations, of course, due to local conditions. Not really, he decided. Julio had tailored an Indian myth for a mute little girl. Master storyteller. And the wind as antagonist, he thought, as his excitement mounted. The whistles, the pipes, the animals that refused to help the boy, all things or creatures of the earth, and the wind that brought disaster, a thing of the Great Chief, just like in Luisa's story. Abruptly he threw himself into the big leather chair and pulled his notebook to his lap and began to write almost feverishly. Later he would put it in the computer, but first in the notebook where all the important things were written.

In her apartment Iris was counting her money, four hundred eighty-five dollars and some change. She had to buy at least one tire. And shoes to work in. The old sandals she had on were coming apart. She knew she could get a job somewhere, but she didn't have any clothes with her, just what she was wearing. More expenses. She had covered a sheet of paper with figures already, allowing for thrift-store bargains for shoes and a skirt and top of some sort. Thank heaven, she thought then, that Bonnie's things had been in the laundry, most of them anyway. Bonnie would be all right for a while. But Iris had to have something to wear to hunt for a job. Pantyhose, she remembered, and bit her lip, added another figure to the column. She couldn't buy pantyhose at a secondhand store.

She put her head down on the desk with her eyes closed, because suddenly she was seeing yet another of the ratty apartments that had been home for six years. Roaches, she thought with disgust, and rats, and dealing in the halls, and the stench. God, the stench!

When she raised her head again, she was dry-eyed and very cold. She would have to change her name, she realized. Iris! And a mute child named Bonnie! Nervously she got up and walked to the door of Bonnie's room; she was sleeping, the new whistle on the nightstand at the bedside.

"Why don't you talk?" Iris whispered. She could, the doctors said. Nothing physiological was wrong with her;

nothing psychological had traumatized her to muteness. Iris bowed her head, her hands clenched. If she would only talk, then they could blend in, go to a regular school and register, not require special classes . . . She tried to think of a new name for her daughter: Betty, Deborah, Sandra . . . Hawk, she thought suddenly, and the child moved slightly in her sleep, not coming awake, but with a new restlessness.

Iris backed away from the door, returned to the table where she had been adding numbers for a long time. She pulled out a clean sheet of paper from the stack she had taken from the desk, and this time she wrote a heading: Names. And Social Security numbers, she thought then, and a new driver's license, and medical records for Bonnie, inoculations, immunizations . . . She stared blindly at the wall behind the table.

In the bay the tide rises with whisper-soft waves; the bony arm of the mountain absorbs the energy of the sea without effort. Moonlight glints off the water and the monolithic shapes on the beach and on the rocky projection across the bay. The sand reflects rays of light in glitter here and there—quartz, mica, possibly grains of gold. Crabs are at work, and a bird, an owl, swoops low, rises, vanishes, all without a sound. The village lights are being turned off—Terry Hayes is looking forward to returning to work in the morning, up at the station, roads and God willing, he thinks. Donna Eccles is at the window of her son's house, thinking how weird it is that whenever one light goes off up at the monstrosity on the point, another seems to go on. Bert Eccles says it's always been like that, go on to bed, Mom. Doc Carmody is in the motel, his back aching with a dull pain that he is used to; he is planning the assault on the buried road the next day.

Far to the south in Stuart Wellington's outer office Wally

Gilman is licking his lips, which keep going too dry. Wellington is not there, and he is glad; this man Lerner is bad enough. He nods. "That's it, all right," he says, glancing from a glossy print of a beach to the tall handsome man who has eyes like holes into an iceberg.

Lerner's expression does not change, but his voice does. It becomes almost inaudible. "Are you absolutely certain?"

"Yeah. Sure. I knew it wasn't Santa Barbara or anywheres around it. That's it." Wally Gilman has no hope of collecting a reward any longer. All he wants now is to be released, allowed to go home, forget any of this ever happened. That bitch, he keeps thinking. That goddamn bitch! "Look," he says, too eagerly he knows, but goddamn, he wants out. "Look. The kid was between those rocks, and that other one was lined up with her. Then, the other picture, the close-up, showed that one really good. It's that rock. I know it is."

In the anteroom of the import office complex a table is covered with photographs, glossies of beaches. Wally has spent hours looking through them, searching for the match with the pictures in his mind, and now they have it. The whole goddamn coast, Wally Gilman thinks, a little awed that they could have been assembled so fast. That's what money can do, he thinks bleakly, and the refrain pounds in his head, That bitch. That goddamn bitch!

"Beat it," Lerner says without looking at him again.

"Hey, how about the reward money? I gave you the lead you wanted."

Lerner glances at him and Wally shifts, rises from the chair he has been in for most of the day. "If you guys find the kid because of my help . . ." Lerner inclines his head toward the door and Wally Gilman leaves, not quite running.

Lerner follows Wally and locks the door, then begins to gather up the photos, keeping out the three of the beach at Cambio Bay. It is eleven at night and he is tired, but, more important, he is worried. In the last thirty hours he has found out where Carolyn Engleman spent the day of the storm, where she holed up when the roads washed out, where she took the pictures of the child the day after the storm. He is certain that there is no other connection between Engleman and Iris Lathan, a chance encounter on a beach, that is all there is to that. But in that case, why has Engleman run now? Why didn't she come forward with the creep Gilman to collect a little spare cash?

He tidies up the office and makes a few notes for Wellington. He cannot reach him tonight. Stuart Wellington and his wife are attending a political function, the dedication of a new art center, fifty-dollar plates, a benefit with the proceeds to go for the relief of teenaged addicts. It will be a late night for them.

He looks over the information he has collected. Quite a bit about Engleman; she has nothing to hide. Less about Iris Lathan; there's little in her life to find. Bonnie Lathan, a mute child, just five, in a special class for exceptional children. Nothing yet about Cambio Bay, it's still just a name, but that will be easy.

Iris could have left there any time yesterday or today, and she might now be in San Francisco, or somewhere else, but it is a start. And thinking this makes him come face to face with his real worry: Why is Stuart Wellington obsessed with the child? The kid, Rick, was right about her. She is not a threat. This makes him more uneasy than anything he can recall in his long employment with Stuart Wellington, eighteen years in all. He has never seen his employer obsessed by anything. Business and emotions don't mix, that has always been Wellington's creed, and he has lived up to it wholly and expects those in his employ to live up to it also. So why is Stuart Wellington acting like a maniac now? Lerner wonders, and he finds that he has been conducting a second line of thought for the past few hours, one in which he cleans out his bank account and hops a plane to France or Italy.

He puts everything away in the office safe and glances about in a final check. He is as meticulous and cautious as Wellington himself. And tonight, for the first time in eighteen years, he believes that he is smarter, because Stuart Wellington is doing the first dumb thing Lerner has ever seen him do. And because Wellington doesn't know why he is doing this thing either. That is the real worry, Lerner admits to himself: Wellington is behaving in an obsessional way that even he does not understand.

A light goes off, another comes on. Iris is sleeping alone in the big bed, dreaming that she hears the pipes again. As before, the music is sad, like an echo of a memory of something lost that is without a name. In her dream she is overcome by the sadness and she is weeping. Someone takes her hand and then draws her close in a warm embrace. "Mother?" Iris whispers in her dream. "Mother, I'm so tired." "I know, dear. I know. It's all right to cry." As she weeps, she is held and comforted.

Carolyn hears the pipes and finds herself dancing to rhythms she has never heard before. The dance is slow and languorous, her movements precise and graceful; she is dancer and observer, and knows it is important to make the right movements, that others are relying on her to make the right movements. She dances now with closed eyes, feeling the music in her body, becoming one with it, dancing in the great ballroom that she always knew how to reach. Others are watching her, shadowy figures making room for her, approving as she dances barefoot in her granny nightgown with blue forget-me-nots embroidered on the front.

Boise dreams that he and Carolyn are walking on the

beach immersed in conversation. She is saying "Other people have goals, great driving ambitions, they want a million dollars, or even just a little place in the country. I've never had a single goal. Isn't that incredible? You create your own future through your dreams and wishes, even your fears. You make them so real that they come into existence. They are amorphous in dreamland, and coalesce in reality and the future then becomes possible. Since I don't have any goals, I have no future."

He says, "I lost my child and my wife. I quit my job and changed my name. Even lost my car. I've been eradicating the past."

The Indian maiden flashes by followed closely by the two warriors. Boise calls out to them, and his voice wakes him on the couch, the dream gone, the music of the pipes in the air all around him.

He is sweating and shaking. He gets up for a drink. The bedroom door is open, the bed empty. The music swells and grows until it is painful.

The bathroom is dark, the door partly open. There is no other place Carolyn can be in the apartment. He runs to the door to the hall and jerks it open. "Carolyn," he calls, not very loud, not wanting to arouse everyone in the house, not yet. With the sound, the music stops abruptly and the house is silent.

Then, from behind him, he hears her voice, frightened, almost plaintive. "Boise? What's wrong?"

He spins to see her in the doorway to the bedroom, holding onto the door frame, swaying slightly.

13

▼ ▼ ▼ ▼

"I heard something," Boise said. "I thought I heard music." He knew he was staring at her idiotically, but he couldn't not stare. "Maybe just the wind. Sorry I woke you up." His voice was strained, unfamiliar to his own ears.

Neither moved until he stepped back into the room and pulled the door closed, his gaze still fixed on her. She was wearing a long-sleeved nightgown, old-fashioned, and she was barefoot.

She shook her head to clear it of the lingering dream; she was sweating, and now began to shiver. "That's all right," she said faintly, and backed into the bedroom again, closed the door, and stood holding the crystal knob with her eyes shut. She wiped sweat from her upper lip, from her forehead, and groped her way to the bed to find the light switch for the lamp, and then sat down on the side of the bed. Although her shivering continued, she did not lie down and pull the blanket over her; not now, not again.

No more dreaming, no more sleeping in this house. The little clock on the nightstand indicated ten past five, a long time before she could expect to find Iris, complete her mission here, and run. Run, she thought.

Boise sat on the couch tensely, dressed except for his boots. He had not expected to fall asleep so soon, he remembered. They had talked; Carolyn had gone to bed and he had sat here with a drink, and then . . . Sleeping and dreaming, and the music.

He rubbed his eyes, no longer certain when the dream had ended. Before he reached the door to the hall, that was as much as he could say now. Obviously he had dreamed that Carolyn was gone from the bedroom earlier. And the music? Part of the dream? The cause of the dream? Separate altogether? He rubbed his eyes again and knew he would not go back to sleep that night—morning, he corrected after glancing at his watch. After five. After eight back in Pennsylvania. In twenty minutes, he decided, he would call his office, his former office, and get Luke Erskine to look up Wellington.

He had told Carolyn about Elaine and Jaime, he was remembering now, surprised at himself, at the inexplicable conversation they had had. Then he said, "I'm not looking for sympathy, you understand."

"I know."

"And I'm not looking for . . . romance, or anything like that," he had added, almost primly, he thought now, embarrassed.

"Me, too, Boise. It's okay. Think you'll go on to sleep now?"

He remembered sitting here with a drink, putting it down, then nothing until the crazy music began. He had slept. He stood up and wandered restlessly about the room, to the window; it was still dark outside, just a glimmer of predawn light on the ocean. Yesterday the phones in the house had not worked; he might have to walk to the village to make his calls, as soon as it grew light. He looked around sharply when the bedroom door opened and Carolyn appeared, also fully dressed now.

"Through sleeping," she said. "Coffee time,"

He pulled on his boots while she made coffee. As they sipped it, she said, "It's going to take time for your person to learn anything about Wellington, and I don't want to hang around here waiting. As soon as it seems a decent hour, I'll find Iris and tell her about the reward, and see what she wants to do. If she wants to go back to Los Angeles, fine. I'll take her. If she needs a tire and wants to go to San Luis Obispo for it, I'll take her there and bring it back and get her car rolling. In either case, I want to do something, not just sit and wait."

He nodded. "Fair enough. It could be tomorrow before we know anything." The difference in time made it awkward. Even if Luke got on it immediately, he couldn't make calls to the West Coast until nine, over three hours from now. "You want to go with me to the village?"

She nodded vigorously. "Do you have a jacket or something? It'll be bloody cold out this early. We can drive my car."

Neither of them suggested that they try the phone in the small lobby first.

Iris folded Bonnie's clothes and put them in the laundry basket, talking as cheerfully as she could manage while the child played with her breakfast of pancakes. "First we have to go to a store that sells tires for the car. And then we'll find a toy store. Let's see, what would you like? A doll? A little car?" Bonnie did not even glance at her. "I know. A new coloring book."

Bonnie dragged a piece of pancake back and forth through syrup, making a clear trail, then crossing it over and over. Iris wanted to take the fork from her and feed her the way she had done when Bonnie was an infant. "Finish up, honey, so I can wash the dishes. Can't leave a hotel room in a mess, you know." Bonnie put the fork down.

Iris sat by her and took her hand. "Look, Bonnie, this is a vacation. We've had a nice vacation in a nice hotel, but now we have to go. I have to get a job and you have to go to school. Vacations are like that. It's fun for a few days and then you have to leave."

Bonnie jerked her hand free and picked up the hummingbird whistle that Iris had strung on a ribbon for her to wear as a necklace. In exasperation Iris took the plate to the sink and scraped out the food. She would take food along to eat in the car. Peanut butter sandwiches, fruit, Cheerios . . . From the corner of her eye she could see Bonnie tracing the hummingbird wings gently. "First we'll go down and tell Martica and Julio good-bye, and Luisa. And we'll go out and pick up your shells. You can play with them in the car . . ." Nothing she said seemed to penetrate; Bonnie ignored her.

A few minutes later they were descending the broad stairs when Carolyn hurried to them. "Iris, I have to talk to you."

"I thought you were gone. What happened?"

Carolyn took Iris by the arm and said to Bonnie, "Wait a minute, honey." The child stopped at the bottom of the steps, wide-eyed and silent.

"What happened?" Iris repeated, hearing fear in her own voice.

Carolyn spoke swiftly, keeping her voice low, almost in a whisper, "When I got home, there was a newscast. Rick Lathan has been killed, and someone named Wellington has offered a reward for information about you and Bonnie."

Iris moaned deep in her throat. She turned paper-pale.

"Rick said to hide her, keep her hidden . . ." She turned stricken eyes to her child who was watching.

"Hide her from Wellington?"

"I don't know. I have to leave. We'll leave right now." She was trembling uncontrollably.

Boise joined them, shaking his head. "Take it easy, Iris. Look, your car has a flat and the tire really can't be fixed. What we'd better do is drive up the coast and stop at the first town that has a garage with tires. Tydall's doesn't, down in the village. We'll bring it back and change it and then you can go on. But you can't drive without a spare. That would be too risky."

Iris stared at him not comprehending.

"Or I can take you and Bonnie to San Luis Obispo, or anywhere you want, and just leave the car here," Carolyn said.

Iris moistened her lips, then shook her head. "I have to have a car. I can't stop around here. They'll find her."

"Okay," Boise said briskly. "Come on. Let's go buy a tire."

Lerner regarded Stuart Wellington without expression, waiting. He had reported everything he had been able to find out about Iris and the child. Now Wellington sat behind his ornate desk and traced the tooled leather figures absently. Finally he folded his hands and looked at his secretary.

"Very good," he said. "Call Windemeer. He can pick up the trail at Cambio Bay and go on from there. They may even still be there, but I doubt it. The woman first."

Lerner felt ice form in his chest. He knew Wellington would brook no insubordination, but always before he had been a reasonable man. Very carefully he said, "Mr. Wellington, everything I've found out indicates that Rick assessed the situation correctly. The child is mute and retarded. She could never be witness to anything."

Wellington looked at him for a long time before he said precisely and without anger, "I seldom play hunches, as you know. The child has to die or she will dance on my grave. Call Windemeer."

Tony Windemeer was the best for certain kinds of jobs. He had had nothing to do with Rick's death; that had not required a specialist, a simple drive-by shooting had been enough. He worked alone and stuck to the thing he could do best. In a career of over twenty years he had never been questioned, never fallen under suspicion. Tony Windemeer specialized in women. The cases he handled always looked like accidents, or assaults, sexual or otherwise, that simply got out of hand; they never appeared to be premeditated murders. He would do the job without leaving a trace that could link it to Wellington, and he would do it swiftly, if that was required, although he liked taking his time. This time he had to work quickly, for Wellington wanted this done with.

Tony Windemeer was a slender man of forty; he looked like an accountant, or a high school teacher, or something equally proper and dull. He traveled with a lot of photographic equipment and took pictures, and even sold one now and then to one of the travel magazines. He had learned that a man with a tripod, an expensive camera or two, and an assortment of lenses and filters could go where he wished, see what he needed to see without question. He was free-lance in both of his chosen occupations, but he had worked for Lerner and his boss in the past and had found them fair and generous enough. This job sounded like a snap to him, a few days, a week at the most, and then he and his wife were scheduled to leave for Maui, a scuba-diving vacation. Diving was his only passion. Later in the summer he was planning to dive in the waters off Alaska, a first for him. He was looking forward to it with great anticipation. Any little job that came his way between now and then would be good; that trip promised to be expensive.

Tony asked only one question about the victims: "Both of them?"

"Yes. Together if possible, otherwise the mother first and the kid whenever you can."

Then the conversation had turned to real information: the make and model of the car (a junker), ages, descriptions of Iris and the kid, the kid's picture, the little that was available about Cambio Bay, the condition of the roads that had washed out and were under repair. Lerner had come up with a brief newspaper item about the convoy that had been led out of Cambio Bay. Neither man believed Iris would have trusted her old car to make it up and over the mountain. She would have waited until the regular road was open, in all likelihood. When Tony left Lerner, he was whistling softly, planning.

Monday they were stranded down in the little town. Tuesday there was the convoy taking some people out; Iris Lathan had not been among them, according to Lerner's contacts. Wednesday in the afternoon a road was opened, but with another detour from 101. She could have left in the afternoon yesterday, or she could leave today, maybe already had left this morning. He visualized the map and nodded to himself. If she had already taken off, she most likely would be on 101 somewhere. He doubted that she would trust driving along the coast after being stranded once. And in a clunker, she probably would not trust I-5—too fast, too dangerous, too far between stops, too far east of where she was. She would want a safe road where she could poke along and that meant that even if she had already left, he could overtake her. It was a long way from Cambio Bay to San Francisco, if that's where she was headed, and traveling with a little kid meant she would be stopping a lot. First he had to find out if she had left Cambio Bay.

Iris wanted to scream over the many delays. The trip to buy tires had taken hours. Carolyn had said there were still detours, but she had not mentioned the miles of one-way road, the many places where the shoulder looked as if it might crumble away even now. At least there were no other cars on most of it. With the southern part still closed, maybe closed forever, there was no place to go on this road except to Cambio Bay. The workers had left their signs and flashing lights, and even some of the equip-ment, but they had gone on to work on the southern end. In the town where they finally had found a garage with tires, she had said, "One," and Boise had said quite firmly, "Two." He had pulled out a credit card and bought the tires.

"Look, Iris, I don't know what's going on, but I do know that you won't make it farther than a hundred or two hundred miles with that other bald tire, and we might as well see to it that you get a decent start, at least."

She had not wept although her eyes felt afire. She had been too nervous for tears. The only thought she had was *Leave!* And then Boise kept making phone calls and they kept having to wait for him.

Now, finally, the car was under the overhang near the side of the house, the new tires had been put on, the laundry basket was in the backseat with Bonnie's clothes folded in it, a lunch was packed for later, and there was nothing else to keep her in Cambio Bay.

Luisa was standing on the porch where she had watched the preparations with an abstracted frown. She had tried to talk Iris into staying, but had not pressured her too hard, as if she recognized the desperation that was driving the young woman.

"You have my card," Carolyn said. "Iris, please let me hear from you."

She nodded. "I promise. And, Boise, I'll pay you back as soon as I can. Carolyn will have an address for you, won't she?"

"As soon as I have one. Don't worry about it." This was all wrong, he kept thinking. There had to be someplace where this kid and her child could stay until they all knew what was up. Luke had told him only that Wellington was powerful, that he had political friends with even more power; he was rich as Croesus, and he inspired rumors that ranged from unsavory to downright criminal, but nothing on the books. Just rumors. Boise had asked him to keep digging, but to what purpose? He had known many men like Wellington and usually they lived and died as rich, respected citizens, and the rumors went to the grave with them, never proven, soon forgotten.

Martica appeared, holding a paper bag, and beckoned to Bonnie who raced to her, smiling. As soon as the child was out of hearing range, Iris said to Carolyn and Boise, "I really don't know why he wants Bonnie, but that's who they're after. Not me. I don't know anything, but she saw or heard something last Monday. That's why Rick told me to hide her. I don't know what it is. But if I just get her away, she'll be safe."

They all turned to look at Bonnie who had on her light-blue denim pants and pink T-shirt; her pale hair was caught up in a ponytail with a pink ribbon. She was examining whatever was in the bag, a delighted grin on her face. Martica was smiling broadly.

"Christ," Boise said suddenly in despair. He couldn't let Iris take that child out alone, not with someone like Wellington after her. Iris was bone ignorant, and broke.

There was absolutely no way she could make it. "Wait a minute, Iris. I'll pick up my gear and drive to San Francisco with you. One direction's as good as another for me right now. I won't be more than a minute or two."

More delays, Iris wanted to scream, as Boise hurried off. But suddenly she wondered, who was Boise Wilkes? Why had he stared at Bonnie like that? Why all those phone calls? Why did he buy her tires? And now offer to go with her? She felt ice water in her veins, and light-headed with fear at the realization that she didn't dare trust him, or Carolyn, Luisa, any of them. There was no one on earth she could trust now. She yanked open the car door and yelled, "Bonnie, come on! We're leaving right now!"

Carolyn reached for her; she shrugged away and darted the few yards to where Bonnie was standing motionless, her eyes too large and puzzled, too frightened. Iris grabbed her arm and pulled her along to the car, shoved her inside, and ran around the front to the driver's seat.

"Tell him good-bye. Good-bye, Carolyn, Luisa, Martica. I'll call or something." She ground the gears when she started the engine, and then sped from the porch, down the driveway onto the street.

The three women stood in silence until the old Dodge Dart was out of sight. Boise appeared seconds later carrying a paper bag with his few possessions.

"She is very confused, and very frightened," Luisa said, and reentered the house.

Boise looked at Carolyn who shook her head. "I don't know what spooked her, all at once she just took off. We could follow her."

It was tentative, a suggestion only. They didn't have the right to interfere, she thought, remembering the look of terror that had appeared on Iris's face. If they followed her, if she saw them coming after her, she might panic even more; Carolyn shuddered to think of that frightened girl driving that awful road too fast, fleeing. Now Carolyn simply felt overcome with fatigue. Presently she would think about returning home, but not yet. She looked at Boise, then glanced about for Martica, Luisa, anyone. The porch was empty, the house silent.

"Buy you some lunch down at the café," she said. "Then I guess I'll take off again."

"You did what you could," Boise said, also very tired, defeated. He put his bag down. "Maybe I'll accept your offer of a lift, after all. Want to walk to town?"

She nodded, and they began to walk slowly, not speaking.

Iris braked as she neared the street through town, and then sped again after she passed the last house. Up ahead, she remembered, there was a viewpoint, a place where she could pull over and fasten Bonnie's seat belt and catch her breath. She could not remember ever having quite so much trouble breathing. Bonnie sat without moving, staring straight ahead.

When Iris reached the lookout, she stopped and fastened both seat belts after getting Bonnie's bag of shells from the backseat. Bonnie clutched the bag, but she continued to look straight ahead, her whole body rigid. Iris started to drive again, carefully now, under the speed limit of twenty-five miles an hour. She did not even see the black car that passed her going the other way.

Tony Windemeer couldn't believe his luck when the Dodge appeared, the woman driving, the child beside her. He whistled softly, made a turn in the lookout space, and went back the way he had just come. Not an accident, not on this stretch of road with all the workers coming and going. Accidents were chancy. You had to go check,

155

make sure no one walked away. No other traffic was visible at the moment, but the highway crew could show up anywhere, any time. He could simply follow her on up the highway and wait for a chance, but as soon as they got past the construction mess, traffic picked up again. He remembered a CLOSED sign at a logging road ahead, and his plan formed itself in the next second. He accelerated and in a minute had passed the Dodge.

At the road where the turnoff to Cambio Bay began there was no choice; the road south was closed. He turned north there and knew that she would have to do the same when she reached it. The next four miles were okay, and then the construction began, and a few miles farther on, there was a logging road or a forest service road posted NO ADMITTANCE.

He stopped his car just past the dirt road, ducked under the sign, and trotted up the road a hundred feet or so. Not too bad here, on the side of canyon that, unfortunately, was not quite deep enough. But the road climbed ahead. He nodded and returned to the highway.

Iris drove cautiously when she reached the construction area, not trusting the shoulders of the road, uncertain where the one-way stretches began. The storm waters had twisted trees out of the ground and carried them down the slope on the left; on the right the dark mountain gave way to eroded hills with stands of stunted oak trees and chaparral that followed erosion gullies. It looked as dry as if there never had been any rain here. There were warning signs everywhere. Ahead were flashing lights and a man with a camera waving to her: A new barrier was across the road.

She slowed to a crawl, trying to see past the barrier; the road curved out of sight beyond a ONE WAY sign.

She opened her window and called, "What's the matter?"

The man with the camera glanced at her, scowling.

"Road caved in up ahead. We're using the detour to get around it."

She glanced at the logging road entrance and tightened her grasp of the steering wheel, began to shake her head.

"It's only a couple hundred feet around," the man said with a shrug. "Some of the guys went to get a detour sign. Or you could turn around and go back the way you came."

He began to sight through his camera, ignoring her. Iris bit her lip and looked again at the dirt road. A couple hundred feet. A couple of minutes at the most. She glanced at Bonnie and thought about going back to Cambio Bay where there was no place to run, and finally she began to inch forward toward the dirt road. Thank God for the new tires, she breathed, eyeing the rocks on the road. She wouldn't have dared attempt such a road with the old tires. And it couldn't be too bad; they wouldn't send anyone off on an impassable road for a detour, she told herself grimly. They wouldn't do that.

Tony waited until her car had gone in a hundred feet and pulled his own car onto the dirt road. Unhurriedly he got out to change the signs around again and then drove on into the canyon after her.

14

▼ ▼ ▼ ▼

Iris knew almost instantly that she had made a mistake. This road was leading her back onto the mountain, and a canyon was dropping away more and more steeply on the left. The road couldn't possibly turn that way to reconnect with the highway. The woods had become thicker here on the north side of the mountain; the understory of scrub sage and vines brushed the side of the car now and then, and the road was deteriorating, little more than a narrow track with many rocks and holes, some of them filled with muddy water that had been captured and had not evaporated or seeped into the hardpan below. The road was too narrow to consider trying to turn around, but she wouldn't dare try in any event. *He* was back there somewhere. He had misdirected her and now was probably following, herding her and Bonnie higher and higher until there would be no escape possible. She felt as if she could not breathe again, and her vision blurred as she accepted that she was helpless; there was nothing she could do, nowhere she could run. Her foot eased on the accelerator as she drew in a shuddering, painful breath.

The car lurched over a rock that shifted with her passing; something scraped the underside with a squeal that sounded shockingly human. The panic that had threatened to immobilize her vanished and she gripped the wheel fiercely. Beside her, Bonnie was rigid, staring ahead.

All right, Iris said under her breath. All right! She tried to remember if she had seen a car or a truck, anything, and the image of a low black sports car came to her. Low, she thought, lower than the Dodge, and very expensive looking. He couldn't drive this road any faster than she was doing, and might be taking it even slower. Also, she had a little bit of a lead. To the right a gully was forming; the road now was on a ridge between the gully on one side and the canyon on the other, neither very deep yet, but the road was climbing. Whatever she could think of had to be soon, before they got much higher, before she came to another barricade, or the road simply ended.

He wasn't after her, she reminded herself then. He was after Bonnie. She had not yet caught a glimpse of the black sports car, but she had no doubt that it was behind her. That meant that he couldn't see her either, she realized, and glanced again at her daughter who looked paralyzed with fear.

She swallowed, but her mouth was too dry and it was a meaningless reflex. "Bonnie," she said in a hoarse whisper, "remember the story about Hawk?" Bonnie looked at her in bewilderment. "Today you are going to be Hawk," Iris said, gripping the wheel so hard her hands ached. "I will stop the car and you have to jump out as fast as you can and scoot down the ditch and hide. The enemy is coming, and you have to hide in the bushes." She glanced quickly at Bonnie, then at the track ahead and fought to keep her voice calm, her eyes dry. "Do you understand what I'm telling you? Just nod."

Bonnie nodded, her eyes fixed and staring.

Faster, Iris thought, faster, but she had to keep her voice calm, tell Bonnie the rest of it. "Honey, remember the man with the camera? He's the enemy, and he is in a black car. Remember that. Don't come out until the black car has gone by you and you can't see it anymore. Remember, don't move until it's gone. And then hurry back to the highway. You know your left hand. That's the way you turn when you get to the highway. There are men working on the road, and Luisa's house is that way. And, Bonnie, remember, you're Hawk. You can hear better than anyone. If you hear the car coming back down this road, hide again and don't come out until the enemy is gone again. Will you remember that? Hide and don't let him see you."

Bonnie's chin was wrinkled; she began to shake her head.

"And when the game's over, we'll tell Julio you're the best Hawk in the world. Better than the girl in his story. No matter what you hear, darling, don't come out, don't let the enemy see you unless I tell you the game's over. Remember that, honey. Remember. I'll tell you the game's over if you can come out."

She kept looking in the rearview mirror, but the road was too curvy; all she could see was the undergrowth and the pale-brown rocky track. It was getting steeper by the minute. Now, she thought. Now. She slowed down.

"Unfasten your safety belt, honey. Unlock your door now. I'm going to stop when I count three, and you jump out and hide as fast as Hawk. Just like Hawk. You're the best Hawk in the world, honey. I love you so much. One." She didn't dare look at the child now. Bonnie's belt was off, the door unlocked, her hand on the handle, her gaze riveted on Iris. "Two." There was another curve in the road. She slowed more, and when she rounded this turn, she came to a stop. "Three," she whispered. "Good-bye, darling. Hide!" Bonnie jumped out and slammed the door after her. Iris started up again and sped a little. When she looked through the rearview mirror there was no sign of the child.

She drove grimly. The odometer read 230, and it meant 116,230 miles. Thirty, she repeated, so that she would know where to start looking for Bonnie if she came back down this way. When! *When!* she muttered. The road kept getting steeper and her temperature gauge needle began to crawl up. When had she checked the water? Added water? She could not remember.

Tony Windemeer was in an icy rage. Lerner should have told him the woman had been alerted. It made a difference. The doll should have driven in a couple hundred feet, a quarter mile at the most, and looked for a place to turn around and get the hell back out. That was scenario 1. Scenario 2 was that she would drive up the mountain to a lookout tower or something and he'd catch up there. Over the side with her and the kid in the heap, dead cargo all the way. No scenario had her driving this fucking road forever, and his car, his *Ferrari* taking a pounding.

His rage extended to Iris Lathan, too. He had heard a story once about a mercenary who had his mark on the ground, with a sword at his throat when the victim spat in his face. The killer put his sword away and left. He couldn't kill someone he was mad at, not according to the game book. Well, Tony Windemeer didn't play by sucker rules like that. Iris had it coming to her and he'd give it to her, and then the kid, or maybe the kid first, just to really get the message across. Let her watch, and then her. And Lerner, he thought coldly. He'd have to pay, too, and his boss. Tony was not supposed to know that Lerner worked for Wellington, but he had found that out years ago. They'd both have to pay for this.

His car scraped bottom and he downshifted and gritted his teeth. No guns. Accident. He could have ended it a long time ago. Shoot out a tire and finish up and get the hell out of this end-of-the-world mountain. No guns. He knew that the Dodge wouldn't be able to make it much farther; it was getting too steep. Four-wheel drive time.

Iris felt as if she had been driving this nightmare road for an eternity. She had stopped once, just to make certain that he was still coming, that he had not seen Bonnie and ended it all back there. When she heard his engine sound, she had sped again, faster, she was certain, than he would be willing to drive. She didn't care what happened to her car. In places she was inches from the drop-off, then several feet, inches again. Rocks jutted up here and there, muddy ruts tilted her this way and that. Her thighs felt on fire, every muscle in her back and arms, in her neck and even in her stomach had gone rigid in her concentration.

When her odometer read 38, the canyon closed up suddenly; Iris had reached a plateau and ahead was a straight stretch of road up to a fire tower. Trees had been cleared in a circle around the structure; there was turnaround space and nothing else. She bit her lip and made the turn at the top. Hide in the woods? The growth was too scant to hide more than a few minutes. And he would be coming so soon. She stared back down the last bit of road, the smoothest in a long time, and very straight, and suddenly she pulled on the hand brake and nodded. She was pointing directly at the road, at the place where he would appear after the last curve. Her car was too overheated to keep driving. It could die on her any second, she knew, but it could still roll.

She was afraid to turn off her motor, for fear it would not start again, but with it on, she doubted that she could hear his car grinding up the last steep section. She opened her door and leaned out, and then she did hear the other car. She waited a few more seconds, trying to visualize that last piece of road, the last few curves. His car sounded louder and she dared wait no longer. She released the hand brake and began to ease down the straight road. The instant she saw the front of the black car appear around at the final curve, she pressed the accelerator all the way down and jumped out the side door.

Tony didn't know the road straightened after this last curve. He couldn't tell that the canyon had closed up and the land flattened here, that he had enough room to avoid the Dodge. When he rounded the curve, there it was barreling toward him, and his actions were reflexes. He spun the wheel hard to turn toward the mountain, not the drop-off, and his other hand undid the safety belt and pushed the door open. He rolled out a second before the Dodge hit the left front end of the Ferrari. Tony landed on his side hard against the last boulder on the forest service road. He raised his head, then let it fall again.

Iris circled him and the two cars warily, hoping he was dead; she didn't dare get close enough to make certain. As soon as she was past him, she started to run back down the road and was beyond the first curve when Tony raised his head a second time and then slowly, painfully pulled himself up, first to a kneeling position, then to his feet, swaying. He leaned against the Dodge and wiped his face; his hand came away bloody, and he began to swear in a low, vicious monotone.

He knew she couldn't be far yet, but there were too many places where she could hide, and he was not in such good shape. His right arm throbbed and pain stabbed through his shoulder with each motion. She would keep, he decided, and added, "But, doll, you're mine."

After a few minutes he was able to look at the two cars, locked in an embrace. His windshield was fractured into a million prisms and the driver's side door was sprung and would not open. His headlight was gone, and the whole front end a mess, but his radiator was okay. He rested and then got to work to try to move the Dodge; when he saw that he couldn't, he rested again, and then squeezed between the Ferrari and the mountainside and wormed his way inside. He crawled from the passenger seat to the driver's side and turned on the engine. Okay, he thought, and he had to rest again. But now he knew that he would be able to shift both cars and get his own turned around and headed back down the mountain. And he would leave, get fixed up. But he would be back, he said under his breath. The doll was his. He heard the mocking crack of a crow and opened his eyes to glare at it. The crow hopped on the road, cried out again, and flung itself into the air. Tony closed his eyes to rest.

Carolyn and Boise were not talking much as she drove out of Cambio Bay and he sat in the passenger seat with an unhappy look on his face. Lunch had been this quiet, and their brief good-byes at the guest house had been subdued; now Carolyn was just wishing she was home, back doing the thing she did fairly well, matching people with houses.

But thinking about going back to work simply added to her discontent, and she admitted silently that she didn't give a damn if she never sold another house in her life, or if all over the world people had to live in tents, or in tar-paper shacks, or just out in the open air. She drove too fast until she came to the construction area and then slowed below the limit posted. Her last look at this godforsaken countryside, she thought with grim satisfaction. What a hell of a week. She started to speak to Boise about what a crazy week it had been, but checked herself and held her breath, listening. Music?

Boise caught her arm in a hard grip and she felt a chill.

Pipes? She looked at him swiftly and slowed to a crawl. "You hear it, too?" she asked in an undertone.

His expression was so strained, the question was pointless. He nodded, leaning forward, peering out the window, scanning the sides of the road.

"Thank God for that," she breathed. "If it was just me . . ."

She pulled off the road onto the shoulder and stopped without turning off the engine yet. The pipes were no louder, but still all around. She edged forward fractionally and stopped again, this time turning off the motor in order to hear better.

Ahead were flashing warning signs. No construction crew was working on this section now, but the signs were everywhere. On the side of the road down the slope twisted trees had been pushed into a heap by bulldozers; a minimountain of dirt edged the road here. And there was no one around. No one, she repeated, but the music continued, the mournful, sweet music of the pipes.

Boise opened his door and got out to stand with his head cocked, trying to find a source. Everywhere, he thought. Nowhere. He began to walk forward slowly, listening.

Suddenly Carolyn thought: *We can't get away from here. They won't let us.*

She turned the engine on and even raced it, just to make a different noise. Boise turned to give her an irritated look, then walked on and she eased the car along after him, partly on the shoulder.

He stopped again, and she could see a barrier posted NO ADMITTANCE across a dirt road. Boise glanced over his shoulder at her, still frowning in concentration. Abruptly the music stopped and in its place they heard a whistle, a plaintive high note that swelled and stopped, then started again.

"Bonnie!" Carolyn yelled. She stopped the car and

jumped out. She ran to Boise and they became motionless, listening. The whistle sounded again.

"Over there!" Boise cried, pointing, and ran around the barrier, up the dirt road, with Carolyn right behind him.

"Bonnie!" she called. "Bonnie, where are you? Iris!"

They ran around a curve, and there was Bonnie standing in the middle of the rough road. She was filthy, her pink shirt torn, her jeans ripped, her hair in wispy snarls, some plastered to her face. Sunlight, tangled in the scant trees here, made a striped pattern on the child. Boise ran to her and caught her up in his arms and held her tightly, his head bowed over her, his eyes closed.

"Is she all right?" Carolyn cried, trying to see the child, the extent of her injuries. "Bonnie, are you all right? Where's Iris?"

Bonnie pulled away from Boise's chest slightly and pointed up the road, her face twisted in her attempt not to cry. Her face was tear-streaked.

"Honey, is someone chasing your mother?" Carolyn asked.

Bonnie nodded, and now her face crumpled and she sobbed great breath-taking sobs that were all the more terrible because her choked breathing was the only sound.

Boise began to disentangle the child. He handed her to Carolyn. "Can you carry her?" Carolyn nodded. "Get her out of here. Back to Luisa's. Tell Luisa . . . I could use some help maybe. I'm going to look for Iris." He didn't wait for her response, but kissed Bonnie's head and turned to trot up the dirt road.

Bonnie began to struggle as Carolyn headed back toward the road and her car.

"It's all right, honey," she murmured in what she hoped was a soothing tone. "Boise will find your mother and we'll go get Julio to come and help him and get you cleaned up and it's going to be all right now. Your mother will come down with Boise and you'll see. Julio and Martica and Luisa will be so glad to see you again . . ." She talked on and Bonnie relaxed in her arms, the sobs diminishing to shuddering gasps now.

Iris ran until she stumbled and fell. She had stepped into one of the mudholes. She pulled herself up and started to run again, and fell almost instantly. The strap of her sandal had broken; the useless bit of leather dangled from her foot. This time she forced herself to rest a few seconds, listening hard. She was still sitting there when she heard a crash, a car tumbling down the canyon with the noise of an avalanche. The thunder echoed and reechoed; when quiet returned, it sounded alarming after so much noise. Iris did not know how far she had come down the mountain, how long it would be before he came after her again. On foot? In his car? Or hers? She bowed her head a moment, then stood up and started to limp on down the rock-covered road.

The ruined sandal was more hindrance than help now; she took it off and carried it, one foot bare, one shod. Very soon she began to leave bloody marks. How much warning would she have if he came in a car? She couldn't think of distance or seconds, only of the need to hide, to have a place picked out where she could duck and hide. *Hide, Bonnie*, she thought, over and over again.

The canyonside was too steep; there was no way to get down and hide there, and then be able to get back to the road. And if she slid and started to fall, she would fall forever, she knew. She backed away from that side and looked into the shallow gully on the other side, a drainage ditch. Farther down, where Bonnie had hidden, it had been deeper, covered with dense bushes, but up here it was shallow and almost barren. In it there were more mudholes, some already cracking open, others still filled with muddy, brown water, and everywhere rocks, some smaller than her fist, others bigger than she was. As she studied that side, she heard the sound of a car from above her. It was making a terrible clanking, grinding noise. Without another glance up the road, she slipped and slid down into the gully, both feet landing in a mudhole.

She started to pull her feet out of the ooze, but then instead slipped into it even farther, covering her legs with mud, then she rolled in it, covering her back, her hair, her breasts and arms. The car noises became louder; something was being dragged, it seemed. It was coming down slowly. When Iris was as muddy as she could make herself, she crawled behind a skimpy clump of sage, half-hidden by a boulder; she curled up, praying she looked like just another rock among many. The last motion she made was to pick up a rock the size of a baseball. If he saw her, if he stopped and came to get her, she had to have a weapon.

Tony had had to break out the fractured windshield, and his sunglasses had been broken in the wreck. Now, every time he came around a curve that turned him west, he had the sun in his face, blinding him. He was cursing monotonously, no longer certain his Ferrari would even make it down the mountain. His door made a grating sound with every bump; the tail pipe was dragging, the muffler busted. He didn't know what other damage had been done, but it sounded like a dying car, groaning and grinding and clanging. He cursed and kept going past Iris trying to look like a rock, on around the next curve.

Iris waited until the noise was subdued by the mountain before she stirred. Cautiously she sat up, straining to hear the car working its way down the mountain. *Hide, Bonnie*, she prayed. *Hide.* In one hand she held her broken sandal, in the other the rock, which looked pitifully small now. She let it drop, and dragged herself from the mudhole, and then considered the sandal. She would have to tear a strip of cloth from her shirt and tie it on; she couldn't walk for miles barefoot, not on these rocks. She yanked off her shirt and began to work at it.

Boise had not covered more than a mile of the road when he heard the clangor of the approaching car. He stepped to one side of the road and took a notebook from his pocket, and a pencil, and pretended to be making notes when the black Ferrari came around a curve into sight. Boise gazed at it in wonder as he waved for it to stop. At Boise's feet was a length of tree limb nearly three feet long, but he realized he would not need it. The man in the car was alone, a bloody mess, but alone.

"Assessing storm damage," Boise said in an authoritative, bureaucratic manner. "How's the road? Looks like you hit an elephant. You need help?"

"It's washed out. Beat it!" Tony shifted into gear and pulled away from the asshole with the notebook, and resumed cursing.

"Hey, fella, you want to show me some ID? You're not supposed to be in here!"

Tony gave him the finger and rounded the next curve. Boise made a note of the license number and resumed his run up the road again.

He felt as if he were running with a lead weight in his chest, lead weights on both feet. He no longer expected to find Iris alive, and he had let the murderer drive away. His hands had itched to pick up the club and batter him to death; then his only concern had been to get away from him and find Iris. But she must be dead already, or the killer wouldn't be leaving. They must have wrecked head-on. She must have fought with him. The image of Bonnie in the dappled sunlight kept swimming before his eyes, the little pink and gold and blue child bloodied, hurt, and in his mind's eye she kept shifting into Jaime, also pink and gold and blue and bloodied.

He had gone along with the lie that absolved Elaine. An accident. Jaime had been riding his tricycle on the second floor and somehow had gone off the stairs. The trail of blood had confirmed her story. And Boise knew she had slapped him up there, had stood watching him tumble, and then had carried his trike up and edged it off the stairs after him, and had watched that, too. Boise knew what had happened because she had told him. Rationally, calmly, even thoughtfully she had told him exactly how it happened. And he had let her father and her lawyer and her doctor lie without interference.

And now he had let another killer go. He fully expected to find Iris's body up there, or down in the canyon.

This time, he promised grimly, he wasn't going to walk away from it, or drive away from it. This time he was going to go after that son of a bitch.

He couldn't keep trotting up the steep grade; he began to pace himself and kept to a brisk stride, not bothering to call her name, certain that no one would answer if he did.

When he finally saw her on the road, a muddy, be-draggled limping figure, hardly recognizable, he thought at first it was of a piece with the eerie music that he kept hearing at odd hours and the specter who had come to him in the middle of the night. Here was yet another ghost.

"Iris?" he called. She lifted her head, poised the way a deer becomes poised before springing away. "Iris, it's me! Boise!" Then he ran and she hobbled toward him as fast as she could.

"Bonnie?" she cried, drawing near.

"She's safe. Carolyn's taking her back to Luisa's."

He had reached her, and now caught her or she would have fallen. She sagged against him; he stood holding her with his head bowed, exactly the same way he had held Bonnie. As she wept against his chest, he kept thinking, Thank you. Thank you. He didn't know to whom he was offering thanks; he was not a religious man, but the phrase repeated again and again.

15

▼ ▼ ▼ ▼

Harold Ritchie was sitting on his balcony with an open
book on his lap, but had not read a word for a long time.
On the wrought-iron table at his elbow there were several
other books, and his notebook, which he also ignored. He
was trying to examine and even to identify the feeling he
associated with the departure first of Iris and Bonnie, and
now Carolyn and Boise. Not disconsolate, he decided; that
was too strong. After all, he hardly knew any of them.
But they had shared an adventure, and that counted for
something. It was the intensity of the feeling that mattered, not duration of acquaintanceship, he thought, and
made a note to look up the word. He didn't believe he
ever had seen it used before. He returned to his line of
thought, remembering the comings and goings of various
professors and assistant professors, the secretaries who
seemed to fade into the landscape with strange regularity.
Someone might have said to Harold something like: "Too
bad about poor old Wagamore, don't you think?" and he

172

would be at a loss. An accident? Illness? His work denounced? Much of the time he couldn't even put a face to the name, which was a variable in the commiserative aside. Often Wagamore, or whoever was to be pitied, had worked in the college for years, sometimes in his department even, but still there was no attachment, no personal sharing of experience although they might have eaten in the cafeteria at the same time, and perhaps even talked at length about a new school policy, or the attitude of this year's students, or something equally forgettable.

None of those people who had passed in and out of his range of interaction had left a gap. Certainly the word he searched for was not inconsolable. Not disconsolate. Morose went off in the wrong direction altogether. Sad seemed almost too feeble, because he felt a terrible gap had opened. A chasm. He knew it was ridiculous, but there was a hole where none had existed before, and he couldn't understand his sense of loss. He never once in his life had found himself peering up and down the school corridors, or casting a searching glance about the quad hoping for a glimpse of old Wagamore, or whoever it was who was gone. He had never given a thought to anyone like that unless reminded by someone else. Departures were a commonplace in colleges, universities; one's customers were always leaving, new ones arriving, none ever left a gap. Yet now there it was and he felt miserable and bereft.

Perhaps he should consider moving his base of operations, he thought then, and forced himself to consider the advantages as well as the disadvantages, although the biggest disadvantage swam to the forefront of his mind instantly. He hated changes. And he was comfortable here. On his last sabbatical he had gone to England, had taken a flat near Oxford, and had virtually never left it except for trips to the library or bookstores. Also, he would have to find another apartment; he had discovered early on this trip that he could not abide motel or hotel rooms for more than a night or two. No, he needed space, and there was no possibility of going back home to his neat apartment. He had sublet it until Labor Day. The search for another apartment, the unlikelihood of finding anything he would not feel was robbery, just packing up his things outweighed any reason for moving on.

The only reason he could find for even considering moving, besides the feeling of loss that had nothing to do with the place after all, was a sense of uneasiness that was as amorphous as the spray that shot up when a wave washed over the barrier where the Indian maiden stood. As soon as he tried to watch it happen, it vanished, and he was aware that the same kind of spray had erupted farther down the outcropping. He had explained to his satisfaction the eerie music and the hallucination of Bonnie at the ruins. That was as simple as anything else having to do with the psychological condition he had found himself in. Enchanted, he mused; by God, he had been enchanted by the stories he had heard, and the rest was the product of his own imagination. Not simply charmed or entertained, but really and truly enchanted. And that, of course, made him uneasy because he never in his life had experienced enchantment before, and he was a sober, middle-aged man, far past the age—

His musings were cut off when the yellow Toyota squealed around the turn from the street below onto the driveway. Carolyn? And she had Bonnie in the front seat! He left his rooms and ran down the broad stairs, out onto the porch where Luisa already had appeared.

Martica hurried around from the side of the house, and the two women reached the car together. Harold hesitated on the porch, uncertain what to do, trying desperately to see around the women, past them, as he looked for Iris. Luisa had the child in her arms before Carolyn was even out of the car, and then they were all talking, and he realized that Iris was missing, in some kind of trouble. An accident, he thought with horror, looking at Bonnie's bloodied arms and teary face.

"Is Julio here? Can he help us?" Carolyn cried, her voice high-pitched and trembling.

Martica shook her head. "He's gone. Where is Iris?"

Carolyn tried to describe the road, but it was just another dirt road up the mountain. She shook her head. "Maybe someone down in the village? Where is the nearest policeman?"

Luisa spoke rapidly to Martica in a language Harold could not understand. Martica took the child from her, nodding, and then began to make soothing sounds to Bonnie and carried her into the house.

"She'll take care of her," Luisa said. "I'll go with you."

Finally Harold came unstuck. "No!" he cried to Luisa. "Not you." He ran to the Toyota. "Up a mountain road? Dirt? I'll take Carolyn in the Buick. We'll need room for Iris and Boise." Iris, he thought despairingly. Iris.

Carolyn didn't think to warn him that it could be dangerous, that a man who was probably a killer was after Iris. She didn't think of it until they were on the dirt road. The barrier had been moved aside; someone had left and had not closed the gate again.

Harold was a good driver; she didn't know why that surprised her, but it did. The Buick rolled over the ruts and rocks with ease; it was high enough that the underside did not get scraped.

Harold felt almost as if he had been caught in an emotional whirlpool: guilt because he felt so, not happy, he thought, because this was Iris's disaster, after all, but vital. Useful. Needed. Yesterday, this morning, even an hour ago he had known there was nothing he could do for such a pretty young woman, nothing he had that she could possibly want or use, nothing he could say that might interest her. And now she needed him. But there was also the agony of fear that she was hurt, lying injured, fallen, tumbled, broken. He drove faster than the road warranted.

They came to Boise and Iris halfway up the mountain road. She was a muddy mess, and Boise was very nearly as dirty. Harold was silent and shaky when he stopped and pulled on the hand brake, and helped them both get in the back. He was afraid to speak, afraid he would start babbling at her. He peered up the narrow road and back the way he had just come and for the first time felt a twinge of doubt. He could back down, he supposed . . .

"There's a turnaround a few miles up," Boise said. "Iris drove all the way. It doesn't get any worse, she said."

Carolyn was twisted in the seat, examining the girl, reassuring her that Bonnie was in the care of Luisa and Martica; then Iris began to tell what had happened, and Harold listened with near-manic joy. They were including him, revealing secrets, talking about plots and threats as if he were really part of them. And Iris, he thought with awe, what a magnificent, brave girl, and just yesterday he had thought she was insignificant somehow, no more than a child.

He kept stealing glances at her through the rearview mirror. Her hair was plastered to her head with mud, her face was muddy with pale streaks left by her tears. She was the most beautiful woman he had ever seen. The gap he had sensed was gone, the hole closed again.

He passed the place where the cars had wrecked; bits of glass and metal were strewn about, and it was clear that the Dodge had gone over the side. He did not stop, but drove on, turned around, and headed back to Luisa's house. He had never felt happier in his life.

That afternoon they all sat on the porch behind the guest house. Iris was wearing a new skirt, a new blouse, new underwear. In her lap she held Bonnie in a new pair of pink pants and a white shirt, new sneakers and pink socks. Iris clung to Bonnie until the child finally squirmed free. Iris was soaking her foot in a shallow basin of hot water that smelled medicinal and felt good on the many cuts and bruises. She had soaked in a long bath that had also smelled medicinal, and her aches had faded almost past recalling.

Bonnie spotted Julio and darted off the porch toward him; he caught her and lifted her and swung her around. They could hear him say, "Hey, little Hawk! You like that? Okay. Now we make a hummingbird feeder. Okay? See, this gourd makes a good feeder, and then you blow your whistle, and we see them come and eat. Okay?" They wandered to the edge of the sunny lawn and sat in the grass.

"Luisa," Iris said then, "all those clothes upstairs, where did they come from? Whose are they?"

"Yours, of course," Luisa said.

"I mean, how did they get here? When? And why? There's a ton of stuff Bonnie's size, and so much that is my size. I can't pay for them all."

"Not now perhaps, but in time. When Bonnie came back so dirty, I just called the store down in the village and told them to send everything a little girl might need for a few weeks. And a big girl," she added with a smile. "If anything doesn't fit, or is the wrong color, or anything at all doesn't suit you, we'll send it back. The rest you'll keep for now. Your clothes are all gone, aren't they?"

"You don't understand," Iris said desperately. "I can't accept presents like that. You don't owe me anything, and I may never be able to pay you back. I don't have anything left. No money, no car, nothing." Her voice broke and she looked down at her hands in her lap and became silent. Her purse with her identification and all her money had gone over the mountain in the Dodge. She would have to call her parents, and whoever was after her could find her through them. She knew this, but she could see no alternative. Her thoughts spun in hopeless circles.

"Dear," Luisa said then, "I don't expect you to take charity. But I thought I might hire you, if you're willing, of course. In time you can pay me back."

"Hire me? For what? I can sell popcorn, or wait on tables, make beds, clean." She heard the bitterness in her voice and clamped her lips tightly together, stared out over the grass at the pink-and-white child with her head bowed over whatever it was that Julio was doing. Little pink-and-white child, little brown man. Bonnie looked up and smiled, and she could see the flash of Julio's brilliant white teeth as he responded to her silent message. *She* deserved better, Iris thought, wanting to weep for her daughter.

"No, no," Luisa said, laughing. "Martica can handle all that very well, except the popcorn part. I doubt that she's ever sold popcorn in her life. What I would like to hire you to do is catalog my library. I've been meaning to do it for many, many years, but somehow I never seem to get around to it, and the books just keep accumulating. In no particular order, I'm afraid." She glanced at Carolyn. "It's almost like having an infinite library. Or an Augean stable. It could take a long time to get done."

Her eyes were so clear, so knowing, Carolyn thought. It was as if she understood exactly that Carolyn had had an infinite library in her make-believe houses years ago. Carolyn had collected dozens, hundreds of ads for books, for bookshelves, for glassed cases and freestanding racks. Her make-believe library had had the ability to expand forever.

Luisa addressed Iris again. "Just think about it. Don't decide right away. We'll have to discuss salary, of course, but in the meantime you and Bonnie are safe here."

Iris shook her head and said in a very low, very intense voice, "I don't think we are. Not here, not anywhere.

178

Luisa, I didn't tell you all of what happened today. Someone is looking for us, for Bonnie and me. They'll come here. They know I don't have a car now. They'll come here looking for us."

Luisa stood up. She said gravely, "No one comes into my house or onto my property uninvited. Let me take that basin. The water has cooled off too much, I'm sure." She felt the water and nodded. "I thought so." She handed Iris a towel and walked away carrying the medicated water that smelled of woods and grasses and spices and herbs.

"Well," Harold said, watching her leave. "Well. I've been thinking, Boise. If you got the license number, and between you and Iris you have a pretty good description of that hood, it seems you might have enough to go to the police with."

Boise shook his head. "Think of the story *he* might tell. He's driving up a mountain road intending to take pictures, when suddenly this crazy lady hits his car with hers and leaves the scene of the accident. Damn near killed him, too." He grinned at Iris and shrugged. "His story might even be more believable than yours."

"I know," she said miserably, watching Bonnie and Julio. Martica had appeared with a bottle. Julio took it and poured from it into the gourd. He had tied a red ribbon to the gourd and used it to fasten his feeder to a tree branch. He took Bonnie's hand and they walked away from the feeder ten or fifteen feet. She put the whistle to her lips and blew the high, clear note once, and then she and Julio sat down again. Martica returned to the porch and reentered the house.

"I can't just stay here and wait for him," Iris said. "I can't go to the police. What could I say? No one's threatened me openly. Rick's dead. And Wellington says he wants to help me and Bonnie." She bit her lip to prevent its trembling. How could she make anyone understand the reality of the look of terror on Rick's face that day, or her absolute conviction that the man in the black car had intended to kill her and Bonnie? How can you make anyone else accept your truth when it sounds insane?

Suddenly Boise said, "I'll be damned!" He was staring at the hummingbird feeder. A tiny, jewellike bird darted to it, flashing green in the sun, then ruby. A second one appeared and they both sipped, hovering, then darted away together.

Bonnie leaped to her feet when the birds were gone; she jumped up and down clapping her hands. Julio remained seated on the grass. She turned to him, threw her arms about his neck, and kissed his cheek.

All afternoon Carolyn kept telling herself that she would not stay here another night, but her Toyota had been moved around the house to the protected parking area, her small suitcase had been carried up to the rooms she had used before, and it seemed impossible to take a position, state her intention, and simply leave. In a few minutes, she found herself saying more than once as the afternoon wore down and darkened into evening.

Boise had been no help. He kept sinking into a deep concentrated study; absent was the only word she could think of that applied to him. Bonnie had eaten in the kitchen, then returned to the porch to crawl into Iris's lap, where she promptly fell asleep. Eventually Boise carried her upstairs for Iris, and now they were all in a dining room where Luisa was serving seafood fettucini. Martica had insisted on staying with Bonnie, and Iris had joined them for dinner.

This was yet another room, not the large, formal dining room, and not the room adjacent to the kitchen. This was more like a family's dining room, with an oak table and chairs, a china cabinet with a bowed front, an oval braided rug on the floor. Homey, Carolyn thought, examining everything warily. The flowers on the table were ordinary garden pinks and daisies with pansies among them. Shining clean windows with white cottage curtains drawn back looked out over the ocean, naturally.

Luisa finished serving the fettucini and picked up her wineglass. "Well, it's been a busy day, hasn't it? To a successful ending of a harrowing day." They all sipped wine to that, and then, without preamble, she said, "Chapter Two."

One day Great Chief called to Squaw, "I am lonesome." Squaw said, "Come to my longhouse and sit by me." They sat side by side as Sun passed overhead. "It pleases me to sit by you again," Great Chief said after a time, and Squaw admitted that it pleased her also. Presently Great Chief said, "I am hungry." She said, "Then we must prepare a feast." And so the preparations started: salmon and deer, rabbit and quail, mushrooms and wild garlic and onions, beans and maize and rice, fruits of the vine and fruits of the trees, and nuts and honey, on and on. Great Chief ate more than he had ever eaten before, and still more delicacies appeared: mussels and oysters and crabs and shrimp. When he would stop, Squaw brought in hot bread from the hearth and cakes from the oven. When he groaned with pleasure that was becoming pain, she brought eggs preserved in sweet pickle juice and candies made with chocolate and pistachio nuts. When he said it was growing late and he should return to his longhouse in the sky, she said, "But look, Sun is still shining," and he lay back on the soft skins she had brought to ease his bones. "Rest," she said, "and I shall sing you the songs from our youth." And she sang the sweet songs they had known before when they lived together and lay together in the longhouse. The sweetness of the music she sang, and the sadness of the separation they now endured made his eyes burn with tears, and she said, "Close your eyes and rest while I sing to you."

He asked, "Is Sun still shining?" And she said it was. Then he asked again, and she answered the same. And yet a third time he asked, and when she told him Sun was shining, he jumped to his feet and cried, "You have betrayed me yet again!" For although Sun was still shining, Sun had almost reached the land of snow and ice and soon would dip down to feel the coldness there, but more, the long shadow of the maiden had been creeping silently across the sand and now was no more than the width of a hair from the warrior of her choice.

Furiously Great Chief called Sun back from his wanderings and he said, "From this day you will be merely a sun, set in a path that I decree, never to stray from it again." And he set the limits north and the limits south that the sun would forever be forced to observe.

Now he said to Squaw, "You have many children on the earth, but you have taken my only daughter from me. Only you can draw forth a child, only you can give me back my daughter." But she would not. The maiden, she said, must be allowed to live as other maidens. He had to let her go. Now Great Chief stormed out in a rage like none ever seen on the face of the earth before. He brought down the snow and ice, and he sent Wind to blow the people away; he withered their crops in summer and tried to wash them away with torrential rains and floods. But no matter how he raged, Squaw walked the earth and brought forth more and more children to join the first people. They were yellow and black, brown and white, tall and short, and their homes were mountaintops and valleys, forests and deserts, shores and plains. Great Chief soon realized that there were so many that he could not rid the earth of them.

Great Chief brooded in his longhouse in the sky. His

daughter stood her lonely vigil and he vowed that if he could not have her for his own, then no one would find the happiness promised by Squaw when she brought forth her children. He sent Wind to whisper in the ears of men and women all over the world: Why does your neighbor have more food than you? Why are the strangers coming? They may steal your women and your livestock. Why share the water with anyone else? And so on.

As the people became fearful and suspicious, they forgot about Crow and Raven and Coyote and Bear. They forgot about Great Chief and Squaw. Now there were just animals and birds. There were many chiefs and many squaws. It was a time of changes, and when it passed, the magic was gone.

Carolyn felt dazed, as if she were just awakening from a profound sleep. They had eaten; the food was gone and now coffee was before her. No one moved yet, as if everyone else was as disjointed, out of time, as she was. Luisa picked up her coffee, made a clattering sound with her spoon when she put it on her saucer, and the spell ended.

Harold cleared his throat, in preparation to say something about the story, but he shook his head and picked up his coffee and sipped it instead.

"Would you like brandy with the coffee?" Luisa asked, glancing around the table at them generally.

Iris refused, but everyone else had brandy, and when she finished passing the glasses, Luisa asked Boise, "Have you formed any plan of action yet?"

He started, then shrugged. So they weren't going to talk about the story, but then he wondered what there could possibly be to say about it. It was just a story, maybe better than the first one she had told them, certainly more compelling, hypnotic even. He said, "I think I should go down to Los Angeles and find out something about Wellington, how big his organization is, just sniff around and see what comes up."

Luisa nodded.

"It could be," Boise said more deliberately, "that the best thing for Iris and Bonnie would be to move all the way out of the West, go to New York, or Boston, someplace like that, depending on how big Wellington's gang is, what resources he's prepared to commit to her."

Iris shook her head. "I can't!" she cried. "Don't you understand? I lost what little money I had. I'll change my name, take my maiden name back, and hide in San Francisco. Bonnie doesn't have to go to school for another year. I can keep her hidden that long, and they'll forget all about us."

She was so pale and pinched-looking, Carolyn wanted to pat her arm, comfort her. Harold, sitting next to Iris, did pat her clenched hand awkwardly.

Calmly Luisa said, "We could get a specialist, a child psychologist, to find out what it is that Bonnie knows, and use that in some way. I'm certain a good psychologist would know how to go about that."

Iris shook her head harder. "No! I want her to forget all this. They wouldn't let us use information like that. It might even put her in more danger!"

"The other possibility is that they will decide to use the resources of the California police to find you, my dear. That man today can bring charges of a hit-and-run accident, can't he? No doubt there will be an insurance investigator sooner or later. If this man Wellington is really above suspicion, various legal actions could be the way he would want to handle this now." Luisa turned to Boise, ignoring the pallor that had spread down Iris's face into her neck. "Could they take Bonnie if they arrest Iris?"

"Probably," he said, his eyes narrowed and watchful. Why was she doing this? Tormenting Iris this way? "They could make a claim of incompetence, get a court order for a foster home, something like that."

Luisa nodded gravely, as if he had confirmed her fears. "And, of course, if the police get involved, her maiden name would be one of the first aliases they would look for. Is it very hard to get new identification, school records, all the necessary papers, do you suppose?"

"Depends on who you know," Boise said. "I could do it back in Pennsylvania. There are people out here who could do it just as easily."

Suddenly Iris jumped up, one hand jammed hard against her mouth. She glared at Boise and Luisa. "Stop it! Stop talking about me as if I weren't even here! Why are you doing this?" she demanded of Luisa desperately.

Luisa stood up also and said quietly, "To impress upon you that you're in a situation you only dimly understand. You are in grave danger, and so is Bonnie, and you are no match for those people."

"And you are, I suppose!"

"Yes, I am. If you'll excuse me now." She turned and left the dining room.

16

▼ ▼ ▼ ▼

The rising tidewater whispers against the sand, a gentle
sound with none of the crash and fury of the waves against
the barrier arm. A gibbous moon rides the easy swells, a
Dali moon stretching, contracting. Most of the lights in
town have gone out now; the residents usually go to bed
early in Cambio Bay. In the motel bar Doc Carmody
finishes his quick one and yawns. "Might as well pack it
in," he says. "See you." On his way to Number Three
he glances up at the guest house in time to see a light go
off somewhere on the third floor maybe, another go on at
ground level, the way they do up there. He goes on to his
room.

"Might be a good time to get some painting done," Syl
Grundy says. "Get ready for the summer like." He eyes
the bar thoughtfully before he turns off the light behind
the counter. Bobby Shehan and Speedy Tydall nod.

"Been thinking we might go down and see the folks,"

Speedy says. "Won't be no tourists for quite a while, looks like." He stands up. "That road, she's a mess."

"She's a mess," Syl echoes.

Earlier, Doc said the engineers from Sacramento would come around in a day or two, or sometime, and they would make the decision about the next step. They all agree she is a mess right now. Be a fool to come down this far, dead end in Cambio Bay, turn around and drive out twelve, fourteen miles. What for? Good time to catch up on things. Paint, see the folks, fix the plumbing, whatever. No point in bellyaching about it, neither, just get on with things.

At the door they pause and glance around, the way people do, and a light in the guest house goes off, another comes on. Syl chuckles. "Bert says his mom's taking off tomorrow. She thinks this is a pretty spooky place. Wants them to move down to San Diego, be close to her."

Speedy laughs. "Bert? Take dynamite to budge him."

They chat, then drift apart. The light in the Morrison house goes off, but Sara Logan's is still on. Sara is reading a murder mystery. She's a real night owl, they tell each other now and then, up all hours night after night reading. In Bobby's grocery store the pale-yellow light flickers uselessly. It isn't to warn off burglars; they don't have any in Cambio Bay, and if he had to say what the light was for, Bobby would be stymied. They just always leave on a light in the store. The blue fluorescent light in Speedy's garage has grown dimmer and dimmer over the years, but he never sees it anyway and doesn't realize this.

Bert Eccles knows his mother is standing at the window staring up at the guest house, and he knows there's nothing he can do about that. She has a thing about the house. He tried to reassure her about Miss Luisa, how when the baby was sick that time and they couldn't get a doctor and were afraid to start to the city with her so sick, Miss Luisa knew exactly what to do, and she probably saved little

187

Wanda's life. His mother, of course, took it the wrong way. He should move his family to a civilized place where there are doctors on hand at all hours, not rely on a . . . naturopath, she ended, but he almost heard the word *witch* form and then be discarded. It isn't like that, he wants to say, but he cannot argue with his mother; she never yields or loses. And she can outwait him, he knows, as finally he is forced to go past her on his way upstairs to bed. "Maybe she's got the lights on timers," he says, and keeps moving upward. For the first time he has said the right thing. His mother relaxes, and he remembers that she keeps her lights on timers when she leaves home for more than a couple of hours. "That must be it," she murmurs, nodding, and she goes to her room and, he hopes, to bed and sleep. Some nights she says she can't sleep at all because of the lights going on and off up there. Her room is in a direct line with the guest house. "It's watching me," she whispered just a few mornings ago, sending a chill down Bert's arms, down his back. Not from fear of the house up there, or anything like that, but fear that his mother might be cracking up, that he might have to care for her for the rest of her life, and that would be hell because his wife Susan can't stand her more than a few days at a time. Next time she comes, he has already decided, she will have a room overlooking the town if they have to move every stick of furniture they own. Then let her talk about hearing music at all hours and a house that watches her.

The whispering water has awakened the creatures in the tide pools. Ghostly crabs, urchins, starfish move in a silent dance celebrating life in a cycle that has turned them to silver and gray and black; the water will sigh as it leaves, and they will go back to sleep; when they awaken the next time with the sun overhead, they will be gaudy again. That is their rhythm.

Harold Ritchie is in bed reading about tectonic plates. He wrote the story Luisa called "Chapter Two" in his notebook, and soaked in a soothing mix of salts and hot water, and now he is waiting for the words to blur, his sign that it is time to turn off his light and bunch up the pillow in a particular way that is comfortable for him, and drift, drift. Falling into sleep is never traumatic for Harold; it is a gentle drifting that overcomes him, that blurs his vision first, then makes his muscles yearn for a certain position, on his side, one leg stretched out fully, the other bent, bone against soft tissue, never bone on bone; one hand open under his pillow as if to cradle his head, the other flat on the bed. It all has to be just so, and then he drifts away. Now that his eyes are blurring, he puts down the book and turns off his light.

To his surprise he doesn't fall asleep. Instead, without effort on his part, images of Iris float before his eyes in the dark room. Iris on the beach barefoot, her delicate feet leaving tracks in the wet sand, tracks that he had not wanted to obliterate with his own big feet. Iris sitting in the sun on the lawn with Bonnie, the sun firing her hair into pure gold, blazing gold. There was a faint blue vein in her temple. So vulnerable. She needs someone to lean on, someone to protect her, not a middle-aged man set in his ways, a born bachelor, fussy . . . He can be a father to her, an uncle perhaps, someone she can confide in when she finds her young man, the way his ex-wife confided in him over the years. That is his role, his only role in her life. He can be mentor, teacher, even to Bonnie. How lovely it would be to have a student who yearned for education, who hungered for books and intelligent talk about them. He can do that. Her uncle, mentor, teacher, friend . . . He remembers how her hand trembled when he patted it at the table, and he knows he is lying to himself.

Iris fell asleep as soon as she crawled under the covers of her bed, and later she woke up suddenly, her heart pounding, her skin clammy in the aftermath of a nightmare that was unrecoverable. She raced from her room to Bonnie's and touched her daughter lightly, then sank to her knees and rested her forehead on Bonnie's bed, until her ragged breathing smoothed out again. Bonnie slept on her stomach, her thumb close to her mouth. She was no longer a thumb-sucker, but it was as if she kept it there for convenience, just in case it was needed during the night.

Now Iris is back in her bed, but she is not sleeping. Scenes from her own childhood flash in and out of her consciousness, out of control. Her mother storms at her.

"Wash that filth off your face!"

"All the girls wear lipstick!"

"And they become as harlots. My daughter is not a harlot!"

"I haven't done anything."

"God knows what is in your heart, the temptations you offer, the temptations you can't resist. God knows you are a sinner!"

"I haven't done anything! I haven't. Everyone wears makeup."

"Sinner! Harlot! You will burn in hell! You have hardened your heart and you will burn in hell. Get down on your knees and beg Him to forgive you! Accept your Lord in your heart. Accept Jesus or you will burn in hell!"

"I haven't done anything. I haven't done anything."

Iris fled up the carpeted stairs, along the upper balcony to her room. It sometimes surprised her when she realized that they were rich, richer than most people she knew. There was an Olympic-size pool, three luxurious cars, a daily maid and cook, a gardener. Her father was important; on committees, on councils, much sought after for his advice. He was busy, busy, busy.

"On your knees!" Her mother followed Iris into her pink-and-white bedroom, into the matching pink-and-white bathroom, where she held Iris by the hair and scrubbed her face until it was raw. "Harlot!"

Iris is sitting up in bed, holding her pillow tightly, rocking back and forth, back and forth. She can hear her mother's shrill voice, feel how hard her hands were, strong hands, large hands. But she cannot see her face. She can see her father's face; he was very handsome, with wavy gray hair and blue eyes, heavy peaked eyebrows, and smooth skin that always smelled of aftershave. He played golf and rode his horse—she forgot about the horses until now. They had two then. She often fled from her mother and ran to her father when she was young, and he would say, "What's the matter, princess? Broke again?" He would hand her a ten-dollar bill, even a twenty sometimes, and then he would go to a meeting. Once she tore the twenty-dollar bill into the smallest scraps she could manage. But only once. After that she kept everything he gave her, hoarded it against the day she would run away.

"You filth! It's that no-good Lathan boy, isn't it? You've been in bed with him, haven't you? Filth! Harlot! Pray to God to forgive—"

Then, as Iris ran out the door: "If you leave this house, don't come back! You hear me! You've chosen the Devil's path! Filth! Filth!"

And this time Iris couldn't say I haven't done anything, because this time she had done it, exactly as her mother knew.

She sits on the bed, rocking back and forth, back and forth, holding the pillow against her breast as hard as she can, her head bowed, eyes closed, and still she cannot pray to her mother's God. He's dead, Mother, she wants to cry out. Does that satisfy you? He's dead. She means Rick, of course, not God, but for her either one could be the *he* she is talking about. One is as dead as the other.

And now, finally, she is remembering Rick, and herself with Rick, and Bonnie with Rick and her. She sees Bonnie like a wriggling worm caught in the middle with both ends in frantic motion, laughing soundlessly, Rick laughing down at her. When do you tell a child that her father is dead? And how? Silent laughter, silent grief? If only she could talk! Iris presses her face into the pillow she is holding, to stifle any sobbing, choking, gasping for breath, but she is not weeping. There are only so many tears to be shed for each person, she thinks, and she used her quota for Rick many years ago; she has none left for him. Tomorrow, she wonders, will she be able to tell Bonnie tomorrow? What difference does it make? she also wonders. Sometimes Rick came for Bonnie every week, then months would pass without him. Bonnie always acted as if he had never gone beyond the next room.

Iris moves the pillow from her face; she is sweaty and thirsty, and nothing ever gets resolved, she thinks in despair. She tries to plan her future, Bonnie's future, tries to plan tomorrow, or even the next hours, and nothing is resolved. She feels adrift in a sea she did not choose to enter and cannot leave.

She leaves her bed and goes to the tiny, immaculate kitchen for a glass of water, which she carries to the door of Bonnie's room to sip, gazing at her beautiful daughter. There is a fish-shaped night-light in the bathroom; the door is open slightly, and Bonnie is bathed in soft golden light. She sleeps peacefully; she always did. Only recently did she give up the raised-fanny posture of her infancy; now she sprawls, sometimes facedown, then on her back, with several stuffed animals and a doll along the wall side of the bed, and her thumb close by her mouth, but hardly ever in it anymore.

Iris tries to picture Bonnie in the house where she grew up, tries to imagine Bonnie's reaction to her grandmother when she screams about filth and repentance and prayers. She shakes her head. Would they even let her in with her child? She doesn't know. And she can't see her mother's face. She can't remember it. She is so tired, she thinks dully, she might even collapse, she could become ill, and then what? The years that Rick wasn't really with them, she always knew how to reach him in case she needed to. The time that Bonnie ran a fever of 103, Iris called him, and he came within the hour. They both sat with Bonnie until the fever broke, until it was obvious that she was recovering. All through that night, the hours of torment, the hours of waiting, she could hear the rumble of Rick's voice, praying for his child, on and on.

Bonnie turns over, flinging out one hand, as if aware of the prolonged scrutiny of her mother. Iris backs away from the door and returns to her bedroom, and suddenly wishes she had a sleeping pill. Normally she is so tired, sleep seems to overtake her even before she has shaped the pillow to her head, the way it did earlier this night, but then the nightmare came, and now sleep is elusive. She knows she has to think, make plans, decide what to do next, and her helplessness is a weight she feels she cannot bear. No car, no money, Bonnie threatened. She wishes for a sleeping pill.

Bonnie is dreaming. She is playing a game with Luisa, Martica, and Julio, even if she can't actually see them. She just knows that they are part of the game.

"Can he hide on the beach?" she asks.

"Not this time. Just in the house and in the garden."

Luisa is out of sight, too, but Bonnie knows who is talking and what she is saying. And now it is time for her to find Julio. She is It. She flits through the house without effort, first in the attic, then the cellar, in the library, the kitchen, wherever her thoughts take her, and everywhere she goes there is light. It is as if she is the light that she carries on her search. She laughs as she nears Julio again and again, always to find him gone by the time she arrives. This is a strange and wonderful game. She knows he was in the kitchen only a moment ago, and now he is gone, but this time she senses him before she moves, before she even thinks about moving, and then, fast as a hawk, she pounces on him, all the way upstairs in a room she has never seen before, a sewing room or something. Julio laughs and lifts her, swings her around, laughing, and she is laughing just as happily. Her laughter is like silver bells, but when she tries to listen to it, the sound is gone, and then she and Julio laugh even more.

When it is her turn to hide, she thinks about the huge piano and finds herself curled up under it. She turns off the light she carries inside herself and holds her breath and pretend/thinks herself somewhere else so Julio won't find her. When he passes nearby, she almost laughs her silver-bell laughter, but she holds her hand over her mouth to still it.

Julio stops and whirls around, and looks straight at her, and she knows the muffled sound she makes in her attempt to still her laughter rings softly, as silver as when she laughs. Before Julio can say anything, she thinks herself away, to the kitchen where Martica and Luisa are drinking tea.

"You win," Luisa says, laughing softly. "Back to bed now. The game's over."

Bonnie rolls over in her bed, smiling in her dream.

Stuart Wellington and Lerner waited for Tony Windemeer in the office. Tony had called Lerner hours before.

"Things to do," he had snapped, "but I want to see you and Wellington. Around ten, his office. Be there!"

"Did you find them?" Lerner had asked blandly, as if talking about stones, or books, giving no sign if he was surprised that Tony knew about Wellington.

"Around ten."

When Tony arrived, Lerner looked at him with interest. Cuts on his face? One hand cut and bandaged. "What happened?"

Tony told them an abbreviated version: Iris had known about him and lured him into a trap that nearly had killed him and wrecked his car. Fifty-two thousand, he added darkly. Totaled. Although he had demanded Wellington's presence, he did not look at him directly as he talked. He kept his gaze locked on Lerner.

Lerner was angry with Tony, and even more so with Wellington. This was turning into a fiasco, and the woman and child were still out there somewhere. Rick must have warned her because apparently she was aware of the danger. He scowled at Tony who was pressing a case for a new car, up front, and payment on completion of the job, as usual.

"You should have told me she was warned," Tony said again, aggrievedly.

"We didn't know," Lerner snapped. "And that seems to me to be part of your job."

"Yeah, but the price goes up if they're warned. Fifty-two thousand!"

"Pay him," Wellington said abruptly, and he stood up and left without a backward glance.

Lerner stared after him.

"No checks," Tony said, grinning now.

"Just shut the fuck up."

Lerner didn't understand any of this. Iris was a kid, a green know-nothing kid, and she had nearly wiped out the best hit man around, and had wiped out his car. Wellington was acting like an old lady over this affair. Lerner had seen the day, and not long ago, when Wellington would have ordered someone like Tony shot before dawn for fumbling the ball like this and then making demands. And it would get around that he had made demands, and they had been met, he brooded, not moving yet toward the office safe. Finally he shrugged and went into the closet where he opened the safe and counted out fifty-two thousand dollars.

"Not another cent before the job's over, and I don't care if she bombs your house," he snapped, and thrust the money at Tony who counted it methodically, turned, and walked out.

But what the devil was the matter with Wellington? Lerner kept wondering after he left the office and went to his town house where Tammi Craymore was waiting for him, and then he didn't think about his employer again all night.

Stuart Wellington sat in the dark in his office at home and looked down at Los Angeles blinking like a Christmas tree below. His wife was out; when he was in, she was out. The only time they even saw each other was when they attended a social or business or political function together. His two daughters knew, of course, and pretended not to, but he doubted that anyone else suspected that he and his wife had been separated for nearly twenty years. They lived in the same house; he paid the bills and gave her a personal allowance that was more generous than she would have demanded, but they were separated.

His problem, he was thinking, staring blindly at the lights of the city, was that he had no idea why he was convinced that Iris and her child had to die. A premonition? An intuition that they spelled his greatest danger? He had said the child would dance on his grave, but he had been speaking nonsense, of course. No image of such clarity or such a nature had imposed itself upon his consciousness, but still there was a feeling that he could think of only as dread, and that feeling was wrapped around the package that had been comprised of Rick, Bonnie, and Iris. One of the three sides down, two to go. And they had to go. That was the only aspect of this stupid affair that gave him no doubt. They had to go.

If Rick hadn't run out instead of waiting as ordered, none of this would be going on now, he thought with some bitterness. He did not like confusion or indecision or bungled jobs; he did not like it that Iris had somehow outsmarted Tony Windemeer. He had an image of himself before a jury, with that silent little girl standing up and pointing her finger at him, and he knew that was insane because she never in her brief life had even seen him. And yet. And yet. He turned away from the wall of glass and touched a button, on a control panel on his desk, that closed drapes, shutting out the city lights. He touched another button and office lights came on, two lamps by a fawn-colored glove-leather couch, a desk lamp that people thought was gold-colored but that was really eighteen-carat gold. He liked gold. Not many things were real, but gold was. Real and forever. He didn't look at the lamp now. He pulled a map from his desk drawer and opened it, studied Cambio Bay once again. He had been studying it off and on all day.

Later, in bed, sinking into the web of sleep, he feels as if the map has been burned into his brain. He rolls over and closes his eyes, trying to rid himself of the bay, the nearby mountain, the remaining road, the ruins on the hill over the town. There seem to be starbursts of color exploding behind his eyelids. And now distantly, faintly, almost unrecognizable as sound, there is music. The sound of pipes, or flutes. The music swells, rises, fills him with an ache that he can't name. The erupting colors, brilliant, uncanny in the purity of color, and the rising and falling music of the pipes hold him immobilized. He can't choose now to open or close his eyes, to try to cover his ears to block the music; he can simply perceive the images and hear the sad, sweet notes rise and fall until he wants to weep with longing.

He sinks into the colors and into the music and dreams of a house on a hill where a stern-faced woman stands and waits for him, her arms crossed over her breast, an expression of haughty disdain on her face.

Suddenly he is released and wide awake. His room is dark and silent. He sits up in his luxurious bed with its silk sheets and vicuña blanket that is as soft as a cloud. Cambio Bay, he thinks clearly. He has to go there himself.

17

▼   ▼   ▼   ▼

By the time Wellington had showered and shaved the next morning, he had dismissed the curious dream. He seldom dreamed, and put no faith in it when he did, but that one had been strangely compelling, and he put it aside as he might have done with a magazine article that displeased him. Breakfast was waiting in his bedroom, the way it always was. Papaya, cut-up oranges, a fig, red finger bananas, cheese, three kinds of breads or rolls, strong black coffee brewed the Colombian way. He had learned to eat these breakfasts in Medellín. Craziest city in the world. You fly in zigzag dodging mountain peaks, and suddenly there it is in a cul-de-sac, with vultures flying circles above it. City of death. He was thinking of Gabriel, who lived in Medellín, or near it, and who found things for him now and then. Gabriel kept a brown boy a few steps behind him at all times, and the boy carried a gallon jug of aguardiente; even at breakfast he was ready to pour it for his master. For a long time, at their meetings, Wellington had thought it was always the same boy, but one day he realized he was wrong. The boys always had that lush wavy black hair so common down there; always had eyelashes that fanned the air; always had slim hips shown off in tight black trousers, but gradually he had become aware of minor differences. There appeared to be a succession of them, clones of some ideal Gabriel had shaped out of clay, according to his own story. Magic clay, he said with a grin, showing three gold teeth, two upper, one lower in the front.

They had been sitting on a terrace surrounded by a high fence that supported rampant growth with orchids here and there. A *finca*, Wellington thought, remembering. A farm of a friend. He never believed anything Gabriel told him, and he supposed then that the place was Gabriel's. On the table that day there had been a skull carved out of flawless, clear crystal and a hideous little fetish. Wellington knew there was another crystal skull like this one in the museum at Bogotá, but this was finer. Gabriel didn't rush him, didn't pressure him in any way; there was time enough, and they both knew the price would be very, very high. Instead, he talked about his beautiful brown boys. That was when he said he had formed the original out of magic clay. He had laughed uproariously at the expression that crossed Wellington's face.

"I tell you this, my friend," he said then, seriously? it was impossible to know about him. "That pretty piece of work, very nice, only two on earth, rare. Junk. You can hire a good craftsman today and have him make you another, and then another. So? Or tomorrow they find a new city buried in the jungle, or hiding in the mountain mists, and they find a hundred more just like it. Again, so? But this," he said then, and there was no mistaking the reverence when he touched the ugly fetish, "this you can't hire anyone to make."

The object was made of stone and sticks. There were

two bulbous sections that looked like a scrotum, two pendulous breastlike lumps, a stick that rose between them that was phallic, or possible a head; it had been tied in place with string that also held an apron of dried grass which hung between the testicles. Looking at it, Wellington had been unable to conceal his aversion. The whole thing was only four inches high, dull brown and gray, hideous.

Wellington made a show of examining the thing, but he didn't touch it. He shook his head. "It's not even old," he protested. "That grass still has color."

Gabriel laughed again. "You think antiquity bestows worth? Made this morning, a thousand years ago, next week, makes no difference. This one has no power remaining. The shaman who created it discarded it, but when he fashioned it . . ." Abruptly he snapped his fingers and his brown boy ran forward with the jug of aguardiente. The conversation was over.

Wellington had brooded over that incident of twenty years ago, and his fingers more than once had twitched with the desire to touch the object, handle it. He wished he had bought it. Even worthless as it must be, he wished he had bought it. Since then he had purchased other fetishes, and he suspected most of them had been made for the tourist trade. He had never seen one quite so ugly, quite so suggestive of answers to questions he had not then known enough to ask. Over the years he had collected a voluminous library about shamans, witch doctors, medicine men, brujos. He had had no idea how extensive the literature was, how extensive the modern interest was. One time he had mentioned the object to Gabriel, years later, and Gabriel had looked at him innocently and said he knew nothing about such a thing.

Now he willed Gabriel and his boys away. The papaya was too ripe. Funny thing about papayas, too ripe and they were foul, too green and they made you sick. Like the three bears and Goldilocks. He frowned absently at himself for the nonstop nonsense that was running through his mind that morning.

All Central America was one great country, he often thought. The boundaries were stupid. What did jungles and mountains know about national borders, or Indians or jaguars or parrots? He collected from the great country of Central America, and more recently from Chile and Peru. All one. All the same. These days he brought in cocaine along with the objects that he preferred to deal in. The coke was almost like a side effect, an afterthought. If he didn't do it, someone else would, and it was his territory, his treasure hunt that had started thirty years ago. At that time there hadn't been any significant coke to bring in, but things change, he thought, things change. He was not political and did not really believe people risked their necks for abstractions. People wanted money and the power it bought, the freedom it bought. That was enough. If freedom meant freedom to overdose, that was not his concern. He was a supplier, not a moralist. He, Wellington, was a collector, that was what he was in it for. He could not understand why it thrilled him to hold an object that someone had made two thousand years ago, five thousand, but it did. The thrill was real. His basement museum would astonish the world, and it thrilled him to wander among his prizes, to touch things, to lift this and that, and think about the great lost empires of the Incas, the Aztecs, the Mayans . . . He felt that they had existed in order to create the objects he owned, that in a sense they had existed for him.

But over the years, there had also been the disquieting feeling that he was missing something, that it had been within his grasp that day on Gabriel's veranda, and he had let it slip through his fingers.

Gabriel sometimes sent a boy, and sometimes just a

message: *Weather is fine. The coffee is exceptional this season.* That meant he had found something of great interest. A condor once, serpentine, with emerald eyes. Another time a gold boat with two fishermen, also gold. A dozen golden ears of corn the size of his little finger. He never had offered another fetish.

The bananas were just right, and the white, crumbly cheese was excellent. He finished eating and rang for the housekeeper to come and clear everything. Because his thoughts had already been running this way, he was not surprised when the housekeeper told him that Gabriel's boy was here. She was feeding him breakfast in the kitchen.

They flitted back and forth across borders as if they were butterflies, he often thought regarding Gabriel's boys. Or maybe they all lived right here in L.A. and communicated by telephone just like everyone else. Maybe this kid was a student at the university, or an usher in a theater, or an extra at a studio. He could have been any of the three, or he could melt into a jungle, or climb a mountain. He was a beautiful boy. Muscular yet slim, the way Gabriel's boys always were. He stood up respectfully when Wellington entered the kitchen.

"What do you have?"

The boy carried a pouch at his belt. Silently he slipped his hand in and brought out something that he passed to Wellington.

Wellington felt the hairs stir on the back of his neck. Peruvian pipes, carved out of dense, dark wood that seemed to have no grain. It was a single object with a series of hollow pipes that were graduated in size, with a narrow mouthpiece. This one was beautifully carved, obviously well used. He stared at it a moment feeling disjointed, more upset than he intended letting the boy know. He would report back to Gabriel that something about the damn pipes bothered Wellington, and then what? He didn't know then what. Finally he looked at the boy and shook his head.

"Not this. Too common. I've seen dozens just like it." It was a lie; he never had seen one this fine.

"He say tell you *del oro*."

The hairs stirred again, stronger. Wellington switched to Spanish now to question the boy, but he apparently had said all he knew, or all he had been instructed to say. Gabriel had golden Peruvian pipes for Wellington.

"When can I see it?"

The boy spread his hands in an I-don't-know gesture, turned and left the kitchen. Wellington still held the wooden pipes in his hand.

He had intended to leave it at the house, he thought later, driving to the shop that was open until noon on Saturday. Today he had an appointment with a good customer who shared his enthusiasms, and after the certain sale, they would have lunch. He drove himself every day, using first one car then another. He had a Lincoln Continental, an MG, a Corvette. In a way, his many cars had made him more sympathetic with Tony Windemeer than he might have been otherwise. He could understand how it would upset a man to have a stupid girl wreck a fine machine. Then his glance happened to light on the passenger seat, on the pipes. Apparently he had carried it out unconsciously after all. He didn't dwell on the matter. It fitted in with everything in his shop. It could go on display and maybe even attract a buyer. He certainly didn't want it, and he knew that Gabriel would collect for it.

Then he forgot to hand it to Teresa Vincente who managed the shop. He placed it on his desk and this time frowned at it. Lerner came in with the mail and he forgot it again.

At lunch with his customer he felt it in his pocket and jerked his hand away as if burned. After lunch he replaced it on his desk and stared at it. Lerner was gone for the rest of the day, or he would have ordered him to get rid of the damn thing. He left it on his desk, collected a few papers from his safe, and walked out of the office.

Driving home, he felt his hands tighten on the steering wheel spasmodically as he realized it was on the passenger seat again. He did not look at it, but he knew it was there. All right, he thought deliberately, figure it out, think it through. He'd had a dream that included music from pipes pretty much like this, and then the thing came into his hands. It was simple coincidence, without any meaning whatever. But he was carrying it around because the dream had made him decide to go have a look at Bonnie and Iris in person, and he had put it out of mind all day. All right, he said again. All right. Why was it important to have a look at them? A snot-nosed kid and a too-young mother. What difference did it make if he ever saw them? He knew they had to die, and with or without his personal attention, the act would be carried out. Ah, he thought in sudden understanding, that was it. He had to go to Cambio Bay now if he wanted to see them personally. Otherwise it would be too late; Tony would move in and do the job and it would be too late.

The fact that he had not answered his own question of why it was important to see them escaped him once more. He couldn't have answered it even if he had thought of it again, but he didn't. Instead, he began to review what he had learned of Cambio Bay. There was a motel. Good. Tomorrow he could drive up in a couple of hours, check into the motel, hang around long enough to get a glimpse of the woman and her child, and then leave. He wouldn't even have to spend the night, but he would check in just to have someplace to go. In a town that size he couldn't simply sit in his car all day. There were Spanish mission ruins, he recalled, and nodded. He would take a camera, make the ruins his apparent destination. Ask around about

205

a chandelier or candlesticks, something he was tracking down. Good.

What if Iris had left the town already? He shook his head. She hadn't. He felt certain that she was there waiting for him, almost as if all her life she had been waiting for him, and he only now had come to realize it. Waiting for each other. He had been waiting for her since long before she was even born. And now he would end the waiting.

He considered ordering Lerner along, and decided against it. He knew Lerner thought he was obsessional about this matter. And he supposed that was correct. How could a child like Bonnie ever hurt him? He didn't know the answer, but he knew with certainty that she could, the same way he knew Christmas would come, and the New Year, and that his wife would be gone for dinner tonight, and that if he called either daughter, she would not be in. There was a measurable amount of certitude in the world, after all.

That morning Carolyn had searched for Iris and finally found her in the library where she stood contemplating the books, thousands of books.

"Taking the job?" Carolyn asked at the doorway.

Iris shrugged. "I don't know. They really are in a mess."

Even if they hadn't been before, Carolyn thought, they would be by now. She did not know exactly what she meant by the thought.

"Can we talk?" She glanced around the room; there was an alcove by a bay window, overlooking the sea, naturally. She motioned toward the seating arrangement. "Where's Bonnie?"

"Helping Luisa plant carrots and beets." Iris walked to the bay window and looked out, then sat down and waited for Carolyn to say it, whatever it was.

"When I'm alone, not asleep yet, or having breakfast, even showering, I know what I want to say, but then I forget again," Carolyn said after a moment. "This morning I made a list." She pulled a slip of paper from her jeans pocket.

The first item was *Coincidence*. She frowned at it. The next thing, in her writing, was *amnesia*. She felt near tears because she didn't know what she had meant by either item. Helplessly she stuffed the paper back into her pocket.

"Can I take you somewhere?" she asked finally. "Wherever you want to go that's drivable."

Iris shook her head and looked down at the table between them. Heavy oak with a golden pattern. She traced a line, then another. "I don't have anywhere to go," she said softly. "A few friends back in L.A., a family who disowned me, Rick's sister in Phoenix. Family is too accessible, you know? Friends? Not the kind of friends you can go to with real trouble. People I worked with here and there." She sounded almost apologetic, almost ashamed, and did not look up as she talked. "You know the kinds of jobs I had? Waiting tables in joints, selling popcorn or movie tickets, fast-food places. All minimum. Time for a raise, and suddenly they make it impossible for you to stay. They change your schedule so you have to work the wrong hours, or too many hours, or somewhere clear out of the city. You leave and hunt for something else. Also at minimum. The others do the same. Work with someone a few months, start a friendship, you leave, or she does, out of touch, can't get together because the hours overlap. Or no baby-sitter, no place to leave a small child. Always something. That's how they keep you in that rat race. Once in, you can't really get out, can't make real friends, can't do anything."

She was staring out the window at the incredibly blue

ocean, calm, brilliant, flashing with light. She glanced across the table at Carolyn, then back at the ocean, and asked softly, "What does Luisa want from me?"

Carolyn felt her hands go moist and she relaxed them both; they had become clenched and she didn't know when. "I don't know."

"There was a day-care center," Iris continued, still looking at the ocean, as if speaking to it, as if unaware that Carolyn could also hear. "I took Bonnie there twice. The next time, she tried to hide under the bed, then in the bathroom in the shower, in my closet. I'd find her and if I turned her loose, she hid again. I didn't take her back there. She wasn't hurt," she added swiftly. "But she knew it wasn't a good place. They know. They do. They'll tell you if you really pay attention." She faced Carolyn again and shook her head. "And here, it's exactly the opposite. She loves Luisa and Martica, Julio. I've never seen her so happy."

Carolyn nodded. "Maybe you should call the state police and talk to someone, or the FBI. Maybe they have a method of helping move people from one state to another, or something." Iris was shaking her head, and impatiently Carolyn said, "How about my family? I have family back in Iowa. I could send you to them, my parents, brothers, sister."

"I don't think we'd arrive," Iris whispered. In the same low voice she said, "I think we were meant to come here and stay awhile. Maybe I'll start on the books today."

Carolyn looked around the large room helplessly. "You need a computer."

"I don't know how to use one."

"I'll teach you," Carolyn said; she heard the words with disbelief, but did not retract them.

"You think she has a computer?"

Carolyn nodded. "If not at this moment, by the time you get around to asking about it."

Iris turned a shade paler. "What do you mean?"

"I don't know what I mean. And that's the honest-to-God truth. I don't know anymore what I mean or what I believe."

Carolyn left Iris wandering down one of the walls of shelves jumbled with fiction, poetry, nonfiction, biographies . . . Carolyn was looking for Boise or Luisa. Either one, she told herself grimly. She found Boise standing on the cliff overlooking the smooth bay. He was regarding the other side thoughtfully.

"Julio says there are great oysters all along a ledge over there," he said when she joined him. "Protected waters, no traffic, they just keep going forever. Problem is you get cut off at high tide. But a little boat . . . Wouldn't take much of a boat. Rowboat, canoe even, skiff . . ."

"Jump in and swim across," Carolyn snapped. "Boise, what the hell is going on here?"

He looked at her blankly, then slowly seemed to focus on her; he shook his head. "I'm hanging around a bit. I guess that guy will be back, or someone else will come around. Thought I'd just hang out awhile. Nothing better to do. If we can find a boat, want to go across with me?"

The problem was, he had decided during the night, he had known Elaine would do it. Not specifically, but something desperate. He had known and had waited in a helpless trancelike state, thinking: Today everything was all right, one more day, and when Jaime is five, he won't be at risk, or when he's four and a half, or four. One more day. Safe. And if she's sick someone else would be able to see it; it has to be my imagination, no more than that. One more day. Safe tonight. Reading *Winnie the Pooh*, the flashing laughter, the bright intensity of the concentration following the stories. One more day.

But he had known, that was the sticking place. He had known, and counted days, inspected his child regularly, counting the days.

Then Bonnie stood in the speckled sunlight, dust motes enveloping her in haze, her face tear-streaked, blood on her scratched arms, her hair as wispy as angel hair, the kind you put on Christmas trees but can't touch without a rash forming, itching.

During the night he had said no. That was all. No threats, no promises. Just *no*. He regarded the bay and nodded. Even a raft would do it.

Carolyn contemplated it also. "Let me know if you find a boat," she said at last.

She walked around the house to the garden area and stood taking deep breaths. The vegetable garden had black loamy dirt in raised beds that were brimming with peas and broccoli, lettuce and onions, carrots and beets. Early vegetables, to be replanted at intervals so that there would always be fresh carrots and beets, fresh salads . . . Over there would be the corn and tomatoes and squash; artichokes already looked like century plants, four feet across, four feet high, with dozens of tight green buds on each plant. Of course, she sometimes had to tell clients, it's hard to raise vegetables on the coast. The salt air, you see. Bad for them. But some people do. Microclimates in pockets here and there. Protection from the sea wind, special care taken.

She was wandering down the rows, not touching, looking only. The sun beat down hotter, the ocean sounds were the only sounds, distant waves crashing out of sight on the other side of the protective barrier where the maiden stood forever. The garden paths branched, turned, twisted; some plants, unfamiliar to her, grew higher than her head. The sun flashed off something on the moist dark earth. She bent to pick it up, a bracelet. When she straightened again, it was to look into the clear dark eyes of Luisa Ravel, who was smiling slightly at her.

"It's lovely, isn't it?" she said.

Carolyn looked beyond her, turned to look the way she

had come, and realized that she had managed to wander back to the grassy space behind the house, the place where the garden started. She looked down at the bracelet she held tightly. Shells and turquoise, pale-blue stones the color of the sky that day, with streaks of midnight blue in a swirling pattern. And tiny silver and gold bead dividers. She looked up from it to Luisa. The bracelet was warm, without a speck of dirt. Silently she extended her hand holding the bracelet. Luisa shook her head.

"I believe it must be yours," she said. "If the clasp is broken, no doubt it can be repaired."

"Who are you?" Carolyn whispered.

Luisa laughed. "I have to go back," she said. "I told Bonnie I'd only be a second."

She turned and took a step around one of the garden beds, and was gone. Carolyn walked to the raised bed and looked; no one was in sight.

She heard her name called and retraced her steps to the edge of the grassy area. Boise was there with Harold Ritchie.

"Hey, where have you been? We were going to leave without you," Boise said. "Julio rounded up a boat for us."

She looked at her watch. Ten minutes before one. She had left Boise on the edge of the cliff at ten-thirty. She moistened her lips and nodded, slipped the bracelet into her pocket, and joined the two men.

"Martica packed up a lunch," Harold said happily. "I really want to get some pictures of the pillar out there, and some pictures of the other two and the house from that vantage point. Isn't this exciting! It's like the scenes in novels set in England where people go off down the rivers and have lunch in some quaint place."

Still Carolyn did not speak. She felt as if she might not be able to even if she tried. She was aware of Boise's curious gaze and ignored it. Harold babbled on and they

Kate Wilhelm

made their way down the trail to the beach. The boat
bobbed gently alongside some rocks, evidently tied to
them. It was a rowboat, with a hamper already in place;
Julio lounged nearby on the sand. The rocks apparently
lined deeper water where a boat could be launched without
anyone having to get in the water, get wet. Had the rocks
been there before? Carolyn couldn't remember. But they
might have been, she told herself distinctly, almost desperately. They could have been there all along.

The bay was smooth, although the current ran strongly
from the mouth of the bay to the dip in the rocks that
made up the northern boundary. At high tide the northern
rocks were completely submerged and the rocky arm became an island. Boise and Harold rowed; Carolyn sat in
the prow and guided them in closer and closer to the
landing point that Julio had suggested. They brought the
small boat in, tied it to a rock, and got out. The arm was
higher than it appeared from shore. Thirty feet, forty?
And it was wider than Carolyn had realized, fifty feet
across, narrowing to a point finally where the mouth of
the bay started. It rose in tiers of dark rock that were like
giant stairs, an easy climb to the top. Nothing grew on
the rocks above the line of barnacles and seaweed. No tide
pools existed here. And the maiden, the pillar of the Indian
maiden, towered over everything. It rose twenty feet, and
was clearly female, a woman looking toward the sandy
beach, forever yearning for her two lovers. They sat in
the shade cast by the maiden and ate the lunch Martica
had provided, and then separated.

Harold scurried about taking pictures, and Boise inves-
tigated the ledge that was underwater now. He waded,
wearing shorts, and sneakers to protect his feet from sharp
rocks. The water was warming up, he said, after an initial

212

shiver. Carolyn gazed at the house on the point opposite them.

It was smaller, seen from here, than it appeared from that side. And it seemed simpler. Or, she thought, maybe the turrets and towers, the balconies and gingerbread vanished with distance. The wind blew in from the sea hard enough to mold her jeans to her legs, to whip her hair, short as it was, into her face. She faced seaward and closed her eyes to the wind, which was fresh and cold.

And suddenly she was thinking of all the impossibilities that she had been accepting, of all the questions that had to be denied, because if asked and answered, they would be terrifying. Freed of bonds that she had not realized held her, she did not dare move, or open her eyes, as if any motion might bring back the enchantment; she stood with the hard wind brutalizing her and thought through the time she had spent at Miss Luisa's Guest House. She knew there was a great evil there, that she, Iris, Bonnie, all of them were in deadly peril.

18

▼ ▼ ▼ ▼

The danger was in the house, not in the village or the motel, she thought, standing with the wind whipping her hair, plastering her clothes to her body. She could taste salt on her lips, and her skin was prickly with the spray. Still she did not move or open her eyes.

Luisa was a magician, a witch, that seemed clear now, but, since Carolyn believed in neither, this was not helpful. A master at trickery, then. But for what purpose? Carolyn could not fathom any reason for the tricks, and left that alone. It didn't matter if she knew why or how. Luisa had fooled Iris completely, had beguiled her, enchanted her. She was using Iris's fear to hold her and Bonnie. Again Carolyn found the why impossible to comprehend; again she sidestepped it. The business about the job was the most blatant trickery of all. No one alone could manage to reduce the chaos in the library to order without spending a year at it, not an untrained person like Iris, no matter how bright she was. That meant that Luisa intended keeping her and Bonnie at the house for the next six months, a year, more than a year? Why?

Impatiently she pushed the why away. She couldn't know why, she reminded herself. Maybe Luisa was mad. Maybe she had lost a daughter in her past and was trying to replace her. Maybe she had a yen for little girls. It didn't matter why. The real question was what should she, Carolyn, do about any of this, if anything. Life had been fairly simple for Carolyn after she left her parents' house. She liked being independent. She liked having friends who demanded very little, and falling in and out of love easily, having all the excitement of love without any of the entanglements. Of course, casual sex could no longer be trusted, and that infuriated her, and frightened her, but there was little she could do about it except be careful. If she took a drink or two now and then, that was okay, too. People did that. Stress, tension, just the goddamn traffic day after day. A drink in the afternoon, a pill now and then. People did that. Nothing out of the ordinary. Nothing to brag about, but that was how it was.

If now and then she thought of all the places she had never seen and never would, it was without great bitterness. Travel would be very nice, but she seemed to have no real talent for making the kind of money it took. No talents at all, in fact, she forced herself to add. She could sell real estate. And she knew that she didn't want to go back to the office, pick up another folder, talk to another client on either end of a deal. Let them live in tents, she said under her breath. But then what?

She had no particular talents, no particular ambitions. She had no burning desire to paint landscapes, or write poetry, or go into politics, or do science. No desire at all to become a housewife, cook dinner for someone every day for the rest of her life, clip coupons, wax the floor. There had been a time when she had thought she might become the well-kept mistress of a wealthy oilman, who

215

more or less promised wonderful things in exchange for the use of her body. When she learned how he wanted to use her body, she had walked out. And now that she was getting on, on the slippery slope of thirty, the body wasn't what it had been at twenty.

Except for leaving her parents' house, she had never actually done anything. Not really. She had been drifting all her life, idly watching the current take her here, there, letting things happen to her, sometimes surprised at them, usually not. Passive, she thought. She could be described as passive, and wouldn't that astonish her friends who thought of her as daring and adventurous, her own woman? But she knew that she didn't go out and cause things to happen; she didn't do things, create events. They happened and she might or might not be there, might or might not be affected, might or might not even react. Coming back to Cambio Bay for no particular reason was one of the few times she had acted instead of reacted. And she no longer knew what she had come back for, what she had thought she could do, or why. Always that damn why, she fretted irritably. Why this, why that, why here, why Iris or Boise or Bonnie, why anyone and not someone else? Why her, Carolyn?

The wind buffeted her, and suddenly she felt as if it had got inside her; the chill now seemed to start deep within her body. She knew how to get the money to make travel possible, she thought clearly then, and turned to regard the house on the point across the bay. She was remembering her first day here, a day that she had forgotten afterward. That day she had looked at the mansion and had thought it would make a fabulous resort. A hundred twenty-five dollars a night, two hundred a night, even more, with horses to ride, a swimming pool, little boats to play with in the bay, golf even. It would make a fortune.

The late-afternoon sun caught on the windows and turned them into fire, a hundred blazing eyes staring at her. Luisa didn't have any record of ownership, or of taxes, she thought, staring back. For how long? What would her back taxes come to?

She was truly free of the spell; she hugged herself against the chill of the wind, thinking thoughts that had eluded her. She had turned into a zombie before, and now she could think again, plan. The first thing she had to do was get away from this place, and not come back this time until all her plans were in order. She nodded to herself. What did she have here? Only a small bag and her purse. She would take only the purse, not stop long enough to pack up anything. Grab her purse and scoot. She nodded again. Tell no one, say nothing. If Luisa suspected, she might try to stop her, have Julio sabotage her car or something. The blazing eyes of the house watched as Carolyn planned.

They rowed back with Harold talking about the maiden and how like a woman the pillar really was. Almost sculpted, he said. He had shot many pictures.

Boise had collected a basket of oysters. "Have dinner with me?" he asked Carolyn.

"Thanks," she murmured, and he took it to mean yes.

Julio was there to help them get the boat secured to the rocks again, and they all walked up the trail to the house. The shadows had lengthened and deepened; the sun was below the rocky arm now, the maiden's shadow reached the sandy beach, midway between the warriors. The air had turned too cool and the chill that Carolyn had felt out there had followed her ashore.

Boise watched Carolyn enter the house, troubled by something he could not identify. She had become so silent, so watchful and withdrawn, her face stiff and unnatural. Nothing had happened out there, he was certain. Harold was still bubbling with happiness, and he, Boise, was wet and cold now. Shrugging, he gave up and went to his rooms to shower and change his clothes.

Carolyn kept her mind as blank as she could, with a simple refrain playing over and over. *Get my purse, go down, get in the car, drive away.* She got the purse and went down again without seeing anyone. The house was so silent it might have been uninhabited. It had the feel of the empty houses she explored in preparation to showing them to clients. She realized she was holding her breath as she went out to the porch. *Get in the car, drive away.* The Toyota was under the wide cover at the side of the house; she had to make a U-turn, and then she was throwing gravel on the driveway, on to the street, and through town. *Drive away. Drive away.* She was tense until she reached the end of the access road to Cambio Bay and turned north, on her way out. She wanted to get past the construction before dark, find a motel, plan. She let out a shuddering breath and realized, believed for the first time, that she was actually going to do it, leave, and not be stopped.

Iris played with Bonnie, bathing her, singing to her, playing silly bath games of losing and finding toes and her belly button and ears. Harold wrote feverishly in his notebook, his impressions of the maiden close up, of the mansion from afar, the way the rest of the town had become invisible from the rocky ledge. Something about the way it was situated, of course. Boise wandered through upstairs corridors and halls and stairways searching for Carolyn's door, feeling more and more foolish as he moved along.

"She left," Luisa said, standing at the head of a staircase that led downward.

"Carolyn?"

"Yes. An hour ago. Come, join us for dinner."

He felt a flush of anger with Carolyn for running out,

and another with Luisa for her attitude, not exactly mockery, or even superiority, but something remote and unknowable. She started down the stairs, obviously expecting him to follow. She was in another of the long skirts she seemed to favor, another silk blouse with long sleeves, tight at the wrists. Ageless, he thought, even her clothes were ageless. He followed her to the stairs.

"I've got oysters to cook," he called after her. "But thanks."

When she looked up at him, she smiled faintly. "Oh, you intended them for yourself? Julio misunderstood, I expect. Martica has prepared them for all of us, an appetizer, I think. I'm sorry."

Her voice was definitely mocking now, musical, soft, and mocking. He tried to remember what he had done with the damn oysters, if he had even seen them again after docking the rowboat. Nothing came.

And a few minutes later, in a different room altogether this time, with Iris, Harold, and Luisa, he started his dinner. And he admitted ungrudgingly that there was nothing he could have done with the oysters that would have matched the Oysters Rockefeller that Martica had prepared.

Luisa served them dinner again, this time pork in pumpkin seed sauce, rice with cheese-stuffed chilies, green beans with slivers of wild mushrooms or maybe even truffles. Boise had never tasted mushrooms like them, and had never tasted truffles at all.

This dining room was intimate, the table barely large enough for the four of them, dark paneling on the walls, a pale thick rug underfoot. There was a marble fireplace with a small fire burning steadily, for comfort and beauty, not warmth, since the room was quite warm. Two gleaming bronze firedogs seemed to move in the shadows of the flames, as if they were breathing.

"Miss Luisa," Harold said after the first few bites that

had drawn a sigh of happiness from him, "why are you doing this for paying guests? I love it, you understand, but I can't figure it out, why, I mean."

Luisa laughed softly. "You're going to write our stories, immortalize them. Isn't that reason enough?"

Harold shifted, suddenly uneasy. She had never seemed mocking before.

In a low voice Boise said, "And Iris is going to straighten out your library. And Bonnie obviously brings joy to anyone she gets near. And I? What about me, Luisa? What's my task?"

"But you're the handsome young hero," Luisa cried, laughing in real amusement now. "Every fairy tale has a hero whose task it is to slay the dragon. The dragon may have many different guises, of course, but it's a dragon nevertheless, and the hero is there to put an end to it."

Harold looked from Boise to Iris, both of them very still now, waiting, watchful. "Miss Luisa," he asked almost timidly, "the story you've been telling us. Is it over yet?"

She took a bite of the beans and shook her head. "In storybook stories, there's always an ending, isn't there? And in real-life stories, there never is. Not even with death, because the cast of characters includes every living creature, and they go on and on. You may think your own story contains just you and one or two others, but not really, my friend. Never. The ripples, the waves go around the world again and again. My story is about real life, so obviously it has not yet ended." She raised her glass and said in a kind voice, "Eat your dinner before it gets cold. Chapter Three."

Great Chief looked out from his longhouse in the sky and saw that the children of the earth were cold and hungry, that they suffered droughts and floods, plagues and insects, and yet they were not vanquished. They refused to be defeated. He yelled, "Squaw, I am lonely." As before, she said, "Come sit by me." They sat side by side and watched the waters rise and fall, watched the clouds form and dissipate, watched the seasons change. "Let us lie together as we used to do," he said after a time. "Chain your evil wind first," she said. "Not until you unchain my daughter," he said, and they both became silent again and watched the waters rise and fall and the seasons change.

"Why do they laugh and sing when the insects eat their corn?" he asked after a time. "Because they are happy yet," she said. "I made them to be happy when I cast down my sticks and clods of dirt." Then he saw that although he might move the sun in the sky, and order the course of the moon, and cause the stars to dim or fall as he chose, what she had done and could do again was greater than all this. He bellowed at Wind to blow down the trees and destroy the longhouses of the people and the tepees and the adobe houses, and when this was done and Wind, exhausted, crept back to his own longhouse, Great Chief watched the people come out from the ruins and cling to one another, and start to build anew. Someone began to sing softly, mournfully, another joined, and another, and presently the mournful song stopped and one of rejoicing replaced it and the people were happy again.

Great Chief turned to say something to Squaw and saw that she was gone, that her longhouse was gone, and he knew that it never had been there. She had created the magic for him so that he could sit by her and ease his loneliness, and now she had taken away the magic and he was alone again. For many days he pondered the problem of the children of Squaw. Then he called Wind again and said, "You must go down one more time and wait until the people have passed through the waking thoughts, passed beyond the dream thoughts, and speak to the shadow of thought that lies beyond reach. Say to it alone: 'Woman, look at man. He has the powerful tool with the magic of the seed to plant in your belly. The creator made him perfect and you inferior, the receptacle for his seed,

221

no more.' " Wind rustled, eager to do the bidding of Great Chief. He stilled Wind and said, "And to the man you say: 'Man, see you that woman covets your power, your magical tool. Without it she is lower than the pale worm that creeps by night. She must be subdued forever and ever, otherwise her envy will make her your adversary to the end of time.' "

Then Great Chief sat in his longhouse in the sky and watched as Wind blew around the world, and then again, and again, and where it blew it waited until the people passed beyond the waking thoughts, passed beyond the dream thoughts, and when they were where the shadow thoughts dwell, Wind whispered the message Great Chief had dictated. He watched as the women smiled at one another and shook their heads at the strange new thoughts, which were ridiculous beyond belief. He watched as men glanced at one another with furrowed brows and glanced at their women with suspicion and even fear. And then he yelled to Squaw to observe what he had done to her children. She wept.

The silence at the table was profound. No one moved; there was not even the sound of breathing until Iris whispered, "Why doesn't she give him back his daughter?"

Luisa stood up, her gaze cool, a professional innkeeper gaze. "I'll see about dessert. Excuse me." She left. She never had seemed to hurry, and she didn't now, but she was there and then not there, as if she had run.

"It's just a story," Harold said anxiously to Iris. "We make up myths to explain the human condition. All people have their own myths to explain mysteries." He sounded too anxious, he realized, and drank his wine. His food was gone although he did not remember eating it.

Iris's eyes were very wide, deep, dark blue in the candlelight, her face as pale as the moon. She stood up. "You're to record what happens," she whispered to Harold. "And you're the hero who must kill the dragon," she said to Boise. "What's my role? The story isn't over yet. There's Chapter Four to come. What's my role?"

Boise got up and threw his napkin to the table. "Let's go to my room for coffee. We can talk there."

Iris shook her head. "I don't want to leave Bonnie that long. You can both come with me, but I have only a little bit of coffee left."

They left the dining room together and went upstairs. At the short flight of stairs to his room, Boise hesitated, then said, "Let's stay together. Come with me for coffee and then on to your room, Iris. Okay?"

They found his room. Harold looked it over appreciatively, nodding. Boise shrugged. He hadn't noticed that it was impossibly situated either until Carolyn had pointed it out. He picked up his coffee can and the pot, and they all went back down, around too many corners to make sense, and ended up at Iris's rooms. She walked on through and in a moment Martica appeared smiling at them all; she murmured good night and left the apartment.

Bonnie was sleeping sweetly, on her back, both arms spread out as if in flight. Iris watched her for a few seconds, then tiptoed out and closed the door softly. Boise had the coffee started by then, and they waited for it in silence at the small kitchen table.

After Boise finished making and pouring coffee, Harold said, "I could take you out of here, Iris. I'm the only one left with a car." He smiled with an effort, and found to his surprise that his heart was racing uncomfortably as he waited for her response.

She looked at her cup and said, "Why? Why would you do that? You know what happened. That man. He'll be back, or someone else will."

"Maybe getting out of here is the only thing to do," Harold said. "And I'm free to come and go. They aren't looking for a rented Buick. We could even drive all the way back to the East Coast, you know. I mean, this man's influence can't extend all the way from coast to coast, can it? Wouldn't we have heard of him if that were so?"

Iris looked at him. "You haven't said why."

"Well, it's evident that you're in danger, you and Bonnie, I mean. And I'm available. And— Damn it all, I don't know why!"

She smiled faintly and looked down at her cup again. "Thank you."

"He's probably right," Boise said then. "You're a sitting duck in this town. Even if you think you're safe in the house, and God knows you could hide here for a long time, you wouldn't dare step outside if a stranger turns up in town; you'd live here in fear. You wouldn't dare let Bonnie outside. And if they're really determined, they could bring in enough people to make a search of the house itself." What he did not add was that determined killers would not be deterred by Harold and his Buick either. But her chances were better that way than just sitting tight and waiting. "I'll go with you, of course."

She turned her gaze to him now, her eyes still too wide, her face too pale. "I'll ask you, too. Why?"

Boise shrugged. "Same answer Harold has. I don't know. We seem to be in this together. Your chances are better with both of us than alone, that's for sure. And they're better back east somewhere than out here on the coast. Do you trust us at all?"

She nodded slowly.

"Then let me ask you why. You don't know us."

She thought about it for a moment and nodded. "Why does she want us to talk like this tonight?" she asked in a voice almost too low to hear.

Boise felt chilled by the question and glanced quickly at Harold, who simply looked bewildered.

Iris lifted her cup and sipped the steaming coffee, holding the cup cradled in both hands as if they were cold. "We can make plans," she said. "They'll seem to be very good plans, and then we'll forget about them. Or something will happen to make us change our minds. Maybe the Buick won't start. Something." She turned her wide blue eyes toward Boise, but it was as if she saw something else, not him. "Or we'll be walking down a hall and one of us will step sideways and be lost for hours. You know," she said, focusing now on Boise. "You know. You said we should stay together to come here to my room. You know." She put her cup down.

He sensed that Harold had stiffened, had become too still, and he studied him thoughtfully. "You know, too?"

"I . . . My God, something strange happens now and then, doesn't it? I thought it was just me. I mean . . . My stomach acting up, or not quite enough sleep, or something." And suddenly he was telling them about the music, about going to the ruins and finding Bonnie, and then watching the house change and change again. He raced through the words, curiously exhilarated to be talking about it at last. He had put it out of mind so many times, and now it all flooded out. Iris blanched even more when he mentioned seeing Bonnie up at the ruins, and he covered her icy hand with his, and talked on.

"But," he finished, "I thought it was probably just a hallucination. Just a hallucination!" He shook his head, baffled. "I never hallucinated before in my life, but as soon as I thought that, I felt it was all right for me to have experienced it. Naming it something made it acceptable."

Iris did not withdraw her hand from his. She was trembling. "I couldn't find Bonnie. She just took a step away and I couldn't find her. And then she was back again."

225

She pulled her hand loose and picked up her cup, and then dropped it as the sound of pipes filled the air. Over and above it and all through the music was another sound, of a child laughing in delight. With a cry, Iris ran to the bedroom door and opened it. The bed was empty.

19

▼ ▼ ▼ ▼

Iris took a step into the room, a scream in her throat not yet uttered, and then she was walking through a wide corridor with Luisa while Bonnie ran on ahead, laughing back at them over her shoulder now and then.

"You see," Luisa said, "true-life stories don't really begin or end. I mean, for example, your story. You could say it started with your birth, but that doesn't take into consideration your mother and father, and then back to their parents, back and back forever. And your story can't end with your death because that fails to consider Bonnie and the new creative fountain that is her life. Life is like that, a fountain of creativity, unpredictable and wonderful, and where the drops touch, new creative processes start. Not one of them is isolated. Think: You act and create ripples that go on and on, in three spatial dimensions, like bubbles without boundaries. They endure through time, true fourth-dimensional creations. Rippling through space and time, reinforcing each other, canceling each other, weakening or strengthening each other until the whole world is shimmering with them. Bubbles without boundaries shimmering all around us forever."

For a moment Iris could see the shimmering world of bubbles. She caught her breath at the beauty of it, involuntarily stopped moving as if afraid of disturbing the shimmers. Luisa laughed gently and reached out with both hands as if to contain the bubbles without boundaries, then blew softly at the empty space she cupped.

"We used to play with a flower called balsam," she said then, as they started to walk again and the shimmers vanished. "Touch-me-nots. Do you know them? When the flowers ripen, the seed pods form like beans, or peas. When they are ready to start their own fountains of creativity, at a touch they explode and send seeds flying out in all directions. We used to wander through the garden with sprays of them, touching the ripe pods here, there, everywhere. Even without the child to help them, the air is enough, the wind, a bird, a bee; at the time of fruition, they explode with new life, and nothing can prevent it."

The corridor was endless. Ahead of the two women Bonnie skipped; when the corridor forked, she chose the new direction and they followed. Now and then the child turned to smile at them, but she did not wait and they did not catch up with her.

"She's a very beautiful child," Luisa said gravely.

"Yes. Can you save her?"

"She can save herself here in this house."

"Will I die?"

"I don't know, Iris. Life is too unpredictable to say. But if you do, I promise to care for her."

Iris nodded. She reached for Luisa's hand, and they walked after the skipping child hand in hand through the endless corridor.

"Iris! For God's sake, what is it?" Harold was shaking her by the arm.

Boise pushed into the room, then looked at Iris in bewilderment. Bonnie was sitting up in the bed, staring at them in wide-eyed silent wonder.

Iris pulled loose from Harold and went to her child, touched her cheek tenderly. She whispered, "Go back to sleep, darling. It's all right."

The music was gone, the house quiet again. Bonnie lay down and didn't move as Iris pulled the blanket up to her chin, tucked it in at the foot of the bed, and then bent low to kiss her.

She returned to the kitchen table with Boise and Harold and they all sat down once more. She looked at the coffee cup she had dropped, spilling the last of her coffee. There had been very little; it made a pattern of swirls, an eruption of coffee; she reached for paper towels to mop it up.

"Iris, what happened?" Harold asked with helpless desperation. "We called to you and you were like a statue, frozen in place."

She shook her head. "I don't know what happened. We can talk some more tomorrow about going away. I think Bonnie may be safer here than anywhere else on earth right now. Let's leave it at that for tonight."

Boise was regarding her narrowly, and Harold was fidgeting with nervousness. "Something happened," Harold muttered. "That music again. Every time I hear it, something happens, something weird. Are you all right?"

She nodded.

Abruptly Boise stood up. "I think it's a form of hypnotism. Somehow there's a cue so that when we hear the music, we enter a trance state. I've read about things like that. It can be done. Carolyn's right. We should all get out of here and then talk, somewhere far from this house."

229

He glanced around the apartment, his gaze coming to rest on the sofa. "And I think we should stay together tonight. All of us. I can take the floor, let Harold have the couch."

Iris felt a great surprise at his words. She couldn't tell them about walking the endless corridor with Luisa; she didn't really believe it herself. But something had happened again, and they had been present. It made no difference if they stayed or left. "You'll just get sore and be too tired for anything tomorrow," she said. "And we all know that no one from outside is going to get in without permission."

They did know that, Boise admitted to himself. Restlessly he went to the window and gazed out at darkness. Even this, standing outlined before a bright window, posed no threat, because from out there no one could see in. Not when all the windows in the house faced the sea. This was a house of mirrors where halls opened and closed, stairs appeared and vanished, and the inhabitants were as fairies among the flowers. Iris and Bonnie would be as safe in this little apartment as Luisa wanted them to be. He swung around to regard Iris soberly. She was too calm, considering that they had all heard her mute child laughing. And none of them doubted for a second that it had been Bonnie. There was no other child in the house. What had Iris seen when she became paralyzed in the doorway to the child's bedroom? Whatever Luisa had wanted her to see, he answered silently.

"I guess you're right," he said then. "There's no point in staying up. Tomorrow is going to be a busy day. We all need some rest."

Harold shook his head. "I want to stay. I won't be a bother or anything, out here on the couch. And if you need something, someone . . ."

Iris took his hand and held it against her cheek for a moment. "Thank you. More than I can tell, I thank you. You're a good man. You're both good men, and I appreciate what you want to do for me. But I want to be alone with Bonnie tonight. If she wakes up again, I may bring her out here and rock her, sing to her. We do that sometimes. But not with company."

Harold was embarrassed now, afraid that unwittingly he had intruded, imposed himself on her. Made a fool of himself, he thought distinctly. He nodded and patted his pockets as if checking for belongings. "Well. Maybe we can get together for breakfast, or sometime early. I guess I should go write up the newest installment of the saga."

Boise went to the door with Harold, troubled by Iris in a way that he had not been before. He hesitated before leaving, studying her calm face. Still pale, but with more color than she had had earlier. But more than that, she had been glazed with fear earlier, had been in fear ever since he first met her, sometimes hiding it better than other times, but always burdened by it. And now she looked unafraid. There was a serenity about her that was more unsettling than her fear had been. Deeply troubled, he bade her good night and left with Harold.

"You want a drink?" he asked.

"Oh, yes. And to talk," Harold said. "Boise, I think you know more about what's been going on around here than I do. But frankly, I know enough to find it all unbelievable."

Boise laughed without humor. "Understatement time," he said. "Come on. I think my room's this way."

"That's what I mean," Harold murmured. "You'd think we'd all know exactly where every room in this house is by now."

They both stopped abruptly. Luisa had stepped around a corner before them. "Gentlemen, would you like to join me in the bar for a nightcap?"

Harold saw the ninety-year-old woman he had seen from the first day here, dressed in her ageless clothes, gracious and straight, and somehow frightening. Boise saw

231

a woman of under forty, with a small waist, high breasts, fragile wrist bones accentuated by the cuffs of her silk blouse. He saw the amusement in her expression as she waited for their reply.

"Will you answer some questions?" he asked brusquely.

"Of course. This way." She turned and led them down stairs that he had not noticed only a moment ago, through the hall on the first floor, and into the small bar that he had not been able to find since the first day he and Carolyn had sat in it.

Luisa went behind the bar. "Brandy? Or whatever you prefer, of course."

They said brandy was fine and sat on stools opposite her, watching, waiting. The brandy snifters were of exceptionally fine crystal, very large; the amber brandy reflected golden lights as she poured and then swirled first one, then the other, and passed the glasses across the bar. She sat behind the bar.

"No one has been threatened in this house," she said meditatively, apparently admiring the swirling brandy in her glass.

"But there are a number of tricks to the house," Boise said, as if commenting on the weather.

"Yes. Tricks. There are places on the earth where things always seem to be in flux, where trickery comes easily. One might even say naturally." There was a faint smile on her face; she was not looking at either man. "Normally we see through the spectacles of our culture. Isn't that so? But in those few places of flux, I believe we see through the spectacles of our needs, our desires perhaps."

Boise tasted his brandy, every bit as good as it looked. "Why are you interested in Iris and Bonnie?"

"Why is anyone? You, Harold, Carolyn. Everyone who meets them feels a compulsion to help them. Isn't that so?"

Suddenly Harold asked, "Who are you really?"

Luisa laughed gently. "You know who I am. Luisa Ravel, proprietor of the house, innkeeper, housekeeper, homemaker." She touched the glass to her lips. "Did you imagine I might say Squaw?"

Harold blushed. "No! I mean, that's just a story. A myth. Are you going to tell us the rest of it?"

"Chapter Four," she said meditatively. "I don't think it's been written yet. There's an outline, of course, but the details are still fuzzy."

"You're making it up as you go?" Harold asked incredulously. "You mean it isn't authentic, after all!"

Luisa shrugged. "What's authentic? I've been telling you a charming story that I clearly labeled a story, and you're behaving as if I cheated you."

Harold knew he had no arguable cause, no complaint due, but the feeling of having been duped was bitter. He thought of the hours he had spent trying to capture her words, not just the words, but the feeling, the nuances, on paper, to be included later in the book that, he realized with dismay, he might never write.

"Why don't you clue us in about the outline of Chapter Four?" Boise said softly.

"If you like," she said with a dismissive shrug. "It is brief, you understand. Now that Great Chief and Squaw have declared open warfare on one another, they are incommunicado. No more sharing the porch and watching the seasons change. No more intimate talks. She knows the agents he works through sometimes, and he recognizes her agents by their deeds, and the agents are at risk, of course. But they can't get at each other directly. The sad thing about it all is that Squaw has become as lonely now as Great Chief. She, like the children she made of sticks and dirt, is incomplete when she is alone, and he is the only companion worthy of her, although now and again she tries to replace him with a mortal. And, of course, he is incomplete in his longhouse in the sky. And their sorrow, their loneliness, their regrets have become too burdensome to bear. Squaw knows she must break the impasse."

Her eyes were the color of rich clear coffee, and now they seemed to shine with golden highlights reflected from the brandy in motion as she turned her glass this way and that, gazing into it.

"Poor little gods," Boise said coldly.

"Indeed. Anyway, she knows no one can put the ill winds back into their containers. No one can scour away the desires the wind has stirred into life in the secret shadow caves of human minds." Harold made a sound and she turned her clear eyes toward him.

"You're talking about Pandora's Box now. The same motif."

"Of course. There's only one myth actually, told in many lands with many shadings, many nuances. But one myth."

Harold shook his head. "Wrong," he said. "There are several that are recognized by all scholars."

"There is only one myth," Luisa repeated firmly.

Harold did not actually smile, but he felt almost as if he had stepped back into a classroom where an untaught student was making an absurd claim about, oh, something like Shakespeare, or Milton. He found himself on familiar and comfortable ground here. "Most scholars believe there are several basic motifs that are repeated endlessly, with thousands of variations," he said, trying not to sound pedantic. He knew he had the tendency to appear pompous if he was not careful.

Luisa shrugged. "One. From it come the three or four that are called basic motifs, and from them come the infinite number of stories, repeating endlessly the same pattern, which is so deeply buried that it has assumed an archetypal status. Without it there would be no literature."

Harold felt his spine tingling now; if he were furred,

he knew his fur would be stiff, at battle-ready condition. "There is the boy meets girl motif," he said, not quite condescendingly. "And the stranger rides into town motif. The brave little tailor. The search for and achievement of enlightenment." Now he smiled. "One could claim the commonality here resides in the cast of characters, that is, all stories finally are about people, human beings, but that is hardly what one generally means by the term 'basic motif.' "

His face burned when Luisa laughed in delight. She, with an apparent effort, restrained her amusement and assumed a more serious expression.

"Consider the stories you have chosen to illustrate your thesis," she said gravely, and he knew she was mocking him gently. He frowned at his brandy as if he were truly considering the stories he had mentioned.

"First," Luisa said, "let me tell the one myth that underlies all others. In the beginning there was Chaos, without form. Chaos was the Great Spirit, that which needs no form, but contains within itself all form. And Chaos created from itself the two principals, one of which we call Great Chief, although he has many other names. You may be more comfortable with Jehovah or Zeus. The other principal we call Squaw, although she too has had many names. In the Jewish legend I believe she was called Lilith. We will leave the semantics for the time being. Great Chief and Squaw shaped the world following the plan instilled in them by the Great Spirit, and they shaped the universe itself according to this plan, and Great Spirit was pleased with the creation. Out of Chaos had come form and pattern, male and female principals, all the creatures of all the worlds, but now Great Chief and Squaw were discontented and they did not know the reason for this. Great Chief and Squaw who had come from the Great Spirit where there can be only wholeness were now incomplete, each of them, and this filled them with unhappiness. But just as the vapor cannot be returned to the drop of rain, neither could they be returned to the Great Spirit; they had been created immortal and eternal, and for all time they were destined to be separate and incomplete. It is their unending struggle to achieve completion once again that has inspired all the stories we know as myths, as romances, as heroic adventure, by however many names they are assigned.

"For instance, the boy meets girl motif is so simple. If there is no completion to be found through deeds and possessions, then perhaps through the other it may be achieved. It is the story of the search for completion, wholeness.

"In the brave little tailor, the man or woman who struggles against overwhelming odds, again it is the need for completion that leads to such heroic deeds. The tailor sees wholeness as the result of conquering fears, enemies, tormentors, whatever or whoever the adversaries are.

"The stranger comes to town on a quest, always the same quest, mind you. Perhaps here he will find the missing part of himself. The people of the town welcome him as the bringer of the other that they sense they too are missing.

"The search for enlightenment and even finding it, of course, needs no further explanation. It is the same story in its most skeletal form." She spread her hands. "See? One truly basic motif permeates all literature."

"But that's a spurious argument," Harold protested, and instantly glanced at Boise, not certain now what the situation required. Good manners suggested that one not argue with the hostess, especially one as aged as Luisa, but etiquette be damned, he thought with a flash of annoyance; he couldn't simply concede the point by silence. "That's spurious because it uses the same grand, sweeping generality that I mentioned at the start of this discussion. Of course, literature is about human beings, and human beings by definition are solitary. Human beings have certain attributes that distinguish them from other creatures, our self-awareness, for example, consciousness, risibility, bipedalism, awareness of mortality, and so on. We are solitary creatures, that's one of the attributes we possess. You can't say that all literatures share that common motif because it isn't a motif at all; it's a common trait that is part of the overall, defining range of characteristics of Homo sapiens. It is subsumed in the statement that literature is about people."

"How strange it is," Luisa murmured, "that humans can accept so readily the attributes of humanity—the position of the nose in the face, memories, the wonderful ability to learn languages and pass on experiences to others through words, all the attributes, in fact, except two. And how bitter the struggle against them, denying them repeatedly through literature, songs, religions. Mortality and that terrible loneliness. It is almost as if everyone knows these two traits are misplaced, that they don't really belong to human beings at all, but have become attached through a horrendous mistake which, if one could but find the correct way, could be rectified."

"You didn't mention mortality as a common motif," Harold said uneasily, feeling that somehow she was slipping sideways through his arguments.

"But the fear of death is subsumed under the terror of our loneliness." Her mockery was gentle. She smiled at him and then deliberately turned to Boise. "But I am being a careless hostess. Would you like more brandy?"

The dialogue was over, that was clear, and Harold was wishing it had not taken place at all. Most unsatisfactory to leave it there, as if she had won points, as if everything had been said that could be said. What about happy stories? he might have demanded. Stories about people who aren't distressed by loneliness and fear? "Denying reality sometimes defines it more clearly than any other method."

He could almost hear her response in his head; he looked sharply at her and she was regarding him with a soft, distant look of amusement.

"Wait a minute," Boise said. "You agreed to answer questions. In the stories I recall, the gods screw each other royally, but it's always the people who get hurt. Real flesh-and-blood people with nerve endings that go twang. They pay the price for war in heaven."

"You have a question?"

"What are you planning for Iris and Bonnie? What are you up to?"

"I told you the details are fuzzy," she said with a faint smile. "Squaw wonders: If the maiden and her warrior consummate their love, will that remove them as the focus of rivalry and bitterness? Perhaps. And Iris and Bonnie have nothing to do with the maiden and the warrior, now do they?"

"Damn you, answer me! What are you up to? I think you're crazy!"

Luisa laughed and turned away from Boise and Harold as if to study the shelves behind the bar, the many-colored bottles there. Slowly she moved away, the shelves parted before her, and she walked through and was gone.

"Oh my God!" Harold moaned.

Angrily Boise went behind the bar and felt the shelves, felt for a control under the counter. "It's just another of her tricks," he snapped. "Ah, here . . ." There was a button. He pressed it and the shelves opened again to reveal a dark area, a storage room of some sort. And, of course, there would be another door that opened to the hallway. He pressed the button a second time and the shelf sections slid together again. "A cheap sideshow trick," he muttered.

Harold looked relieved, gulped his brandy, and stood up. "Too many tricks. Why? What are they for? Why is she playing with us like this?"

"I think she's mad," Boise said flatly, and now he felt a tingle of fear. If she was mad, she suddenly became something else, he thought, not just the beautiful owner of a guest house, enigmatic and mysterious, but another Elaine. A simple madwoman with no inhibitions, no fear of punishment or retribution. The image of Bonnie in sunlight appeared before his eyes again, and he found himself shaking his head.

When Jaime died, rage and guilt had welled up from the shadow caves of his mind, and he had forced them back, walled them off again, sealed them in, as if to imprison them forever. All his driving, traveling blindly, days, nights, weeks, a blur of motion on the white paths to nowhere, had been his effort to deny his personal devils of the shadow caves, and now the stones had rolled away. The caves yielded a rage more intense than he thought possible, guilt more agonizing than he thought bearable. Not again! Not again.

"Boise," Harold said in a low intense voice, leaning forward on the bar. "We have to get Iris and Bonnie out of here. Tonight, if we can."

Boise nodded. "Let's see if we can find their apartment." His voice was just as low. It was as if they both thought every word was being listened to, weighed, measured. As if every word ordered up a counterpoint of action. With the thought came the realization that he didn't believe they would be allowed to find Iris again that night. "Come on," he said brusquely.

They started to go to the door, but Harold paused, his hand on Boise's arm. He was reluctant to speak out loud and searched his pockets for a scrap of paper, and wrote: *If we don't do it tonight, as soon as we find them tomorrow. The way Carolyn did it. Just get in the car and drive out.* He showed the note to Boise, who looked startled, then nodded, and they stepped into the hall.

The corridor stretched out in both directions. This was

the wide, carpeted main hall with the beautiful chandeliers, and the open library door with the lights that were
never turned off. All the other doors were closed. They
walked side by side to the main stairs and started to ascend
when Harold saw the diminutive figure of Bonnie at the
back of the hall. He took a step toward her, opened his mouth
to tell Boise, and found that he was alone. Boise must have
gone on up, he thought uneasily, trying not to let himself
voice the awareness that there hadn't been time enough
for Boise to vanish up the flight of stairs, not that fast.
Now there was no one in sight in the hall or on the stairs.

Harold stood unmoving for several seconds. He was a
solitary man, he was thinking unaccountably. He had lived
alone all his adult life except for the brief trial of marriage.
He liked living alone. He knew he had quirks that would
make it difficult for someone else to adjust to him, and he
was comfortable enough with himself that he did not even
consider trying to change to make any adjustment possible.
There never had been a need to change since his divorce.
He was not an adventurous man. When he traveled he
kept to the well-guided paths, the documented vacation
spots, the recommended hotels and restaurants. He was
prudent; he believed in avoiding trouble, going down a
different street to avoid it, going back home and waiting
it out if that was necessary. He could never become part
of a mob because his dislike of crowds made it impossible
for him to linger long enough in one to become part of it.
And here he was considering his many cowardices and
quirks at the bottom of a staircase in a handsome house,
unmoving because he was afraid to move.

He found himself walking toward the entrance to the
guest house. He could leave right now. He could get in
the Buick and drive out of here, come back tomorrow for
his things, for Iris and Bonnie, if they would go with him.
Carolyn had been right, and smart. She had done it exactly
the right way, not announcing it to anyone, not lingering

once she had her mind made up. He had seen her make the decision to go away; of course, he had not known then what it was, but he had seen it. One minute as troubled as the rest of them, and frightened, and the next minute quietly determined.

He had his hand on the crystal knob, then drew back with a shudder, and now he was thinking of Iris, how she had outwitted the killer on the mountain, how she had won, saved herself and Bonnie. The bravest woman he had ever seen, he thought, as he had thought then. She was the one in danger, not he. Even more unaccountably, he was thinking that she could be his daughter, the age difference was so great. She was a child still. A beautiful, brave child who could behave like a tiger protecting her young. He half smiled at his image of her turning into a tiger, but the image stayed in spite of the mockery he now attached to it. And he realized that in spite of himself, knowing he was being a foolish middle-aged incompetent male, he loved Iris.

He was frozen in place again, this time by wonder, disbelief, and fear that he had admitted those words into his mind. But, of course, he would never mention what he felt; the fear was unjustified. She would never have cause to laugh at him, or, worse, be kind and gentle and dismissive, because she would never know.

He returned to the wide stairs and started to go up, thinking of his unsatisfactory life. He was a good teacher, not brilliant, but good and tolerant, patient with his students even if he did not like them all that much. He was surprised at that thought because he never had expressed it before. He was not a brilliant scholar who did brilliant papers or books, and the small college where he taught did not demand that of him. In fact, it might have made his colleagues uneasy if he had displayed real brilliance. What the school administration wanted, demanded, was steadiness and reliability. Precisely his qualities.

What he liked was pursuing an elusive line that led from one book to another by way of an allusion, or a brief reference, a footnote. He liked to read, and even write papers, but the papers he liked to write were not papers anyone else was ever interested in. The trails he liked to follow led nowhere in particular, just to another little chink in the wall of his own ignorance. The things he liked to do, and could do well, could be done right here in Luisa's house, in her library. He found himself outside Iris's door; he knocked softly.

She was surprised to see him. She looked past him, then opened the door wider. "Is something wrong?" she asked, moving aside to permit him to enter.

He shook his head. In confusion he said, "I just didn't want you to be alone all night. May I sleep on your couch?"

It was the Iris-child who opened the door for him, but it was the woman who now studied his face and slowly nodded. "If you want to."

Helplessly he entered the apartment.

Sometimes in the village they hear the pipes, and they say it's the wind blowing through small openings in the rocky barrier that gentles the bay. Tonight the moon is nearly full; the bay is silvered by it, the rocks seem to glow. On the beach the sand is gleaming silver, and the wind blows through the many openings in the rocks. Or the pipes are being played.

North of Cambio Bay Carolyn tosses restlessly in a motel bed that is too soft. The air smells like chemicals, like canned air poorly preserved. She has a mild headache. In her head she keeps hearing the pipes, and she remembers dancing in the big ballroom in her nightgown. The music is melancholy, then gay as it swells and ebbs. It is hauntingly beautiful, achingly beautiful. She imagines the little girl Hawk circling her ruined village, piping the people back, and tears burn her eyes. Angrily she jumps from the bed and turns on the light at the standard-issue table. On it are sheets of paper that she has covered with sketches of the guest house. This time she will do the figures, she thinks with determination. But the activity, the resolution, picking up the pencil and shifting the paper in order to start, none of it dims the music of the pipes in her head, all around her.

She has to go home, before her boss, Laurence Banning, becomes alarmed enough to call the police, or a friend does. Susan Wright or Ethel Krueger or someone will notice that she has been missing longer than usual without leaving word. Someone will begin asking questions. She shakes her head, doubting it. Why would anyone? No one owes her anything, any more than she owes anything to anyone. Live and let live. More than likely what they will all assume is that she has found a new irresistible man and eventually she will return, haggard and a bit more cynical than before, and Susan or Ethel will say let's have lunch, meaning forget it.

You must want something out of life, her mother said the last time Carolyn was home. She sits at the standard-issue table and tries to think what it can be that she wants out of life. Her shoe boxes of furniture, her imaginary houses.

She lets the pencil drop to the table and leans back with her eyes closed, yielding to the music that won't go away, listening to it intently, trying to understand the strange harmonies, the strange melodies, the poignancy and the gaiety. It wants her to go back to Cambio Bay. It is calling her home.

20

▼　▼　▼　▼

At seven in the morning the next day Boise called Luke Erskine, his former colleague in Scranton, Pennsylvania.

"Hey, that phone company's something else out there," Luke said disparagingly. "I called back a couple of times. Line's down. What gives?"

"Called about what?"

"Your pal out there. The one you asked about. Word is leave him alone. A friend who has perfect deniability passed it on."

Boise shrugged, gazing out the window of the lobby of the guest house. Today the phone was fine. This minute the phone was fine. He said, "More."

"Imports. Legit. Imports not so legit. Mucho land in Colombia, Brazil, Peru, Guatemala. Probably other places. Keeps a low profile, never tabbed with anything, but there are things lurking. Disappearances, killings. Pals in high places—local, state, federal. Generous campaign

244

donor. What makes him a hands-off candidate is arms deals. That buys him protection in a big way. More?"

"I'm getting the picture," Boise said sourly.

"Thought you might," Luke said; he sounded cheerful. He could afford to be cheerful; he was in Pennsylvania where the apple trees probably were in bloom. He continued, "Step on his toes on his own turf and you get slapped down so hard you bounce until Christmas. When are you coming home?"

The question was almost meaningless. Boise had not even thought of returning for a long time. "Don't know. What's new?"

Luke chatted politics and gossiped, and presently they hung up. Nothing really was new, except that it now seemed that Boise had underestimated Wellington's circle of power. Years before, Jimmy Kamisky, Elaine's father, had told him, "Son, there's no mystery to politics. It's who's got the power and how he uses it. Them that's out want in, them that's in want to stay in. And the real politician will fight like a stud mutt to get to the bitch in heat. That simple." But it was a little more complicated, he had come to realize. People like Wellington had to be included in the equations. Who did he own? Who held the strings and who jumped when the strings were tugged, those were the big questions Luke had raised, and it appeared that Wellington was a master puppeteer. Iris had insisted on not calling the police, and she had been right, obviously. But with this enlarged circle of influence, and the kind of influence Luke suggested, it was doubtful that running was an answer. Not if his circle included national figures, federal government figures.

Boise's office had been involved in researching the constitutionality of proposed legislation, not exactly in the path of the big wheels, but no one could work at any level of government and be unaware of the centered figures in those spheres of influence. If you tried to get near them you would be deflected off to the side, very soon if you were in the category of Iris and her child. They couldn't penetrate the outermost ring. Eventually most people got shunted off, down the slippery slope to the outside looking in. The higher the spheres rose, the more rarefied the atmosphere, the fewer of them there were in collision orbits. And Wellington apparently had little to fear at the altitude he called home. Why would someone like that go after a mute child? He knew as well as Boise did that he was untouchable where she was concerned, even if she could talk and sing and dance like a pro. Boise had seen too many legitimate attempts to unseat the king get the brush-off treatment or worse if the contestants for power underestimated the opponent or overextended their own resources. For a time the challengers might experience the illusion of closing in, then whammo, they found themselves on the outside again. He shook his head, bewildered by Wellington and his hired killer. Could Iris have been mistaken?

He considered the scene on the mountain, assuming the role of attorney for the other one, the driver whose car had been destroyed. He had a case, Boise admitted. A hell of a lot better case than Iris. All he had to do was deny he knew anything about why the road barrier had not been in place, his word against hers. A very expensive car, no doubt expensive cameras, not hiding anything, an affluent professional out doing his job. A good story. The cool, methodical approach was very troubling to Boise. A real professional, he repeated to himself. If he had connected up there on the mountain, Iris and Bonnie and the old Dodge would all be strewn on the side of the canyon to be found sometime, with no possibility of ever proving anything at all. But it still didn't make any sense for Wellington to be after them in the first place.

If Wellington had known Boise's thoughts that morning, he would have agreed. It made no sense at all. At seven he called Lerner at home and said, "If your man has located those objects we've been looking for, tell him to wait for further orders."

Lerner blinked sleepily and made a note that made no sense at all to him either. Why wait? Now what? "Anything else? Chances are I won't be able to contact him. Especially on a Sunday. He said he would be in touch."

"Try," Wellington said. He hung up, and looked over his breakfast, exactly the same as yesterday's, and last week's, last month's. He hoped the papaya was properly ripened.

He chose his clothes carefully after breakfast—tan slacks, nice, but not too nice. A pinwale corduroy coat, tan crepe-soled shoes much scuffed. A sports shirt, open at the throat. He took from his safe a wallet that went with the outfit, and with it in his pocket he became Stephen J. Whorley. He was going antique hunting today. Mission bells, bowls, shards, ornaments, books, anything left over from the mission at Cambio Bay. A camera and notebook completed Stephen J. Whorley; he started to leave, then turned back and picked up the Peruvian pipes and slipped it into his pocket. Now he was ready.

Today he drove a four-year-old Celica, nice car, but not too nice, not nice enough to be memorable, to draw attention to itself or its driver. He liked driving, even in L.A.; he found it soothing, a place to think, to be detached in a way that was pleasing to him, part of the half-million drivers a day that passed through this stretch of road, and yet apart from them. Always apart from them. Half a million a day, he mused. Too damn many people here these days. Off and on for fifteen years he had thought about getting out, going somewhere else where half a million cars did not drive through any given section of road a day, where half a million a year would be high, but even when he entertained those fantasies, he did it abstractedly. He would never leave.

Although he liked to drive and found it relaxing, today he was tired already by nine as he drove north on the Santa Barbara Freeway. Not enough sleep last night. Damn dreams of pipes and whistles all night, waking up, drifting off, hearing the music rise and fall like waves on the beach, as monotonous as waves on the beach, as hypnotic.

Damn Gabriel, he had thought last night, tossing, covering his ears with his pillow. Why had he sent the wooden pipes when he had the golden item? Did he think that Wellington wouldn't know what a Peruvian pipes was? That he had to be reminded? That was probably it. Not too many people knew, actually, not gringos anyway. He had heard a variation of the Hawk story; there were more variations of all the stories than anyone could track down, of course. In the story he had been told, Hawk piped back her people after a disastrous storm wiped out the village. And there was another version that had her pipe back only her father. Essentially the story centered always on that one element: The girl had piped back the dead. And during the night the damn pipes had called him, sad, joyous, discordant at times, melodic at other times, on and on, calling him all night. He tried to picture the golden pipes, gleaming, intricately carved. The bastards had all been master carvers of everything, stone, wood, gemstones, gold, silver. He wondered if the golden pipes could be played, what sound would come out? Hollow, metallic, trumpetlike, dull?

He drove well, exceeding the speed limit slightly, staying with the flow, comfortable with the flow, and mused about the golden pipes, about Tony Windemeer. Had he made it back to Cambio Bay already? Had he already found Iris and the child? Was this trip, Wellington's trip, as stupid as he had called it repeatedly last night, and again this morning—as he was calling it right now, in fact? Stupid thing to do. No reason. This was the sort of compulsive behavior that got people sent away to the funny farm.

Maybe the sound would be one of those pure sounds he had read about. A compelling pure sound. He was smiling a tight little smile, wanting the golden pipes more than he would have revealed to Gabriel. He began to think about the price, what his ceiling would be, what Gabriel's floor would be. High, he knew, very, very high. But that was what the coke money was for.

North of Cambio Bay, Tony Windemeer was reading *The Times* as he ate breakfast. He glanced up when Carolyn entered the small restaurant; he looked her over, then returned to his paper, not interested.

Carolyn didn't even see him. She felt stupid and heavy, heavy legs and arms, heavy head, as if she had suddenly acquired a sensitivity to gravity and could feel its pull throughout her body. She could imagine telling her shrink about it: You see, Barry, this invisible ray, gravity, has found me and is pulling me into the center of the earth. She ordered coffee and toast and let her mind play with the idea of telling Barry about Cambio Bay, the strange things she had seen, heard, felt there. Barry was a psychologist, not a real doctor, she reminded herself sometimes, but he was her counselor, advisor, what? She didn't know exactly what to call him and usually settled for "my shrink," exactly the same as most people she knew did. There were more shrinks in Los Angeles than ingenues, she thought sometimes. They called themselves advisors, counselors, therapists, doctors . . . She had forgotten the line of thought that she had been following.

That was because she had not been able to go to sleep

until dawn, and then had not slept well, had not awakened feeling rested even a little. The second night in a row that she had gone unsleeping, she grumbled to herself, and now she was heavy-limbed and could not hold a thought through to the end. That damn music, she thought bleakly. That goddamn music all night. She yearned for twelve or fifteen hours of unbroken sleep, dreamless, fathomless sleep.

Her coffee and toast were served by a young Chicano woman in a green uniform that was too tight across her hips. Carolyn watched her cross over to the other customer and pour more coffee for him. He barely glanced at her. Carolyn had waited tables during one of her college years, and in fact had made more money doing that than at any of the other part-time jobs she had held. But she had flirted outrageously with the guys and they had tipped well. This young woman didn't look like the flirtatious sort, but rather more like Iris, worried, fearful, careful. Did she have a child, more than one whom she had to support? Probably. The train of thought had come around to the point where Carolyn was forced to think about Iris. She had managed to avoid worrying about her all night, and until this moment this morning. But now Iris swam before her mind's eye, hand in hand with Bonnie, the beautiful pink, blue, and white silent child.

Not her worry, Carolyn reminded herself. Iris was grown-up; she could handle whatever trouble she found herself in. She had proved that already. Carolyn added strawberry jam to her toast. The coffee was surprisingly good. She held up a finger and the young waitress came back with the coffeepot.

The other customer was finished. He folded his newspaper, glanced at his check, tossed some bills down, and left the restaurant. A paper, Carolyn thought suddenly. She could sit here and linger over coffee with a paper while she waited for the heaviness to ease out of her body.

She went out to the newspaper racks and looked over the choices, only vaguely aware that the man was consulting a map in his car. She was depositing her coins when the other customer made a sweeping U-turn and headed out of town. For a moment Carolyn watched the long, handsome Thunderbird, then she finished putting coins in the slot and withdrew her paper, returned to her booth. But something was niggling on her mind.

Quite suddenly, in detail, she remembered coming down the mountain with Harold driving his Buick, Boise and Iris in the backseat, and Iris answering questions about the man who had pursued her up the dirt road. Sharp faced, she had said, slender, dark hair, about forty. And Boise had added, "And a long scrape on his left cheek."

Carolyn went cold all over, matching item for item, as if she had mental columns to compare, the description they had given with the description of the man who had just left the restaurant and headed away on the road to Cambio Bay. There wasn't anything else down that road. It dead-ended at the construction beyond the turn-off to Cambio Bay.

She signaled the waitress for her check and asked for a container of coffee to go, paid her bill, and walked back to the motel adjacent to the restaurant. She had to check out, but first, she would call someone in Cambio Bay, anyone to give Boise a message for her. What message? She bit her lip. Return her call. She would wait for him to return her call. What she wouldn't do was go back to deliver the message personally. She searched the motel room for a regional phone book, and when that failed, she called information for a number for Bob's Market and one for Tydall's Garage.

She sipped the coffee as she waited for a ring, first for Bob's Market. She got a recording; that line was out of service. She dialed Tydall's Garage number and after a moment heard the same recording. She dialed the operator

251

then and asked for anyone in Cambio Bay, she didn't care who, and was told that the lines were down to Cambio Bay.

She hung up and finished the coffee. Of course, she said under her breath. Of course.

Moving slowly, deliberately in her strange heavy body, she checked the room for her scant belongings, and went to the office to return her room key and pay for the phone calls. Then she started to drive north, away from Cambio Bay, toward the turn that would take her to Highway 101, south, and home again.

After a few minutes she came to the first vineyard with neat rows of grapevines stretching to the horizon and felt almost as if she had driven back in time, back to an afternoon of the previous fall. She had gone to a friend's vineyard to celebrate the festival of the new wine. That was what they had called the event, a day-long party with more than forty people gathered under wide-spreading oak trees at picnic tables. Rotund, bald, sloe-eyed, with incredibly small teeth, Ahmad Jarel, owner of the vineyard, had stood up to give a short benediction, a prayer of thanksgiving. It had been simple, eloquent, sincere. "Thank you for the bounty, for the creatures who walk the earth, for the fruits and grains that spring forth. Thank you for friends to love, for those who love us." There had been little more; the party had become quiet, respectful, thankful, as if a layer of superficial irrelevance had been stripped away from each one of them, revealing a different self, perhaps even a truer self.

Carolyn had been driving more and more slowly as that day grew sharper in her memory; the respectful silence that followed the short prayer had moved her as much as the prayer itself.

Friends to love, she thought. She came to a stop at the side of the road, her gaze on the straight rows of grapevines, carefully tended, nurtured. The fruits and grains that spring forth. Friends to love. She took a deep breath, glanced in her mirror, then made a U-turn and headed back.

Boise stood on the edge of the cliff watching a game being played below on the beach. Apparently Bonnie was It. She stood in thought, her head tilted, and then ran a few steps. She stopped, extended both arms straight out and began to twirl around, pulled her arms in tight, dropped to the sand and rolled several times; she came up laughing. Watching her were Iris, Harold, and Julio. Julio began to shake his head when Bonnie pointed to him. She nodded vigorously, and clumsily he mimicked her, ran a few steps in a parody of her grace, spun around and fell. Bonnie jumped up and down clapping, then pointed to Iris. She was as graceful as her daughter, and when her turn ended, she was laughing helplessly. Harold looked embarrassed, but he had to take a turn also, and was even more awkward than Julio had been.

The sunlight on Bonnie's head turned her hair silver-white, nimbuslike. She was barefoot, in pink shorts, a pink top this time. She was joyous in her play. Now she pointed to Iris, her turn to be It.

Iris, also in pink shorts and top, stood in thought as Bonnie had done, then ran to the edge of the water, dipped her bare toe in, then waded a few steps, and ran back out. It was clear even from the hundred feet above them, and the distance of several hundred feet, that Bonnie was disdainful of this pitiful effort. She raced to the water and copied Iris, but then became distracted by something. In a moment Julio joined her and they squatted at the water's edge, engrossed. Iris and Harold withdrew and started to stroll, their heads lowered in conversation.

In the hierarchy that Iris envisioned, on the right hand of God there were the creators of all sorts, God's true heirs—the poets and philosophers, playwrights and novelists, sculptors and painters . . . On the left were the interpreters, the performers who made the works accessible to the rest of humanity—the dancers and musicians, the translators, conductors . . . On a tier below this dwelled the teachers who straddled the line between the sublime and the ordinary, who, at their best, opened the door to the miracle of creation, and at their worst built roadblocks between the initiates and heaven. Iris would have blushed and denied any such elevated position for any person alive if she had been challenged. Now, walking with Harold, talking with him, she was oppressed by the feeling of inadequacy, inferiority in the light of his education and wisdom. And yet, she had to admit to herself, there was another side of this unlikely association in which she clearly was superior. It was Harold who appeared tongue-tied and stumbling, who seemed at a loss, with only blushes to compensate for a lack of words, a lack of coherence.

Three times he had referred to their ages, the thirty years that separated them, and yet, she thought again, and yet. There were times, such as this one, walking with him on the beach in quiet conversation, when it was clearly she who was the wiser, and he the blushing, stammering adolescent.

With Rick, life had been little more than sex. Their love life had been intense, their bodies demanding sexual release at any hour of the day or night, and, surfeited, they had ignored each other for the most part until they tumbled into bed again. It had seemed enough for a while, and then for another while she had pleaded chores, fatigue, her periods, Bonnie's demands, anything to excuse herself. *Talk to me*, she had cried, *say something!* But there had been nothing to talk about, nothing to say, and finally he had come home with too much money, wanting only the tumble into bed, and she had thrown him out.

There had been no one since then; there actually hadn't been time for anyone, or opportunity, or, she had to admit, desire. But now, with this older man, this teacher, professor, this traveler and sophisticated intellectual, when his arm brushed hers, when his hand touched hers, when his gaze encountered hers, he blushed like a boy, and she felt a throbbing within her that she had thought dead for a long time.

She knew she was too thin, too pale, ignorant, and she sensed that he knew none of those things about her. When she caught his gaze fixed on her, she knew she was lovely and desirable, and for that reason alone she would have responded to his timid advances. But it went deeper than that, she admitted. Deeper, or at least in a different direction. She could apply reason, caution herself that it was a mismatch, and warn herself that he was being avuncular, not romantic, and none of that mattered either. She cast a sidelong glance at him as they walked, and caught him eyeing her surreptitiously. They both blushed, and that, she knew, was what this feeling was all about, whether or not she could ever explain it or justify it.

Boise was just turning away from his observation of the party on the beach, to resume the walk he had begun, when Luisa touched his arm, suddenly at his side, although he had not seen her approach.

"Watch," she said softly.

Below, Julio said something to Bonnie, who nodded. He stood up in thought. Apparently that was part of the game. Then he nodded, knelt again at the water and reached in. He drew his hands out, cupped; sunlight flashed on silvery, squirmy fish, as small as a finger. Gradually he opened his hands and the fish fell back into the water, twisting and turning. He nodded at Bonnie. Without hesitation she reached both hands into the water and brought them out filled with fish.

Boise felt the edge of the cliff tilt, and he closed his eyes

255

hard. When he opened them again, Bonnie was laughing up at Julio, her hands opened over the water, droplets flashing like diamonds in the sunlight as they fell.

Luisa's hand was very firm on his arm as she drew him back from the cliff. "Let's walk," she said.

He felt stiff, moved like a sleepwalker, and allowed her to guide him for several minutes until his heart was normal again, his breathing regular.

"I read," Luisa said, "that some children in Africa, I forget the tribe, were tested when very young and were found to have eidetic memories, right up until they learned to read. After that they lost their marvelous memories and became civilized."

"Who are you?"

"It doesn't really matter, does it? You've seen Bonnie. You know that she is a magical child. She hasn't learned yet that she can't do things, you see. No one has taught her that."

Elaine had said, "Of course he has to go to nursery school. Children need to be socialized. He needs to learn to get along with other children, to be disciplined if necessary. They're born little beasts, absolutely *non*human, you see, and they have to be taught how to become human. It doesn't just happen."

Boise rubbed his eyes hard, rubbed away the sharp memory complete with visual details and even smells. Elaine had worn a particularly musky perfume. That day she had been wearing a red silk dress, and had warned Jaime away so he wouldn't smear it.

Luisa was leading him up the rocky cliff behind the guest house. It was not especially steep or hard going, but already they had reached a point that let him see over the arm of the cliff that held the bay water protectively; he could see the ocean stretching out to the horizon, blue, calm, brilliant under the morning sun. Looking the other

way, the village dwindled, the houses had become min-
iaturized, doll houses, with toy cars, Lilliputian people.

"Here we are," Luisa said a few minutes later. She was
not even breathing hard, although Boise was winded from
the last section of the climb. She sat down on a smooth
rock, with another smooth rock wall behind her back. She
patted the rock for him to sit by her.

"I didn't realize this cliff was so high," he said after a
minute.

She smiled slightly. "How far were we from Bonnie and
Julio, do you suppose?"

He narrowed his eyes, thinking about it, and then looked
at her angrily. "Too damn far. Weren't we?" He couldn't
have seen tiny fish from that distance, he realized. Another
trick!

She sighed. "You and Harold want to take them away,
don't you?"

"Not just want to. We intend to. That man who's after
Bonnie is coming back. We all know that. The man who
hired him is powerful, and he thinks Bonnie's a threat for
some reason. We intend to take them someplace where
they'll both be safe. And you really can't stop us, you
know. You couldn't stop Iris from running out before.
You couldn't stop Carolyn from leaving. We've been grant-
ing you powers that are as imaginary as the fish were."
His voice was hard and grating, filled with bitterness.
"You just listen to me a minute," he went on, although
she had made no motion. "I saw one child die too young.
I know what that's like. And I have no intention of letting
it happen again. We're leaving in the morning. I plan to
stop to buy a gun at the first place that sells them, and
then we'll see."

"You can't save her with a gun, Boise."

"And you can't save her with your tricks!"

"You want her to be cured, to play with other children,

to be a happy, carefree child, and you think your way is the only way. There are other ways. There really are."

"What the hell do you want for her? What's wrong with wanting her to be normal, to be like other little girls?"

"What I want . . ." she said musingly. "I want to save the magic in her if I can. To nurture it, let it expand, not teach her *no* too many times too soon, to teach her some of the other ways to see the world, teach her some of the knowledge that is being lost. Look." She stood up, pointing back over the village.

He turned to see a tiny black car pulling up to the mission ruins. It was too far away to make out details; simply a black object moving against the ocher hillside, the ocher walls that were still standing. A man got out and walked around the car, looking at the village, at the guest house. When he turned toward the sea, Boise suddenly saw his face, as if he were no more than fifteen feet away, the sharp features, the dark hair, the long scrape on his cheek, the narrowed eyes that were taking in the grounds of the guest house, searching for Iris and Bonnie.

Boise leaped to his feet, both hands clenched, and the other man dwindled again, became indistinct with distance. Boise swung around to face Luisa. He was alone on the high point overlooking the ocean.

21

▼ ▼ ▼ ▼

Tony Windemeer drove down the access road to Cambio
Bay whistling between his teeth, not for the music, or
because he was enjoying himself, but because this was a
fucked-up mess and there was no one around to yell at,
hit, or even blame. Three miles of this road, the village
at the end of it, and in the village he would stand out like
a whore in a red dress at a Sunday School picnic. On the
other hand, he no longer believed Iris and the kid were
still here, not now, not after she knew someone was coming
for her. Too exposed. A shooting gallery, that's how she
would see this hole-in-the-wall, he felt certain, because
that was how he saw it.

He pulled in at the overlook and stood at the railing to
study the scene below: the town of Cambio Bay, the little
protected bay itself, the ocean, and nothing else. There
was cover up here, a hundred feet higher than the town
—oak trees, some pines, broom or something, chaparral,
enough. He should have done it here, when he had her

259

alone on the road before, he thought with disgust, and got back in his car and continued driving. It was only another half mile to the town, and most of it was closed down tight. Sunday tight. All he hoped for now was to learn when she had left, if she had said where she was heading, and how. Bus probably. Got a ride up to the highway, to the first place to catch a bus and got the hell out of here. That was the only scenario he could imagine after the chase up the mountain.

He stopped before a grocery store, picked up a magazine he had pictures in, and entered.

"Hiya," the man behind the counter said. He was bald, and very tan.

Tony got a Coke and leaned against the counter to drink it. He laid the magazine on the counter and glanced about the store. A café was attached, but there was a CLOSED sign propped up on a chair in the doorway.

"One thing we know here," the man said to him. "You sure ain't just passing through." He laughed.

Tony grinned and nodded. "Nope. Came for some pictures, maybe get a writer out this way, have an article like that one about Playa Negra." He flicked the magazine to the pictures he had taken of the black beach and then turned away to gaze out the windows. He acted unaware that the other guy was scanning the article.

"Not much here to take pictures of," the man said. "Course there's the Tres Indios and the mission ruins."

"I'll have a look. A little news item caught my eye about this place. Said a lot of people got stranded here by the storm."

They chatted about the storm and the convoy and the guest house, and when Tony decided he had learned all he was going to here, he wandered outside and began to take pictures of the town itself. The bitch was still hanging around, staying at the guest house, he thought with disbelief. What for? Gradually he talked to several other people, and then made his way to the overlook at the beach and took pictures of the pillars that people here seemed to make so much of. Just rocks. As he was turning to focus on the guest house, his real target now, he stopped all movements. There they were, the woman and the kid, down there on the beach with an Indian and another guy.

The Indian picked up the child and swung her to his shoulders, and they all started up the trail to the guest house. He watched them out of sight around a curve in the trail.

Shooting gallery, he thought again, and shook the thought away; no guns. It had to look like an accident or uncontrollable passion. He didn't quite grin at the thought. Passion was what he felt about Iris Lathan at that moment. But for now, he had to finish up and get the hell out of here, not let her see him and get spooked, and he had to make sure people knew he was on his way out, and then . . . He wasn't sure yet what followed, but this time, the dolls were his. Both of them.

He drove by the mission ruins without getting out of his car, and then stopped at a high point to study the guest house from across the expanse of the town. Just a big house, windows and balconies everywhere, accessible. An army could walk in, apparently. He nodded and drove back into town. He returned to the store and got another Coke and a ready-made sandwich from the cooler, and said maybe it was a bust after all. One motel couldn't take care of tourists even if there was anything here to bring them in.

"I'll develop the film, see how it looks," he said disparagingly, and the guy in the store shrugged in a philosophical way. Tony drove out of town, aware that several people were watching.

At the lookout, he pulled over again, and this time he consulted his topographical map, located Cambio Bay and the lookout, and then whistled softly. A trail led from the end of the parking area to the rear of the ruins. About a half mile through the woods, then another half mile around the end of the town and he'd be at the guest house. He grinned and folded the map, tucked it away in the glove box, and got out of the car to inspect the trail. It looked more like an old abandoned road than a trail, maybe the original road to the mission, and it was wide enough to pull his car in around a curve and get it out of sight. He walked down the trail for a hundred yards or so and was satisfied. It was strewn with boulders, unused. Of course, anyone parking at the lookout who happened to stroll in that direction might see the car, but who would park there? Dead end, no tourists, and the townspeople sure didn't need to come up here to look over their dump of a town. He moved a few of the bigger rocks out of the way so that he could back in without causing damage to the underbody of his car, and then he maneuvered the car out of sight and sat behind the wheel thinking. It was one o'clock. Lunchtime. He ate his sandwich and drank the Coke as he thought of his actions to come, step by step.

He would have to reconnoiter first, make sure he could get all the way through. He would be there before dark, and leave after dark, but it didn't look too bad, not dangerous, and he had a good little flashlight. In a bag in the trunk of his car he had old jeans, a ratty sweatshirt, sneakers. He knew what laboratories could do with samples of fibers, and he intended to leave samples. The beach towel he carried would do. It was from a K Mart. As were the cotton gloves he carried, and a coil of rope. Okay, he thought, after mentally checking his inventory, the gods were smiling, all was well. He locked his car and started down the trail to the ruins. He still didn't know how he would get to Iris and Bonnie, but he knew that he would. And if he got his hands on the kid, the mother would do whatever he said without a peep. Two very quiet little dolls.

"You've come back," Luisa said to Carolyn when she walked up to the porch.

"Yes. Where is Iris? Bonnie?"

"They were down on the beach a few minutes ago. Maybe they're showering. Why did you come back?"

They stood on the wide porch, Luisa in her calf-length skirt, her silk blouse, exactly the same as every other time. She looked serene, untroubled, pleased to see Carolyn again.

"I'm not sure why. That man who tried to . . . hurt Iris and Bonnie is in town."

"He tried to kill them," Luisa corrected.

"Iris has to be warned. Now."

"You don't love her the way Harold does. You don't have a burden of guilt to assuage, as Boise does. Yet you're here, possibly exposing yourself to danger. Why, Carolyn?"

"I told you, I don't know why. I haven't done the self-analysis bit. Next week I'll ask my shrink why. I have to find Iris."

"You know you can't," Luisa said gently. "I'll tell her as soon as she comes down. We have to talk about the library work after lunch."

"I think I can find her," Carolyn said slowly. She looked past Luisa at the house and she could see the branching corridors, the stairs going up and down, the many doors. She knew which door opened to Iris's apartment.

Luisa moved to her side and took her hand. The bracelet Carolyn had found sparkled on her wrist. She had not realized she was wearing it, and could not remember when she had put it on.

"Yes, I think you could," Luisa said. "But look, another guest! How busy we've become suddenly. Will you show him the house, dear? I'll go talk to Iris."

Carolyn looked over her shoulder as a car came to a stop under the overhang. When she turned back to Luisa, she was gone. Carolyn felt no surprise at all.

"Hello," Wellington said, leaving the car. "They tell me in town that the motel's closed for remodeling and this is the only place to get a room." He looked up, then in one direction, the other, and whistled. "I'd say there's room here. My name's Whorley, Stephen Whorley."

Carolyn nodded. "There's room. I'm Carolyn Engleman. Would you like to look around first?"

Wellington did not pause, but hearing her name gave him a start; he remembered that she had been here last week, she had taken the pictures of Bonnie, and now here she was again. He held out his hand and they shook.

His handshake was firm, not too hard, not a contest; his gaze was direct; his interest in the house appeared very genuine, and yet, Carolyn thought warily, he was lying. She could not have said how she knew he was lying, but she had no doubt that he was. If asked, she would have insisted that she never had seen him before; she was simply uneasy and cautious with him.

"Your place?" he asked then, waving toward the house.

"I wish," she said with a shrug. "I'm in real estate, back in Los Angeles. I'm hoping the owner and I can talk business concerning it on this trip. What's your business, Mr. Whorley? Real estate, too? I hope not."

"Oh, dear no! I collect." He laughed, a dry-grass crackling sound. "Little things, things I can carry. I'm here on a hunting expedition. How I usually spend my Sundays, out browsing, always hoping. My God, this is a marvelous house!"

Without warning he darted to the large side door and began to examine the stained-glass panels.

"I have permission to show you the house," Carolyn said, more bewildered than before. Whatever he was lying about, it was not about being a collector. He was absorbed in the doorknob, was down on one knee studying it.

"Brass," he murmured finally. "Carved brass, not molded. My God!"

They entered, and he froze in place, staring wide-eyed. At length he whispered, "Dear God! Look! A Betancort!" He rushed to the sideboard where a statuette was centered. It was a male figure, wearing a short cape and a plumed headdress, shorts or a pleated short skirt. His chest was bare. It looked like gold, but obviously it must have been gilded, Carolyn thought.

She had not noticed it before. She nodded at it now. Of course, a Betancort. She had never heard of him. She saw other statuettes, some on the wall, some on stands, all appeared gilded. She amended that: She assumed they were gilded; they all appeared to be gold. Silently she crossed her arms over her chest and prepared to be occupied for as long as Luisa decided to keep this man busy.

Boise stood on the cliff at the farthest point of the land curving around the bay. From here to the other point, the end of the protective rock arm, was no more than twenty feet; below, he could see the submerged rocks that made up the barrier to the ocean. The water broke in white wavelets over the barrier and was calmed before it entered the bay. Toward the left, seaward, and several hundred feet down, waves crashed into the rock cliff and spray shot high into the air. The problem was that he didn't know how he had got to this point.

He had been heading back toward the house, toward Iris and Bonnie, to alert them to the killer in the mission ruins, and his feet had brought him here instead.

Boise had been in a wreck once. The car he was a passenger in, driven by his high-school friend Les, had come to a stop at a red light, and a truck behind them hadn't. What Boise always remembered most clearly about that wreck was the calm that had descended on him, the way time had changed and had gone into slow motion. They had been driven forward by the impact, toward oncoming traffic, and he could still hear his own voice saying quietly "Pull on the emergency brake." He could still see how his own hands had moved to check his momentum, how he had examined the traffic that was not stopped by the red light which governed the turn lane only, the lane they were in. He had seen the faces of other drivers, grimaces, open mouths; he had even seen their clothing, sweaters, coats, a red-and-green plaid scarf. His insides had turned to ice, but the world had stopped, had become a jumble of discrete objects, each one frozen in place, frozen in time, each one examinable.

That moment and this one, he thought suddenly, were linked, were one moment somehow. He had taken two, three running steps back to the house and had come here instead. That other day nearly twenty years ago he had been shown a glimpse of a different world that was still this world, and he had denied that world because he could not come to terms with it, could not explain it to himself, recall it, talk about it to anyone else, or ever find it again. But it was there. It was here. All those intersecting lines, linkages, spheres, whatever they were, were still there. And he, anyone, could choose to be anywhere within his own sphere, just as Luisa appeared in hers where she wished, when she wished. But he hadn't chosen to arrive at this point, he reminded himself, and knew that didn't matter. Luisa had chosen for him.

The calm he felt was precisely the same as the great calm that had befallen him on the day of the wreck, and yet that day he had been in deadly peril. His friend Les had suffered a broken neck, and never had recovered fully. He, Boise, could have been killed, or desperately injured, and he had been unscathed. But the danger had been there; it had opened his eyes to the other world that he then worked so hard to banish again. Now, in the calm that allowed no fear, he looked back the way he had come and saw that it was much too steep to climb easily, or to descend safely. He looked past the rocks to the guest house and saw Iris and Bonnie in the library with Harold, examining picture books. He saw Carolyn standing near a man who was running his finger over the pattern on a large beaten copper plate. Across the village, the ruins were empty. He nodded. He would see the killer there later, at a much closer range, fifteen feet, twenty, close enough to see the scrape on his cheek, the flatness of his eyes.

He looked at the garden and saw Luisa regarding him thoughtfully. She reached out her hand, and he took it.

"I thought you might like to see the medicine plants," she said.

The calm shattered and Boise was violently sick.

"You don't understand," Wellington was saying furiously to Carolyn. "This is copper, but it's priceless, more valuable than all the gold in this house maybe. Look, it's a replica of the medicine wheel at Medicine Bow, Wyoming. Maybe it was even the blueprint they used. My God!"

"I take your word for it," Carolyn said.

He was too absorbed in the disk to pay any more attention to her. The copper had come from Manitoba, he was certain. It had that green cast. And from there to the Great Lakes. The Eries had had a hand in it. That was their signature, the imprint of a stone mallet. And the Cheyenne, of course . . .

Carolyn was studying the room with interest. She had not been here before. Today she had been in several rooms she had not entered before. On one wall in this room was the great copper disk that had stunned Wellington, a weaving hung on the opposite wall, a blanket of many flowers and wildflowers in a circular pattern, unlike any she had seen in the past. There was a long table, a conference table? It appeared to be, with a dozen heavy dark chairs arranged around it. There was a low chest covered with another woven spread, and a basket decorated with feathers and shells and beads. And of course, wide French windows with an ocean view. She nodded at the windows just as Luisa appeared on the balcony outside.

Luisa opened the window and said, "Lunch is ready on the back porch. Would you both like to join us?"

Wellington would have been content to wander for the next few hours, but the invitation could not be turned down cold, he thought almost aggrievedly, and he supposed he couldn't ask permission to roam unattended.

Carolyn introduced them, and she and Wellington stepped out.

"Mr. Whorley," Luisa said, "you like my assortment of knickknacks?"

"You have some interesting material," he said cautiously. He could not decide how to treat this treasure house. Did she know what she had? He studied Luisa covertly as they walked along the porch, turned at the back, and approached the wider area where a table had been laid. Luisa Ravel was seventy or a little more, he decided, but in good health. She could live another twenty years, sitting on all this museum-quality art. Not a sign of security here. Anyone could walk in and take anything. Someone could bring a truck and load up. She might decide on a garage sale, with hand-drawn signs on the road, no offer refused. Or vandals could walk in with sledgehammers or spray paint. He shuddered at the thought.

Carolyn was paying no more attention to Wellington now; she had turned him over to Luisa. She moved ahead of them, glad to see that Harold and Boise were already on the porch, and beyond them Iris and Bonnie were looking at something at the edge of the grassy area near the garden. Carolyn went to Boise and said in a low voice, "That man, the killer, is in town."

He nodded. "I know. You came back. Why?"

She shrugged helplessly. "I don't know." She wished she could say for Iris, out of altruism, out of friendship, love for the other, the helpless, but she knew it would be a lie and she didn't bother. For Boise? She shook that off impatiently. He would be good in bed, she knew intuitively; his body and hers were good for lovemaking, but that had not drawn her back. She glanced at the house itself and that was closer; this was the house of her childhood dreams, a house such as she might have put together out of fantasies and dreams; she understood this house, she realized with a feeling of belonging, a proprietary feeling that was totally unjustified. In her mind an image formed, an image that defied language. They had all been dropped into space, into time at birth, and each of them was the leading edge of a shock wave that sent out ripples that diminished gradually but never died altogether. The ripples intersected, deformed other ripples, merged, strengthened and waned. Iris and Harold and Bonnie formed a tight system now, circling each other, their forward thrust forgotten, all attention focused on each other. And into the larger configuration that was made up of them, of Boise and Carolyn, Wellington and his hired killer, the members of Luisa's household, there had come a streak of something else, cometlike, not to be denied, something from elsewhere, headed to elsewhere, something to upset every other orbit without being disturbed in its own trajectory. That other, that something else, the mover who was not moved, that was what had drawn her back, but to find it, to discover what it meant to her, she had to befriend Iris, befriend Boise, Bonnie. All this was beyond words, beyond her comprehension, her ability to express. It was not conversion; she would have welcomed conversion, the certitude that her actions were correct, the outcome blessed. She had nothing to give her that kind of confidence. She had no more than an urge to do this and not that, a feeling that this way was preferred to that way, an increasing tension or a lessening of tension.

Luisa and Wellington had drawn near by then and in relief from her tumultuous go-nowhere thoughts, she turned away from Boise as Luisa made the introductions.

Harold mumbled something to Wellington, not really rude, but paying little heed to him, his gaze on Iris. The sunlight on her hair made it shine like silver, hers and Bonnie's. His knees still felt weak as he remembered his hesitant suggestion that he could help her with the cataloging and her equally hesitant acceptance. But he would not say anything beyond that, he told himself. It meant nothing at all, just a friendly gesture, and he really didn't have anything better to do now.

"You're writing a book about local customs?" the new-comer asked.

Harold blinked, trying to remember his name, Worthy, something like that. "I may. Right now I'm just gathering information." His gaze returned to Iris and Bonnie who were approaching the group.

When Wellington realized who they were, he felt another mild start, but it passed swiftly, and he shook hands with Iris and smiled at the child. Iris and Carolyn moved away a few feet speaking in low intense voices. The child stood before Wellington and looked at him. Her eyes were very large and very blue. No one else moved or spoke. Very slowly Bonnie reached out her hand, as if to receive something that he had not offered. The elephants, he thought distantly with a chill. She wanted her elephants back.

"Bonnie!" Iris cried, and hurried to the child to take her hand, draw her away. Bonnie did not resist.

"Wait a second," Wellington said heartily. "It just happens that I do have something she might like. Look." He withdrew the Peruvian pipes and handed it to the child. She nodded gravely; Iris looked embarrassed. "It's all right," he said. "I have kids of my own. I know how they are."

"Thank you," Iris said then. "I just wanted to say hello to Carolyn. We've already had our lunches. We'll see you a bit later."

She walked off with the child who was studying the pipes, turning it this way and that to examine the carvings.

"Well," Luisa said. "Let's have some lunch. What is it today, Martica?"

It was bouillabaisse and a spinach salad, with warm, crusty bread; it was all delicious.

"Sometimes," Luisa said, after a sip of a fine white wine, "it seems that as one grows older, and the pleasures of life fewer, that all that remains is good food, good weather, and health. Nothing else makes much difference."

Wellington brought up the topic of the storm and for several minutes they discussed that, and then conversation lagged. Luisa Ravel, he decided, was going on senile; the food was her only interest apparently. And Boise Wilkes was an Easterner, as was Harold Ritchie. Neither of them mattered. Carolyn Engleman was a California real estate hustler. He knew the type well; they could sniff out bargain houses, lots, foreclosures to come, anything that promised to make them a buck. She had landed here during the storm and was back like a vulture slavering for the carcass. Carolyn Engleman was the one to talk to, he decided. She had shown virtually no interest in the priceless objects scattered about like dime-store trinkets; she was interested in the house and land, and he was interested in the contents of the house. They could deal. She had moved right in here with the old woman, who obviously already trusted her. Lonely, looking for anyone who took an interest, no doubt. He had seen her kind before often enough. They could sit on a fortune and never see it, never appreciate it.

Because no one else seemed inclined to talk, Wellington filled in the silence with lies about his other self, Stephen Whorley. He had used Whorley before; it took very little attention to flesh him out now. And he was thinking that if Windemeer appeared, he would have to be turned off for the time being. He couldn't do the job here. He would have to get Iris and the child as far away from here as possible, not have any suspicion descend on this house and the museum inside. No reporters here, no cops. He struggled with the laughter that wanted to escape when he realized that he might have to protect Iris Lathan and her little girl Bonnie.

22

▼ ▼ ▼ ▼

Conversation lagged, trailed off, was revived, only to lag again. Harold merely toyed with his food, although he knew it was excellent, and in fact he was hungry. But he wanted to be done with it, be away from the table, find Iris and sit near her. They didn't even have to talk. It was enough just to be near her.

Boise was trying desperately to make sense of this morning, and once more was reaching the conclusion that Luisa was drugging him, hypnotizing him, somehow controlling him, making him see what she chose for whatever reason she had. At the back porch, he had turned to study the top of the cliff that made the southern boundary of the bay, and he knew he had not been up there. A mountain goat possibly could climb those rocks, but not he, not any man. And yet . . . He sipped wine and didn't even pretend to eat the soup or bread.

If Iris wouldn't leave, he thought suddenly, then he could take Bonnie alone. No one would suspect he had smuggled out a child, and she would be safe. He would see to it that she was safe. He realized this was the only plan he could carry out; Iris was enchanted, incapable of leaving here now. And if she and Bonnie stayed, the child would die again. He clattered his wineglass against silverware and saw that his hand was shaking. He set the glass down.

Harold looked sharply at Boise, then at Carolyn who was just as distant and removed; he frowned at them each in turn. Luisa was playing a new role, and he saw that it was up to him to make conversation if there was to be any. Not having any talk was strangely ominous, as if everyone was listening too hard; it was nerve-racking.

He mentioned his college and his project for this sabbatical. "There are a number of books on the subject, of course—folklore, mythology, campfire stories—so I'm searching for something original, a new approach."

Wellington glanced at him without interest, his mind on the copper disk, the biggest one he ever had seen, and in the best condition. Almost lazily he said, "You know, whole histories are told in the blankets, the historical blankets? And in the patterns of the disks?"

"I thought all the knowledge, the interpretations of those artifacts was lost," Harold said after a pause, trying to recall what he knew about disks, coming up with very little.

"Much is gone, but there are fragments still. A good researcher could piece them together, perhaps." Wellington drank the coffee that the Indian woman poured and then put his napkin down. "What a wonderful luncheon! You have a gem of a cook, my dear Miss Ravel."

She nodded, then said with a little frown, "It is said that the site of this house has been in constant use for thousands of years. I don't know if it's true, of course, but it is also said that the garden behind the house here was laid out the first time centuries before any white man set foot on the continent. It's been maintained in much the same pattern ever since. Of course, some things are now overgrown, and I expect some have died out, but still . . ."

"Circular pattern?" Wellington asked, aware that his heart was thudding again. A medicine-wheel garden? He had read of them, had even seem some reproductions, but nothing satisfactory, nothing that even hinted of the power that supposedly was attached to them.

Luisa shrugged. "Basically. I think circular is not quite right, but you can judge for yourself. Now, it is time for my nap. If you will excuse me."

They all rose with her and watched her leave the porch, her back very straight. Boise resisted the temptation to run after her, catch her by the shoulders and shake the truth out of her. Later it might come to that, but for now he needed to talk to Harold, arrange to borrow the Buick, find Bonnie . . .

Carolyn watched Wellington stroll through the grass, hesitate at the garden entrance, then step over the border and vanish.

Boise followed Harold to the library. "I want to borrow the Buick," he said, standing in the doorway.

Harold looked surprised. "Of course. I talked to Iris and she is reluctant to trust the roads, you see. She feels safer here than out there."

"I know. But if Bonnie lies down on the backseat, covered with a blanket or something, just until we get out to the highway, I can take her to San Francisco, get a flight from there to Pennsylvania, anywhere. No one will even suspect that she's gone. I'll send the car back with a hired driver."

Harold was shaking his head. "Iris won't permit anything like that, I'm certain. She'll be down in a few minutes; you can ask her."

"Help me talk her into it," Boise demanded harshly. He took a breath, went on in a more reasonable voice. "You know she can't even think right now. She's too terrified for Bonnie. After she knows the child is safe, she'll come to her senses, and then the two of you can beat it, join me back east."

"But she isn't like that any longer," Harold said. "I mean . . . I don't know what I mean, but she's changed, she's more certain of what to do, that this is the place to stay. See for yourself when she comes down."

Carolyn was the last one to leave the porch. At the entrance to the house she paused for a moment and took a step forward to find herself outside her apartment door. She laughed softly and opened the door. She could hear her brother's question: "How do you get from one room to another if there aren't any walls?" And her answer, "You just think yourself there." She laughed again inside her apartment.

She crossed the room to the rocking chair before the windows overlooking the sea. A book lay on the table beside the chair. She picked it up: *Magic Gardens of the World*. She sat down and opened the book. Hanging cliff gardens of Greece. Terraced gardens of China. Lush tropical gardens of Polynesia. Formal gardens of England. Ah, she thought finally: Medicine gardens of the American Indians. She began to read.

Tony Windemeer had taken a nap in the car, and now the shadows were lengthening, the air cooling off. Time to get to work, earn scuba-diving money, holiday money. Time to show the doll it wasn't nice to wreck people's cars. He changed his clothes first, the old jeans, older sweatshirt, sneakers with holes in them. Two or three cars had gone past the overlook during the afternoon, none had stopped. Just as he had expected. Town of 203, all bored to tears with the scenery by now, and no tourists, not until they patched up the road, so this wasn't the end of the world.

The trail to the mission ruins was a snap, he had learned, and there were dozens of good places among the falling walls, hidden from view. Good places to hide them afterward, not for long, just overnight, time enough for him to get back home, make a couple of phone calls, set up his alibi, and get some sleep.

He carried the oversized beach towel and the rope under his arm and started down the trail. He had spotted their room already, had seen the kid on the balcony, stairs nearby, no guards in sight. What for? He knew that once he had the kid by the hand, the mother would heel like a well-trained bitch. No problems there. And he would go in after them if he had to.

In the house Boise was looking at Iris with despair. "For God's sake, let me try to get her out of here!"

Iris shook her head, as she had been doing ever since he started urging her to send Bonnie away. They were in the library; beyond the windows she could see Bonnie and Julio collecting rocks. Julio had made her a carrying pouch with two compartments, one for the pipes, one for other things. She was trying to fill it. From here it looked as if Julio was naming every rock the child picked up. They both examined each one; he said something, Bonnie looked again, nodded, and put it in her pouch, and they moved on. Julio was the grandfather Bonnie never had had; Martica and Luisa the grandmothers. At last she had a family to love, to love her. If Iris, as a child, had been offered the chance to stay here forever, or go on to the other world out there, she knew what her decision would have been. She had made it for Bonnie.

Besides, she thought, if anything happened to her, Luisa would take care of Bonnie. She could not tell anyone about this because she was not certain when or how it had happened. She was not even certain how she knew it, but the knowledge was absolute, not to be questioned.

Harold had drawn away from Iris and Boise, unwilling to add his voice to Boise's arguments; he could not explain why, unless it was his very selfish desire to keep Iris here, to stay like this forever. At least until he had to go back to school in the fall. And then they would see, he added, but already he was brooding about the change that was inevitable and unwelcome.

Iris looked at him, as if for support, and he joined them with some reluctance. No doubt Boise was right; it was madness to remain here and be targets, but he could not bring himself to pressure her.

"If they stay in the house, or within the immediate grounds . . ." he started. Boise looked disgusted and faced away from him.

Now Luisa appeared beyond the window, walking toward the cliff that overlooked the bay. She paused to speak to Julio and touch Bonnie's head, then moved on.

"I'd better bring her in," Iris said stiffly, not looking at Boise or Harold now. She left both men in the library, walked out to the hall and out of sight.

"Boise, relax," Harold said.

"Relax! What I want to do is grab that kid and run! Don't you feel it? Something's happening right now. Something's going to happen! He's up there at the ruins! What if he has a rifle, a telescopic sight or something like that? Where are they safe from a bullet? Do you have a gun?"

"Good Lord! A rifle! I never even thought of that."

Wildly Harold turned toward the windows. Iris and Bonnie were walking toward the rear of the house with Julio. Out of sight from the ruins, but for how long? "You're right!" he cried then. "We have to get them away now, tonight. Let's make her leave now!"

Grimly Boise nodded, and they hurried from the library, down the hall to the back porch to wait for Iris and Bonnie.

Wellington had been feeling the power wax and wane. He knew this garden was real, a real medicine garden, with real power at the center. The realization first struck in the form of a surge of charged air that made him stagger, nearly fall down; it had taken his breath away, filled him with fear and awe, and it was undeniable. Undeniable, he repeated. Now he was moving deliberately, letting the power guide him to the center. This could not be done rationally; logic didn't work in the garden. The problem was that the forks and branches made no sense. Each path seemed like every other one, and he could not even tell the difference between the plants any longer. At first he had been able to. Thyme creeping over a low stone wall, violets, a straggly tall plant with scarlet blooms, then vegetables. The vegetables were wrong, he thought without conviction. Had he seen them before? Beets? Carrots? Not in a medicine garden, surely. Then he came to a bed of plants he couldn't identify, gray-green leaves, small lavender flowers nodding. More thyme. More beets. Some of the intersections were simple choices, straight through, or to the left or to the right. But some were branches where several paths came together, and none of them led straight through. Twice he had come to a shady lawn, with a stone bench one time, a wooden bench the next; he had rested both times, trying to make the directions make sense, trying to orient himself by the shadows, which were noticeably longer and denser now than they had been only minutes ago. He did not want to be in the garden when it became dark. It would not be a good place after dark.

Deliberately he avoided the curved paths, certain the straight ones would lead to the center, but although he chose a straight path again and again, it always began to curve as he trod upon it. More plants with the scarlet blooms, or was it the same clump? He should make a map, he thought, and stopped to search his pockets for paper, pencil.

He knew he had edged in closer; he could feel it in his nerve endings, a new awareness, almost a tingling sensation, as if he had come upon a field of electricity, charged air. He moved more slowly, letting the power draw him along toward itself, and he forgot the map he had started; that was logic, rationality, and neither worked here. Just feel it, he thought, let it direct him. Once he reached the center, he knew he would never need a map again, the power could not be denied him if he found it, invoked it. He thought fleetingly of all the objects he had held over the years in which power had once resided. After so many of them, it was unmistakable, the feeling of emptiness that normal objects never had, the feeling that something had been there and had been drained away, recalled. Never had he felt anything as powerful as the presence he sensed here in the medicine garden, a presence that was nearly palpable, that was watching, observing to see if he was worthy.

He came to another of the grassy areas with a bench and saw Carolyn Engleman seated there. The sensation of power fled.

"What are you doing here?" he demanded, enraged.

"I thought we might stroll together, talk."

"Not now. Later."

She shook her head. "Why not now, before it gets dark?"

"I have to be alone now," he said brusquely. "I need to think. Leave me alone."

She shook her head again. "I can't leave you alone."

His fists clenched; furiously he turned and strode away from her. After a few steps he saw her ahead of him, leaning against a tree.

"White oak," she said, pointing at the canopy of leaves above her. "Very rare this close to the ocean. The vine is bittersweet nightshade. Pretty, isn't it?" She pointed to a delicate tracery of leaves climbing the tree. "The flowers form bright-red berries later. Deadly, I'm afraid."

"You're crazy! Get out of here!"

Carolyn glanced at the sky. "It will be dark soon. If you get caught here at dark, you may never find your way out. Did you know that? I shall be your guide, your Beatrice."

"What do you want? What's your price?"

"See up there, nearly to the top of the oak tree? Mistletoe. The golden bough, the key to the gates of death. Gift from heaven, sent to earth on a lightning bolt."

He glared at her, both of them unmoving. "Do you understand the paths?" he demanded finally.

She nodded. "Let us stroll together. The center is this way."

Helplessly Wellington began to walk with her at his side.

One minute Iris and Bonnie had been on the sea side of the house, and the next they were walking above the southernmost edge of the valley that enclosed the town. Iris looked about in bewilderment; Julio had vanished, but Bonnie was running ahead. Iris hurried to catch up.

"Bonnie! Stop! Wait for me!" It was as if the wind swallowed her words.

Tony Windemeer was disbelieving at first. The old Indian man with the cotton-candy hair had sent the dolls to him! He watched until he was certain that the kid was intent on something or other that would bring her to the edge of the mission grounds. He picked up a piece of dry wood, hefted it thoughtfully, and nodded. Then he positioned himself behind a thicket of chaparral and waited. The kid came into sight first, fifteen feet in the lead, darting along like a butterfly.

He waited until she drew even with him, then sprang out and grabbed her up in one arm, turned, and said softly to Iris who had just then appeared, "One peep and I break her neck."

The blood drained so fast from Iris's face, it was as if someone had pulled a plug. Her hand flew to her mouth to stifle the scream, and she swayed, her eyes turning white.

"Doll, you faint on me and I'll drag you by the ankle. Now come on."

He raised the club, made sure she saw it, and understood how easy it would be to bring it down on the kid's head; he watched her narrowly as she stumbled forward a step. "Good," he said softly. "Now move the other foot, doll. Let's go!"

He held Bonnie by the waist, his arm pressing her against his body, exactly the way Rick had carried her just a week ago. For an insane moment Iris thought it was Rick, that he had come to take Bonnie to the zoo, except this time Bonnie was unmoving, her eyes wide with fear. Iris managed another step, then another, and haltingly, in silence, she followed Tony Windemeer as he led her to the mission ruins.

"God, where are they?" Harold moaned at the back of the house, looking around like a madman. "They must have gone in already."

Boise stopped moving, listening, hearing nothing, not

even the wind. "At the ruins," he said then, and started to run. He could hear Harold pounding behind him.

The shadows had grown so long that the land was in stripes, dark, light, dark. It would be dark very soon, as soon as the sun dipped just a bit lower. They would need lights, help. Boise ran faster.

"Do you understand what you're talking about?" Wellington demanded of Carolyn. "You say you know where the center is, but do you know what that means?"

"Enough." She understood nothing. In her room she had put down the book about magic gardens and had stood up, with her eyes closed, visualizing the garden paths. Wellington, she had thought then, knowing finally who he was. Wellington making his way to the center of the garden where one might call upon . . . What was never specifically stated in the book, but it was enough to know that something could be called there, and that Wellington was looking for it. She had known only that he must not reach the center until nearly sunset, and she could delay him until then. She had taken one step—out of the house; another step—into the garden to wait for him.

Now she felt something all around her, stirring in the air, almost crackling, almost hissing, but subliminally. She could feel the hissing and crackling even though the silence had become profound. She took a step; Wellington followed.

"It's the wrong way!" he wanted to scream at her, but he could feel the power again, not as strong as before, and the shadows had lengthened alarmingly. They had to be done with it before dark. He feared being in here in the darkness more than he had ever feared anything. She took another step. He followed, certain that they were circling it, not drawing closer, circling it only. But he could not see a path that led inward. She took another step. The low sun turned her cheek red, turned her hair to fire, then she was in shadows again. Another step. Afterward he would have to kill her. He knew this as a simple fact that needed no explanation or examination. She had to die for what she would witness here, for the knowledge that had been granted to her.

Carolyn stopped again, this time with her face turned toward the sun directly. She looked inhuman with the red sunlight on her like that. She pointed and did not move again. She could feel it, something testing her, probing, flowing through her; she neither resisted nor called upon it. She understood at last that if Wellington called it and failed in any way, it could flare and destroy both of them, more than just the two of them. She did not move.

Wellington was afraid to break the silence with a question, but there was no need to ask anything. Now he could feel it swirling around him, touching him with electricity, making his heart race. It was surging through him, welcoming him, accepting him, flooding his body, overwhelming his mind, promising, promising. He flung his arms wide and stepped forward to the center.

The low sun had burnished the ruins into gold, like a picture in a storybook, Tony thought, pleased with the timing. Magic time, sunset. The dull ocher glowed. Behind the ruins the shadows were almost night dark. That pleased him also. Iris made a soft sound and he looked at her in surprise. The sight of the beach towel spread out on the ground had broken her finally. The length of rope looked like a slumbering snake on the towel. He grinned at her.

"We'll have a little party, doll. You, me, the kid. A little private party. You'll like it."

Iris shook her head, tears coursing down her cheeks,

but the kid was as inert as a sack of potatoes, just the way he wanted her to be.

"No noise," he reminded Iris, and squeezed Bonnie a little, enough to make her writhe.

They had reached the towel; suddenly Iris collapsed to her knees, her head bowed, moaning, clutching the ground with both hands, as if she were trying to hang on. It was nice, her on her knees for him, but too soon. He took a step toward her, lifted his foot to give her a kick, and she straightened and threw two hands full of dirt into his face and sprang at him like a cat. As if on cue Bonnie began to struggle; she turned into a writhing snakelike creature, clawing at him, kicking, twisting crazily. His reactions were all reflex now. As soon as Iris threw the dirt, his head had started to twist away. He dropped the kid and clutched at his eyes with that hand, and swung the club with the other.

"Bonnie, run!" Iris screamed. He smashed the club down on the side of her head at the same moment she reached him and drove him back with the force of her body. He staggered, and she sprawled facedown in the dirt.

One eye was blinded by the dirt, tearing, burning with agonizing pain. He cupped his hand over it and pressed it closed, and then looked for the kid. She couldn't have gotten far yet. Bash the kid and get out was all he could think of now. That was what Lerner had ordered, first the woman, then the kid. And then just get the hell out. He stumbled to the side of the ruins, and there she was, standing up in full sight, not running, waiting for him. She lifted something to her mouth; he stopped as she began to play some kind of pipes. Crazy kid! He started toward her again, but the ground began to shake, and behind him there was too much movement, as of feet running, doors slamming. He looked beyond the kid and saw the house across the way rising and falling, and the ground rising and falling with thunderous roars. The kid just stood there playing the pipes in the middle of an earthquake. For an insane moment he thought she was the cause of the earthquake. He took a step toward her; the ground lurched and he was flung down in the rubble of rocks and bricks. His eye was on fire; a deep groan shook him as he pulled himself to his knees, then to his feet. He had lost the club when he fell and he could no longer see anything on that side without turning his head, but he could not stop staring at the crazy kid. He groped in his pocket for his knife. He had to get her; he could think of nothing else. He had to make her stop!

Boise and Harold pounded up the path to the ruins, breathing in wrenching, tortured breaths, and all around them the music swelled and ebbed, soul-searing music rising and falling. Suddenly the ground seemed to move in time to the music, and it too was rising and falling. Boise saw them first, Bonnie standing as if impaled by a slanting beam of sunlight, playing the pipes, and the killer swaying on his feet, trying to move toward her, jerking, lurching, nearly falling. The ground rose and fell, bricks tumbled and thudded against other bricks, shattered into dust that was caught by a small whirlwind, spun faster and faster up into the air, away. Other whirlwinds formed and disappeared.

Harold ran past Boise, in the direction Bonnie was pointing, but Boise kept his gaze on the other man, the man with the scrape on his face, the man he had seen exactly like this earlier.

Tony knew it was over as soon as the two guys appeared. That crazy kid, he kept thinking, that crazy kid standing there blowing the pipes. Crazy. He tried to move, but the ground jerked him again and he staggered, and now he saw Boise, and felt a cold breath start at his neck and flash down his back, down his arms and legs. He was crazy, too. They were all crazy, but Boise was killer-crazy. Tony knew that look, that whole attitude. Killer-crazy. He got a firmer grasp on the knife, held it out low in front of him, and tried to back away as Boise reached down and picked up the club Tony had dropped. All Tony wanted now was out, just to get the hell out. And the goddamn music beating in his ears, the sun swelling and burning, swelling in time to the goddamn music. Boise moved in close enough to swing the club, missed, not quite close enough yet. Tony staggered backward a step, another. He was being driven toward the wall behind him, into a trap, he knew. A whirlwind spun by him, a column of black air, dust-filled, rose like a snake. The ground heaved again; Boise lurched, teetered before he caught his balance. Tony reeled into the ruined wall; more bricks fell, a new dust devil swirled, and this time he was spun around with it, to fall into the wall, through the wall, and everywhere around him the bricks were falling.

Bosie stopped. The wall crashed down, burying the man under it. Abruptly, as suddenly as it had started, the movement ceased, the ground was still again, the air stopped swirling. Dirt and dust pattered to the ground like raindrops and were still. Only the music continued.

Carolyn watched Wellington enter the middle of the garden, a small space with paths radiating out like spokes of a wheel, and that was exactly right, she thought. Medicine wheel. Wellington stood with his arms outspread, his face lifted; lightninglike flashes ran over his body, his face, danced on his arms and fingers. He was exultant, transfixed. Then all she could see was the inhuman brilliance of a cloud, a whirlwind, swirling and pulsating.

Wellington felt it building, building, accepting him, loving him, giving him the power to know, to see, to be everything he wanted. The emptiness was being washed away with the electric current surging through him, wholeness, completion, holiness taking its place. He was being transformed into godhood, his fears banished, his heart, his mind, his entire being erupting with joy.

Then, all at once, he was awash with a rage so intense it was monumental, demonic, totally consuming. He was flung to his knees and twisted in agony as the power was wrenched from him.

Carolyn watched unmoving as the brilliant cloud settled over his body, lit by interior fires, kindled by the last rays of the sun, too brilliant to gaze at; then darkness swirled in the place of the lights, and the colors tarnished and turned into shadows. Wellington dropped to his knees with his hands over his face, sobbing.

She went to him. The center was calm, empty now, merely another section of the garden. He was unresisting as she took his arm and helped him rise, and walked him to one of the spokes that radiated from the center, where she gave him a barely perceptible push. He stumbled forward blindly. She turned and took a step on the opposite ray, and walked into the mission ruins.

Harold was kneeling by Iris, crying her name over and over. Boise was standing hunched near the ruins of a wall, his hands clenched, his face drawn and white. Bonnie stood playing her pipes. The shadows were gone; the sun had dipped into the sea. Violet twilight lay over the land now.

Harold started to gather Iris up into his arms, and Carolyn said, "Don't move her."

The music was somber and gay by turns, poignant and merry; it rose and fell and rose. Echoes of the music repeated, returned by the mission walls, by the trees and rocks and hills. Iris stirred and made a soft sound; she moved her hand, the other hand, and looked up at Harold in puzzlement.

Boise started to move toward Bonnie, and Carolyn caught his arm in a grasp that was too firm. He stopped. Bonnie played the mournful, joyous, magical music until Iris sat up and, with Harold's help, rose to her feet.

At last Bonnie stopped playing. The silence that descended was uncanny, as if nothing in the world lived or moved. Julio walked into the clearing and went to Bonnie.

"Little Hawk," he murmured. He picked her up, swung her to his shoulder, and led the way toward the house. Boise reached for her when Julio lifted the child, but Carolyn's hand was on his arm, and even without its restraining pressure, he would not have touched Bonnie, would not have tried to claim her.

"She isn't Jaime," Carolyn said softly. "She can't be your child."

"I know." He looked back at the ruins, but the gold had faded and the bricks were simply old ocher, the color of the hill behind them. It was over, he thought dully, and he didn't know what he meant by that.

23

▼　▼　▼　▼

Sundays in Cambio Bay are lazy. The Shehans go up to San Luis Obispo to attend church with his parents, and have early dinner with them, argue some about politics, or the best way to dry fish, or something else that doesn't make much difference and that no one will change anyway. Bert Eccles and Syl Grundy toss a few horseshoes, and talk a bit about maybe buying a boat this year, and wait for Bobby Shehan to come home and Terry Hayes to stop fiddling with his old truck that never was any good and time hasn't helped any. They will play pinochle, the way they do most Sunday evenings. Some of the kids spend the afternoon on the beach, building and tearing down forts, having sand fights, testing the water—warming up nicely. Along about sunset a dozen people or more might find themselves walking along the cliff over the beach. You can't really see the sunset from down there. The sun dips behind the outcropping out of sight long before it sets. From up on the cliff some people have seen the green flash, that moment when the sun has plunged into the sea and for an eye blink there is the Emerald City itself lighted up, dome and all. Some have seen it, and some who haven't say they have because they feel they should have as long as they've been watching for it.

Sara Logan and Rita Cronen are among those walking on the cliff to watch the sunset, talking about the latest book that Sara has read. They pause when the shadow of the maiden touches the sand of the beach and creeps inward inch by inch, midway between the warriors, always falling short of either of them. Her shadow will come in ten feet, and then the sun will vanish; everyone in Cambio Bay knows the schedule. They walk on, slowly, in no hurry. The bay is as smooth as it ever gets, rising and falling so slightly that the motion has to be known or it would not be noticeable. Farther down the cliff Luisa Ravel has come out to watch the sunset, as she does many evenings. Sara and Rita are too distant to call to her, but they wave; she waves back and then faces seaward. The warriors' shadows are climbing the cliff behind them, as if they are trying yet again to escape the prison of the beach. They never make it to the top. The sun sinks into the sea before that can happen. The maiden's shadow is now far enough onto the sand that if she were positioned a few feet farther south, it would lie on one of the warriors.

Everyone in Cambio Bay will have a different story to tell about the next few minutes.

The Emerson boy is thrown off his bicycle and lies on the newly unquiet ground, thrilled with the excitement of earthquake.

Sara and Rita run away from the cliff edge, fall, get up and run again, and then hold each other until the ground settles.

Bobby Shehan and Syl Grundy see a strange man stagger to the edge of the cliff, beyond Luisa; they see the cliff crumble under his feet, taking five feet of land down to the beach, taking the stranger with it. Bobby and Syl lose their footing, are thrown facedown on the lawn near the motel beach access, and they stay there until it's over.

Speedy Tydall watches his fluorescent light twist, then explode into fragments, and he throws himself through the doorway of his garage, out to the grass, and down flat, holding the land with both hands as if to make it stop.

The water from the bay surges back and forth like water in a basin that is being tilted, and tilted again. Two teen-aged boys are caught in a surge when five-foot waves wash over the beach. They are rolled and rolled, coughing and spitting water; when the water surges the other way they heave themselves up and run.

There is the noise. Some will say like thunder, or an avalanche, or drums being pounded, crashing, earth crack-ing, rocks being crushed, sonic booms that follow one another too fast, ear-hurting, head-hurting, bone-hurting noise. A few windows break, glass shatters, dishes rattle, pans clatter and crash, plaster cracks and falls. Everywhere the noise. And through all the noise, over it, overwhelming it, then subsiding, there is the music of the pipes. Not everyone will admit to that; most of them will decide it was their imagination, but some of them will know forever that they heard the pipes over all the other noise. They won't talk about it.

No one sees the rocky arm reach out to narrow the gap in the bay where the ocean enters. When the arm moves, the shadow of the maiden crosses the pillar of the warrior, and all three pillars topple; now they are no more than heaps of rocks, with whirlwinds dancing around them, as the sun sinks into the sea.

The cliff where Luisa stood watching is empty now.

24

▼ ▼ ▼ ▼

In the house they have washed and are seated at the kitchen table where Martica placed the soup tureen before Carolyn. She serves the soup.

"Where the hell is Luisa?" Boise demands. "She couldn't have left during the earthquake."

"No one seems to know where she is," Harold says.

From across the kitchen Martica says, "She comes and goes. She'll be back one day."

Boise thinks he hears her add, "They fight. And he'll be mad, but even if he gets over it, she can't stand to stay away long. She'll be back." He looks at her sharply, but she is busy at the stove.

Cambio Bay is sleeping now. The talk of the earthquake kept the residents up later than usual, the damage check, the minor injuries that needed attending to, the state police who had to come for the two bodies, but now it is over and the lights have gone out. Couples are entwined more closely than usual, some children are in their parents' beds, all drawn together tighter because they are aware of what could have happened. The pale-yellow light in the grocery store is on, and the flickering NO VACANCY sign at the motel. The blue light in the garage is gone and Speedy won't replace it; he never saw it anyway.

The bay has changed. The arm has narrowed the gap that allows the sea to enter; it is only ten feet wide now, and the water boils passing through from sea to bay. At the north end, the arm appears detached, but under the surface of the water, out of sight now at high tide, it is still connected, as all things must be.

Up at the house one light goes off and another goes on, the way they do up there, the way they have always done.

W24
LC-9/22/15

Add -9/11/00
cc-6

DISCARD

5-90